Comments on novels by Paul A. Myers

Greek Bonds and French Ladies

Love and money are both at risk in Myers' politically driven novel of intrigue and betrayal…told with humor and sophistication.
> —Kirkus Reviews

It has French charm and romance intertwined with a feeling of extravagance and elegance.
> —Jennie, Goodreads review

A Farewell in Paris

In this lively novel, Myers clearly demonstrates his familiarity with the intellectual culture of Paris in the 1920s.
> — Publishers Weekly

Few places evoke nostalgia like the City of Light in the 1920s, and Myers doesn't skimp on the literary and historical details in his latest novel.
> —Kirkus Reviews

…excellent historical perspective regarding the failed peace between the two great wars of the last century. It's the historical research that makes this book interesting.
> —Al, Goodreads review

Paris 1935: Destiny's Crossroads

…takes us into the back rooms of high-level officials, writers, and media stars in order to understand why events happened as they did…involved and intriguing, Myers' work definitely is worth reading.
> —Historical Novel Society Online Review

What were the diplomatic and political actions in France leading up to the start of WWII? What treaties and alliances in Europe set the wheels in motion for Hitler to get Germany moving? …the true story is the political intrigue …
    —Barbara Ell, Goodreads review

Paris 1934: Victory in Retreat

…descriptive and thoroughly researched narrative feels true to the era; the "City of Light" shines through the page.
    —Historical Novel Society Online Review

I fell in love with this book as I was reading it. First of all I love historical fiction and the author was amazing with the plot and the details…
    —Brittany Tedder-Bixlar, Goodreads review

Vienna 1934: Betrayal at the Ballplatz

Myers' characters feel true to the era…an excellent job of making the story real due to his good research and fine storytelling. The interweaving of fact, fiction, real, and fictional people makes this book exciting and romantic.
    —Historical Novel Society Online Review

…found this story to be very informative about the pre-war situation in Europe, but especially in Austria…I found this book interesting, well written in most instances and full of intrigue, suspense, and romance.
    —Twin Two, Amazon customer review

Greek Bonds and French Ladies

A Novel

Paul A. Myers

CreateSpace edition
Imprint: CreateSpace Independent Publishing Platform
Produced by Paul A. Myers Books
Copyright © Paul A. Myers 2013
ISBN-13: 978-1494325985
ISBN-10: 1494325985

Revision 2/10/14

Dedication

To Minche

Also by Paul A. Myers

Novels

A Farewell in Paris
Paris 1935: Destiny's Crossroads
Paris 1934: Victory in Retreat
Vienna 1934: Betrayal at the Ballplatz

Cultural profiles

French Sketches: Cap d'Antibes and the Murphys
French Sketches: Cap Ferrat and Somerset Maugham
French Sketches: Monaco, Onassis, and Prince Rainier

History

North to California: The Spanish Discovery of California 1533–1603
Clerk! The Vietnam Memoir of Paul A. Myers

All titles available in e-book editions.

Somerset Maugham The Summing Up about maugham strickly personal his life at cap Ferrat

Contents

Dedication v
Also by Paul A. Myers vi
Contents vii
Cast of Characters ix
Epigraph xi
1. Paris 1
2. Geneva 4
3. Computer Intel 10
4. Moscow 13
5. Lunch at La Défense 15
6. A Business Arrangement 19
7. Le Bistro de la Banque 32
8. Monaco 35
9. Île St-Louis 39
10. Nice 51
11. Auverne 55
12. Dinner in the Bois 68
13. A Visit to Geneva 75
14. The Alpha Dogs 78
15. Bookshop 90
16. Café le Rostand 98
17. Dinner at Antibes 101
18. Bastille 118
19. Berlin 127
20. A Small Bank Scandal 130
21. Weekend Rendezvous 141
22. Majorca 145
23. Russians in Geneva 161
24. Hackers at the Gate 166
25. Antibes 173
26. Banque Genève Crédit Suisse 183
27. The Rubber Room 190
28. Gare de Cornavin 196
29. Vienna 198
30. Brasserie Lipp 205

31. Encore, Auverne...219
Sources 224
Author...230

Cast of Characters

[handwritten: "good editors should do this"]

Gentlemen

Jim Schiller—the American managing partner of Bermuda Triangle Ltd., a hedge fund based in Geneva, Switzerland

Jack Hawkins—the British partner of Bermuda Triangle Ltd.

Jürgen Kretschmer—the German partner of Bermuda Triangle Ltd.

Dieter—the German computer geek for Bermuda Triangle Ltd.

Édouard Soissons—an investigator *[handwritten: Head of Computer Operations]* for Strategic Intelligence International, a Paris-based international consultancy

Alain Renier—a former French finance ministry official and expert on banking now employed by a big French bank

French Ladies

Sophie d'Auverne—a former high official at the French finance ministry and current consultant for Strategic Intelligence International, a Paris-based international consultancy

Inès d'Auverne—*grand-mère*, the elderly grandmother of Sophie

Martine d'Auverne—mother of Sophie and widow of Inès's only son, Jean-Pierre

Marie-Hélène d'Auverne—daughter of Sophie and about ten years old

[handwritten: Christine Lagarde, pg 6]

Epigraph

The so-called "Lagarde List"—the name given by the Greek press to a list containing 1,991 names of wealthy, Swiss-bank-account-possessing Greeks...is causing a major stir in Greece right now. Since Friday, two men suspected to be on the list have turned up dead in apparent suicides.

Business Insider, October 8, 2012

1. Paris

Ministry of Finance, June 2011. Waiters glided across the reception hall balancing trays of slender flutes of champagne on upraised palms. With ballet-like precision, the waiters swept the flutes off the trays and into the hands of well-dressed men and women gathered in the brilliantly-lit room of the vast finance ministry at Bercy. Far below, beyond floor-to-ceiling glass windows, lay the Seine River flowing towards downtown Paris. The neighborhoods of Paris stretched away in the distance; the finance ministry commanded all it surveyed.

In the center of the room, an elegantly dressed woman in her late thirties held forth to three women in their late twenties about her experiences working in the prime minister's office at the Hôtel Matignon. The woman had worked for the prime minister before becoming a high aide to the finance minister, a discreet emissary entrusted with carrying out cabinet-level negotiations of great delicacy and sensitivity. The three younger women, dazzlingly dressed and in high spiked heels putting fine turns to well-shaped legs, listened with rapt attention. "When you're a top budget analyst for the prime minister," the older woman intoned, "you should be able to come up with a billion euros in budget savings before he puts his cup of coffee down on the desk at the beginning of a budget meeting."

"For starters?" one of the young women asked.

"Yes, the prime minister has an endless need for a billion here, a billion there..."

"And if you deliver?" asked another young women.

"You become the prime minister's trusted colleague. He's no longer looking up your dress."

The three young women all laughed. They took sips from their champagne glasses.

"You're always so much fun, Sophie," said the third young woman.

1

Sophie looked over the shoulder of one of the women and saw a tall silver-haired lady, sheathed in elegant Paris couture, walking across the reception area towards her.

"Excuse me," said Sophie, and she broke away and walked towards the approaching silver-haired woman.

"Madame Lagarde, congratulations on your appointment to the International Monetary Fund," said Sophie to Christine Lagarde, the French finance minister who had just been appointed director of the IMF in Washington D.C.

"Thank you, Sophie," said Lagarde. "Do you have the information? A second copy of the list must be protected."

"Yes, it's right here," replied Sophie, pulling an iPhone out of her Chanel handbag and holding it up to make the point.

"Good. Please keep it somewhere away from the ministry. Somewhere safe and secure."

"I'm taking it to my family chateau today. I'll bury it deep in the family library."

Lagarde laughed. "Good. You've been such a help, Sophie. I'll keep in touch."

"Thank you, madame."

Across the room stood a late middle-aged woman in a frumpy wool skirt, ill-fitting silk blouse, and a jacket sitting unevenly on sagging shoulders. Under broad brown bangs coming down to her eyes she watched Christine Lagarde speak with Sophie d'Auverne, a top aide to the finance minister. She paid particular attention to the iPhone but her brow furrowed; she appeared perplexed about what it might all mean. She sighed; there's something she's not getting, she thought. There's always something she did not understand, some dots that never quite connected in her mind, the story of her life. She sighed.

The woman watched as Christine Lagarde took her leave of Sophie d'Auverne. Then she scurried across the room heading for the ladies restroom. She fumbled and pulled a smartphone out of her handbag as she barged through the lavatory door. She was nicknamed The Mouse by the other women in the ministry, a holdover from decades long past, rumored to be kept on in her sinecure upon the mysterious request of some other ministry. The other women in the ministry had slowly pulled away from her over time, embarrassed by her coffee-break stories about romantic trysts with exciting foreign gentlemen on weekend getaways.

Figure 1 The French Ministry of Finance at Bercy in the 12th arrondissement of Paris. Two ministers have offices in the massive edifice.

2. Geneva

One year later. May, 2012. Geneva, Switzerland. Three men are sitting at a conference table overlooking downtown Geneva and the lake beyond.

"There's blood in the streets of Athens," said the American, referring to the Greek capital racked by massive street riots in May 2012. He looked at his partners. "What was it the Rothschilds said?"

"The time to invest is when there's blood in the streets," said one partner in a strong British accent. The reference was to the legendary European banking family, and the quote was from the revolutionary times of the nineteenth century.

The American put the newspaper down on the conference-room table and massaged his chin, deep in thought. He was troubled. Europe was troubled. He looked vacantly out the window at Lake Geneva a couple of blocks away. You were supposed to make money when there was trouble.

He glanced at his two partners and said, "Tough question—should we buy a couple billion more in Greek bonds?" The doubt in Jim Schiller's voice contrasted with the sleek and self-assured look of the New York investment banker he had once been.

"Well, following the Rothschilds' rule, I would say it's a good time to buy in," said Jack Hawkins with a jocular touch of cynicism. Jack was in his sixties; a full head of gray hair went with the hearty and bluff manner of a longtime British banker.

"*Ja*," the other partner said in a German accent, "but will the bet make money? Not so easy to tell. Maybe the hard Left will overthrow the Greek government in next month's elections. Maybe the Germans will really say *nein* this time." Jürgen Kretschmer's dour manner contrasted with his outward appearance as an elegant German executive with a polished boardroom manner.

"Yeah, a lot of risks," said Jim as he mused about other possibilities. "Maybe François will go wobbly," he said, referring to François Hollande, the recently elected French president. He smiled at the word "wobbly," remembering that great phrase from Margaret Thatcher as she counseled the first President Bush on standing up to the Iraqi invasion of Kuwait in 1990. The Iron Lady herself had gone down and given the Argentines a good thrashing at the Falkland Islands a half dozen years before.

Sitting at a small conference table with his partners in the corner meeting room of the Geneva office building, Jim glanced up at the wall and the beautiful poster print of Hamilton, Bermuda. Above that was a graying timber from some long-ago shipwreck emblazoned with the name of their hedge fund, Bermuda Triangle, Ltd.

Yes, Bermuda—where it all came together. That last year of the Bush administration had been like a banana republic with money. It had been so easy betting the house against the American mortgage-bond market, riding the derivatives into the big money. Then the American banks went down like ten pins in a cheap bowling alley. It was a short seller's paradise. Jürgen, the German partner, called it the "Happy Time" after the famous turkey shoot the German U-boats had off the eastern coast of America in early 1942. Was it only four years ago? The Happy Time?

Yes, four long years ago, he said to himself. Not that Europe had been bad. But you had to work at it. And you could see the dark shadows of unknown risks out there, circling around like wolves in the Russian winter.

Jim came back to the present and back to business. Something else in the newspaper bothered him. He jabbed a finger at the picture of a dark-eyed, silver-haired lady on the newspaper page, just under the headline, "It's Payback Time: Don't Expect Sympathy—Lagarde to Greeks." The subhead went on to say "Take responsibility, and stop trying to avoid taxes, International Monetary Fund chief tells Athens." He tapped the picture staccato-like and looked at his two partners. They knew he was getting ready to say something.

"She knows something," he said with conviction and tapped the picture one more time for emphasis. He paused, and his tone changed. "But what?" he asked. His voice had taken on a soft whisper of almost childlike perplexity. Was there some hidden risk out there?

Greek Bonds and French Ladies

Figure 2 Christine Lagarde, director of the International Monetary Fund and former French finance minister.

"What's the issue?" asked Jürgen.

"It's about Greece," answered Jack. "How big a position in Greek bonds do we take? When? What are the risks?"

"Yeah, should we even go in this round, or is it game over?" said Jim. The risks were clearly on his mind.

"Well, we really cleaned up on the last round," said Jürgen, referring to the structured buyback of Greek debt engineered by the troika earlier in 2012, a buyback deal that had been a hedge-fund gold mine. The Germans had not been amused; paying off speculators—American and British—caused teeth to gnash in Berlin. The Germans felt they'd almost been swindled by the hedge funds.

The troika referred to the European Central Bank, known as the ECB; another entity called the European Stability Mechanism; a big bailout fund created by the Eurozone, whose name didn't translate well into any language—probably on purpose; and the International Monetary Fund in Washington DC, the big international agency headed by Christine Lagarde. She had previously been finance minister in the just-defeated center-right government of Nicholas Sarkozy.

"Maybe we should sit this round out?" said Jürgen.

"The investors expect results. If we sit this out and the other guys win big, we'll look stupid," said Jack.

"Worse," said Jim. "We'll have made a mistake. Not good. Greek debt is touching thirteen cents on the euro. Too much upside...too good to pass up."

"Shitty little country," said Jürgen in a voice dripping contempt.

Jim laughed and said, "Jürgen, you're responsible for Frankfurt. You tell us what the *über-führers* think of the shitty little country." Frankfurt was the headquarters of the European Central Bank and the mighty Bundesbank, Germany's long-respected central bank and the *éminence grise* of European finance.

"If the French stay with Germany," said Jürgen, hitting the table with his palm for emphasis, "and the IMF stays with Europe, then Angela will make sure Greece gets bailed out again." Angela Merkel was the German chancellor, the decisive voice in European economic affairs. "She won't risk a meltdown before the German elections next year."

"In for a penny, in for the pound," cheerfully added Jack.

"*Ja*," grunted Jürgen, somewhat less happily.

"And Lagarde is the IMF," said Jim, rubbing his chin in rumination. "She has the last say in these negotiations—smart lady."

"We need more information," said Jürgen. "I can predict what the Germans are going to do but not the French and the IMF."

"We need to know more about the IMF," said Jack.

"Lagarde's power base is Paris," said Jim.

"Well, France is your bailiwick, mate," said Jack. "You've always done well in Paris."

"So Lagarde and Paris it is," said Jim.

Jürgen shook his head slowly back and forth in consternation. "Who would have ever thought that a French finance minister would wind up somewhere important?"

"Yeah," said Jim with a laugh. "We need to find someone who has been close to Lagarde."

"I see a trip to Paris coming," said Jack with a wink at Jürgen.

"Yeah, Paris is the next stop," said Jim. He had spent a year at a Paris lycée on a high-school exchange program and then had done a junior year abroad at Nanterre, the big university just west of Paris. He could speak passing French.

"For now, let's keep buying Greek bonds, particularly on the dips. Build up our position," said Jim. "We can always play the investment two ways—interest income to Dubai and capital gains to New York." He swung his chair around so he faced the inside wall and looked at the large poster print of a big, squat pressure cooker painted in a funny, surrealist manner. It was a Max Ernst painting from the 1920s, from the era the French called *Les Années Folles*—the crazy years. A couple of pipes protruded from the big, squat pressure cooker. Above the picture was their handwritten title, *The Sausage Cooker*.

Figure 3 *The Elephant Celebes* by Max Ernst.

"The American clients want all the fifteen percent money we can funnel to them," said Jim, nodding at a big pipe coming out of the side of the pressure cooker. The fifteen percent money was capital gains and dividends subject to the low fifteen percent tax rate created by the Bush tax cuts. The low rates ended in December.

"The Dubai guys just want money—as long as it's green," added Jim, nodding at another pipe coming out of the cooker. Gains and income that could not be funneled to New York were packaged to Dubai by a process of skillful finagling nicknamed "the sausage cooker" by Jim and his two partners.

Jack followed Jim's gaze to the Max Ernst print and said in admiration, "Do we have the best lawyers and accountants or what?"

"Yeah, the keys to modern hedge-fund management," said Jim. "Plus computers."

"And a little footwork," added Jack. "I think I'll go visit Monaco. Check out the shorts. They've been making money as Greece falls."

"I'll be in Paris. Let me know what you find out."

"Speaking of computers," interjected Jürgen, and he looked at Jim. "Maybe before you go we should check with the computer geeks?"

"Yes," said Jim. "So many angles." He looked out the window toward the brilliant blue of Lake Geneva and then glanced at the poster print of Bermuda. He sighed then smiled and said to his partners, "This is the moment; I feel it. The big money."

3. Computer Intel

The three men walked down the hall from the conference room. Jürgen held his hand out and ushered Jim through the entrance, where the big, padded door stood open leading into the interior office they called the Rubber Room. Over the entrance was a large hand-painted sign emblazoned, "The Alpha Dogs," alpha being the investment world's shorthand slang word for the elusive goal of above average returns. The one-meter-thick walls to the Rubber Room were insulated, with high-tech materials making the interior impenetrable to microwaves and other intrusive surveillance techniques. You didn't want the secrets to any elusive alpha to slip away to the competitors.

"Good morning, Dieter," said Jürgen, greeting Bermuda Triangle's head of computer operations.

"And what's on the real world's mind this morning?" asked Dieter. He was a young man, with stringy dishwater-blond hair, sitting in front of a huge computer console. He wore a clean rainbow-dyed T-shirt with "Free Assange" silk-screened across the back, a reference to the *über*-geek Julian Assange of WikiLeaks fame.

"Boss needs a briefing on where we stand on the Greek bond position," said Jürgen, and he stopped and sighed. "And our lack of solid, quantitative support for our trading position."

Dieter waved his hand for Jim to take a seat in the center of the room; Jürgen sat next to him. Jack stood behind them.

"Hey, I understand the present difficulty—politics," said Jim. "With investments, your work has been beyond reproach." Jim had approved all the purchase orders for Triangle's state-of-the-art computer operations. He knew about the high-frequency filtering software they used to monitor worldwide trading activity, the pattern-recognition software that could tease out the tiniest of meanings from the torrents of data racing across the trading screens. He had sat in on careful discussions where signal-to-noise ratios of various data streams were scrutinized for meaning, looking for a ghost of significance. Jürgen had built a magnificent

10

operation, completely German in its thoroughness. Jim addressed the present situation. "Greece is an extreme case of large discontinuities brought about by political decisions, not market forces."

"Yes, we see the political data build up into waves, but then the waves break in unpredictable ways," replied Dieter.

"We appreciate your understanding, Jim," said Jürgen.

"Every tool has its place," responded Jim.

"Jim," said Dieter, getting to business, "we tested your idea that maybe there was a political sentiment that could be sifted out of television finance news to tell us where the next political decision would go. But no luck, nothing. Just like everything else on cable finance TV." Dieter made a long face and shook his head in the negative.

"What happened?" asked Jim.

"We analyzed the leading cable finance channel backward and forward, round the world," said Dieter. "Remarkable, almost all noise…little signal."

"Really?" said Jim.

"Yes. We analyzed all the satellite outtakes and uplinks, too. Thought maybe they were hiding the good stuff. Same thing—no signal."

"Well, what does correlate?"

"What we found—and it's hugely exciting," said Dieter, his face bubbling with enthusiasm while he flipped his hands up at the surprise of his finding, "is that the S&P 500 correlates much better with the data stream coming back from the Mars rover than with cable finance news."

"Good for the Mars rover. So what can we conclude about cable finance news?" asked Jim.

"Most days, a dead planet," said Dieter, and he turned his palms up, signifying emptiness.

"Not all was wasted," added Jürgen. "We built a public-relations model for each finance ministry in the Eurozone. Each one has a unique signature. What's more; each finance ministry has a public-relations party line that can be identified and its direction and momentum tracked. You can literally see any abrupt departures from the party line. For example, when the French finance ministry is presenting a party line originally crafted in Berlin, we can detect it."

"I thought they all came from Berlin," said Jim.

"No, not all. For example, in Paris we can see when the political leadership is controlling the message coming out of the finance ministry. It's too soon to have a signature on François Hollande." Jürgen paused and turned thoughtful. "And he's so bland he will probably always be a weak echo. But when Sarkozy was in the Élysée Palace, well, the bling-bling came right through. Lit up the whole screen."

Jim smiled.

"These efforts will pay off for us in the future," concluded Jürgen.

"I'm sure they will," said Jim, and he turned to Jack. "What now?"

"HUMINT," replied Jack, rattling off the acronym for human intelligence. "Get the word from on high in Paris."

"Recommendations?"

"Strategic Intelligence International in Paris," said Jack. "A consultancy."

"When we're able to penetrate their encryption…strong signal," added Dieter, admiration in his voice,

Jack gave a thumbs-up to Jim.

Jim stood and started walking to the door with Jürgen and Jack; he stopped and turned around and looked at Dieter.

"Yeah, boss?" said Dieter.

"Remember; don't let the algorithms just chase the momentum. It's like the dog and the fire truck. What happens when the dog catches the truck?" Jim held his hands in a cupped fashion and rapidly separated them and said, "Boom."

Everyone laughed.

"Free Assange," said Jim, pumping his fist in the air over his head.

Dieter beamed.

"Paris it is. I'm on my way," said Jim to his partners as he walked out the door.

4. Moscow

The energy minister sat in his chair with his back to the window, which was filled with the stark silhouette of the Kremlin just across the square. He was in an expansive mood. "I was just telling the president that real foreign policy was made in the energy ministry, not by the aging apparatchiks in the foreign ministry," said the energy minister to two underlings sitting across from his desk.

"Did the president let you win at arm wrestling?" asked one of the underlings with the eager-to-please eyes of a well-trained lapdog.

"No, of course not. He always wins at arm wrestling, always gets the girl," said the energy minister with a chuckle.

"Yes, number one always gets his way," said the other underling.

"Back to business," said the energy minister with characteristic brusqueness as he leaned forward across his desk. He jabbed a pudgy finger at the picture of a dark-eyed, silver-haired lady on the page of the English newspaper lying on the desktop. The newspaper had been air freighted in that morning. The headline read "It's Payback Time: Don't Expect Sympathy— Lagarde to Greeks." The subhead went on to say "Take responsibility, and stop trying to avoid taxes, International Monetary Fund chief tells Athens." The minister tapped the picture staccato-like and looked at his two underlings. They knew he was getting ready to say something.

"She knows something," he said with conviction and tapped the picture one more time for emphasis. He paused and looked at his underlings with a twisted glance and asked, "Tell me one more time what the rumors say?"

"The lady is Christine Lagarde, now the director of the International Monetary Fund. Two years ago, she was the finance minister of France. The rumor was that she sent a CD to Athens with the names of more than two thousand Greeks with Swiss bank accounts. She thought they should be investigated for tax evasion."

"So?"

"Well, we have been paying generous commissions to a lot of Greeks for arms deals, pipeline approvals—all the usual stuff...some of their names might be on the list...bad publicity—"

"Bad publicity? Do I care? Do I look like a sissy?"

"No...of course not."

"So what else?"

"Well, there's a rumor that the French have an even bigger list...with more than a hundred thousand names on it of Swiss bank-account holders across all of Europe—"

The minister interrupted. "Now we're getting somewhere. If we had that list, we could really lean on some people this fall when we're renegotiating the gas and oil contracts...get our price. OK, how do we know this?"

"We've had a source in the French finance ministry for years."

"Is he any good?"

"It's a she. Well, she's a real tyro...the older she gets, the younger the men we have to send in. She really tires them out, but they do come back with a little information...but two years ago we may have hit it big..."

"You sent in someone big?" said the energy minister.

The two underlings guffawed. "The Mouse—that's her code name—said there were rumors of a big list and that a second copy went missing just as Christine Lagarde was leaving for the International Monetary Fund."

The energy minister rubbed his hands together. "Good, we're looking for a CD with more than a hundred thousand names on it...some of that has to be pure gold. You can always find a frog that wants a half million euros in a Swiss bank account...for a small favor. Put some agents on it. Find the frog."

"At which end of the cabinet room do we start?" joked the second underling.

"They sell themselves so cheaply," said the other underling.

The energy minister laughed and said, "The French are so easy to work with—bribe the boys; bang the broads."

5. Lunch at La Défense

Jim sat at a small table at the far end of the terrace under a shiny white umbrella, its plastic surface buffed to a high gloss. The terrace was set a couple of feet below the level of the sidewalk, which was separated from the broad esplanade beyond by green-tinged glass partitions. All along the esplanade the giant, modern skyscrapers of La Défense reached into the bright spring sky, mostly big French banks and headquarters of French multinational corporations. The terrace itself was a gray-brown expanse of large flagstones seamlessly mortared into a flat surface, over which glided waiters in black pants, fronted with white aprons and starched white shirts. The café was at the base of a huge, blocklike glass-and-steel skyscraper, which cast a soft shadow over the luncheon crowd chatting away on the terrace.

Figure 4 La Défense—the modern business district across the river from Paris.

Jim scanned the entrance area to the café, watching the sleekly dressed business people approach the maître d' and whisper the name of a reservation. A sheet of paper was consulted on the podium, a waiting hostess stepped forward, and the business people were whisked to a reserved table. Presently, a young man in

15

his midthirties, with thinning brown hair and the small, rectangular spectacles of an Ivy League grad student, came up to the maître d' and furtively whispered a question. The maître d' smiled and pointed over toward Jim. The young man reached out and pushed the maître d's arm down so as not to attract attention.

"No need to point," cautioned the young man.

"Of course," said the maître d', embarrassed by his momentary indiscretion.

The young man gave thanks and walked over toward Jim.

As the young man approached, Jim stood up and held out his hand. The young man shook the outstretched hand and said, "Alain Renier."

"Jim Schiller," replied Jim as he extended his hand toward the other chair. Alain sat down, and Jim followed.

"A colleague at an international conference suggested I speak with you."

"Yes, Emilio—"

"No need to mention names," interrupted Alain.

"Yes, I agree."

"He described the arrangement he had with your firm. Would something similar be available to me?"

"Why, yes," replied Jim. "My partners have approved the same arrangement. We'll start with one million euros, no short transactions, fifty percent margin."

"That would be nice." Alain sat back and smiled. "Other details?"

"We will watch what you do. We won't front run any of your picks." Jim meant that Bermuda Triangle would not buy or sell stocks or bonds in front of executing Alain's orders. "And we'll follow discreetly behind and with safe volumes. Don't want to attract attention from the surveillance software."

"Yes, quite so. That's important to me, considering my position."

"Yes, just what is your position?"

"I'm the director of policy planning at Crédit Générale," he said, nodding toward one of the skyscrapers across the esplanade. Crédit Générale was one of the half dozen largest banks in France.

"And?"

"Up to the election, I was working on European-wide banking regulation at the finance ministry. Mostly with my German counterparts."

"Yes, we are interested in the German connection. We are long Greek bonds and don't want to get surprised by any risk bombs."

"Greece will be kept together. It would be inconvenient for the big French banks if there were any unexpected events; you know, like a missed interest payment."

"Understood. But it's the attitude toward private investors that concerns us."

"Yes, the Germans hate to pay off speculators."

Jim flinched. "Our term of choice is 'investor.'"

"Yes, of course. I was just telling you how they feel about it in Frankfurt."

"Who do you know in Frankfurt?"

"Good source at Deutsche Bank. Near the top...well connected to European Central Bank...the Bundesbank is family to him."

"Good. If you could keep us informed of any change in sentiment..."

"I will."

"We have a completely anonymous server site tucked away down in the Mediterranean. Completely nontraceable."

"They all say that."

"Well, then, how do you plan to communicate with us?"

"Not by e-mail."

"No e-evidence," said Jim, and he laughed.

"And no formal correspondence either."

"Just how do you plan to contact us?" asked Jim, a mild look of perplexity on his face.

Alain pulled a cocktail napkin over and pulled out his pen. He wrote some notes on the napkin and handed it to Jim. "By cocktail napkin. Just tell me the name of your favorite bar in Geneva, and I will get the napkins to you."

Jim laughed and pulled over another napkin and wrote the name of the little bistro just down the street from Bermuda Triangle's office. He said, "They know us. What is your opening move?"

17

"My first position is the same as yours—long Greek, all in."

"Best intelligence I've heard all day. We're either all smart or all dumb together."

"I assure you—it's not dumb." Alain smiled smugly, confident in his inside knowledge.

"How about French banks?"

"BNP Paribas," whispered Alain.

"Your bank?"

Alain slowly swung his head back and forth in the negative.

"Short?"

"Too soon."

"I see."

"Watch the napkins. OK?"

"*D'accord.*" OK.

The two men ordered a *demi-bouteille* of wine and light salads for lunch. Alain regaled Jim with stories about life in the French ministry of finance. Then Alain added cryptically, "Remember, they," and he let the word hang there mysteriously, "know a lot about you. And if they know, then other people know."

Later that afternoon, back in his hotel room, Jim sent an encrypted e-mail, routed through the Triangle server hub at Majorca: "BNP validated; Greek strategy validated; source solid."

6. A Business Arrangement

The elevator stopped about halfway up the skyscraper. Jim stepped out and walked down the narrow corridor to the plate-glass window at the end. He looked down the treelined esplanade of La Défense and across the River Seine; he let his eyes travel up Avenue Charles De Gaulle to the Arc de Triomphe in the far distance. He glanced back in the other direction and saw the massive La Grande Arche to the west. It was a grand view of one of the most stylish business districts in the world. He walked back half a dozen steps, looked at the small bronze plaque on the door, pushed the door open, and entered the reception area.

"Jim Schiller," he said to the receptionist.

"*Un moment*," she said and pushed on an intercom button. "M. Schiller."

A pleasant man of late middle age opened a door and came up and held out his hand. "Édouard Soisson."

He has a head of thick gray hair like Jack's, observed Jim.

"Could you follow me?" said the gentleman.

"Sure," said Jim. He couldn't quite place Soisson; he didn't seem like a consultant, more like a policeman. Jim followed the man down the hall, and they entered a small corner conference room. Again Jim admired the magnificent view down the esplanade toward the river; he glanced across the green space to the skyscrapers lining the far side.

"Our European finance expert will join us shortly. That's your interest?"

"Yes," replied Jim.

The door opened, and an attractive woman in her early forties came in holding a leather-bound note pad and a businesslike Longchamps handbag. She smiled warmly at Jim and sized him up in a glance—the gentleman was pleasingly slim and dark haired, about her age, but seemed more like an investment banker than a buccaneering international speculator. "This must be Mr. Jim

Schiller, the new client," she said in an aside to Édouard as she kept her eyes on Jim.

"Yes, I am. Pleased to meet you," said Jim. He stood and held out his hand.

"Sophie d'Auverne," the woman replied. She squeezed his hand.

Jim looked at her with almost open-eyed wonder: the beautiful auburn hair, the silky crème-colored blouse over a softly rounded figure, the trim skirt over slender hips. She sat down, and Jim followed.

"Mme d'Auverne—" said Édouard

"Please…let's use Sophie." She flashed a winsome smile at Jim.

"Jim, by all means. I charm easily."

Sophie laughed. She turned and nodded at her colleague and said, "Édouard. Now that's all settled. *Allons-y.*" (Let's go.)

Jim liked her smooth assurance, the subtle way she took command of the meeting.

"Sophie held high-level positions in the finance ministry—up until last month's election," said Édouard. "She started her career with the City of Paris. She has many acquaintances in the ministries and the UMP party." He was referring to the big French center-right political party, *Union pour un Mouvement Populaire.*

"That's what we're looking for. Insight into what the French government is thinking—at the highest levels—and also what the French government thinks the German government is thinking."

"Shrewd," said Sophie. "The German government ultimately drives policy. The French only nudge at the edges."

"It's simple. My partners and I are running a hedge fund out of Geneva. We're long Greek bonds. We think in the coming weeks we should add to our position, but…"

"Were you in the last round?" asked Sophie.

"Yes," said Jim.

"You must have done well." Sophie raised her eyebrows, obviously impressed.

"OK, but since then Greek bonds have fallen. They're down to twelve to thirteen cents on the euro. So we started to wonder whether we could do it a second time. We've been making big bets."

"Yes, I can see your apprehension. And the Germans hate paying off speculators."

"We prefer the term 'investors,'" said Jim and laughed. "Everyone I meet in Paris calls us speculators."

Sophie let out a laugh and smiled at Jim. She wondered who else he had met in Paris. She continued. "Let's look at two dimensions of the dilemma from the perspective of European leaders, how it looks from the ministerial level."

"That's exactly what we're looking for."

"Of course I cannot divulge confidential information from my time at the ministry. I've only been away for a couple of weeks."

"Understood," said Jim. "We're looking for simple insights on how the second round might play out."

"Oh, you have your calculator with you," said Sophie, upbeat in tone. "Let's play a game."

Jim pulled his HP finance calculator out of his shirt pocket.

"Input a hundred for the bond, annual interest payments of four, a four percent interest rate, and a ten-year term. That's the bond of choice, I believe?"

"Yes, it is. Greek ten-year at four percent," said Jim as he punched the numbers in with his index finger for the widely tracked Greek bond, almost a permanent video on Bloomberg terminals across Europe.

"Now, just hypothetically mind you, let's cut the annual interest payment in half to two. What do *we*," said Sophie with an air of inclusion, "get?"

"About fifty. The bond's lost half its value."

"Did you buy any bonds at fifty?" Sophie asked.

"Are you kidding? Last round, we averaged in at sixteen."

"Yes, that is what I would have guessed."

Édouard watched Sophie volley the numbers around the table with keen appreciation for her talents; he hadn't really seen her in action before. He wasn't sure which she handled with more assurance: the numbers or the man.

"Now put in a forty-year term."

Jim punched in the number and said, "*Voila*, less than twenty."

"And over a span of forty years, inflation takes care of the rest."

"Less than a dime on the dollar," said Jim.

21

"Less than a nickel, I would say," she said with self-assurance.

Jim looked at her with interest. The lady knew her numbers.

"How does the European Central Bank eventually get out of this?" he asked.

"There are whispers in the ministries about a future exchange of sovereign bonds for zero-coupon perpetuities."

Jim savored the words and then repeated them. "Zero-coupon perpetuities...the complete perfection of worthlessness...so no loss on the books?"

"Exactly. No high official ever has to make a public admission of loss," she added, capturing the political dimension.

"And the real value of a zero-coupon perpetuity is, of course, zero," said Jim, a twinkle in his eye and a smile broadening across his face. "Alchemy."

"Sorcery, I would say."

"Clever."

"So, there, you see?" said Sophie. "Those are the kinds of numbers that bounce around in the ministers' heads." She looked across at Jim and said disarmingly, "When they're dreaming."

Jim laughed.

"So that's the first half of what the European leaders think," said Sophie. "They want to reduce the annual debt service while extending the terms of the bonds."

"We call it 'extend and pretend' back in the States."

"Ah, yes, the always colorful Anglo-Saxons," said Sophie. She reached over to her handbag and pulled out a little notebook. "Let me jot that down. I'm capturing all the cowboy capitalism quotes I come across—for my memoir."

"You may be capitalism's most beautiful chronicler," added Jim.

"Thank you." Sophie dipped her head at the compliment. "Now let's discuss the other half of your worries: some sort of default or forced conversion on the Greek bonds you own and are thinking about buying."

"That's the money question."

"You are concerned that Athens will set off the collective-action clauses in the bond contracts and investors, such as yourself, will be forced to take a lot less."

"Yes, that's it exactly. Jürgen, our German partner, says that Deutsche Bank is pushing this hard."

"You would have to settle for less?" An ironic smile spread across Sophie's face.

"Maybe worse. We might not"—Jim paused, a pained look coming over his face, and he spit out the word—"break even." He said it as if it were an obscenity.

"Yes, our sources agree on Deutsche Bank. However, we believe the German position will be to offer the investors way more than they paid"—she paused—"but less than they would like. Investors would still make a lot of money. Wouldn't you?"

"Anything north of twenty cents and we're OK. Above thirty cents, we double our money and ship big capital gains back to New York plus pay the Dubai investors a generous chunk of interest income. A double win."

"We think the collective-action clauses are there so that the preponderance of investors will all come on board around thirty-five. Above thirty-five, the Germans start to gag."

"If that's how it plays out, we win big," said Jim.

"Yes," said Sophie slowly. "That's how we see it playing out." She was truly impressed that Jim and his partners had set themselves up so well. She made a mental note to find out in some future conversation how the gains were split between New York and Dubai.

"Why?"

"This year, the European leaders are concerned about Italy and Spain. They need private-investor money in those markets to help stabilize what could become—and I want to stress this word—*precarious* situations. Every European leader fears contagion from Greece."

"You don't think the Europeans will try a cram down when the next Greek debt financing comes up? Play hardball?"

"Oh, so American. Hardball, really," said Sophie in a gently mocking manner. "They need you."

"I hadn't really looked at it that way."

"Our firm believes the deal will get sweeter the closer the deadline comes. The European leaders don't like the word 'precarious.' They back away from the word almost as if it were a cliff."

"That's what Jack, our English partner, says."

"So why are you retaining Strategic Intelligence International to advise you when you have such good counsel inside?"

"Big money, big risks. We always like to go for outside validation of inside conclusions. We don't want to get hit by any unexpected risk bombs."

"Risk bombs?"

"You know, sudden, unexpected happenings. When you're long and you're wrong...boom." Jim held his hands out in front of him and then rapidly moved his open palms away from each other in the universal pantomime of a blowup.

"How charming," said Sophie under arched eyebrows. She reached over and wrote the phrase down in her notebook.

"Well, some bureaucrat pulls a clause out of some agreement, forcing investors to take pennies on the euro—or worse." Jim shrugged his shoulders. "A lot of people would lose money."

"Yes, we would not want investors to lose money on other people's misfortune," said Sophie, and she gave Jim a thin smile.

"They hired the money, didn't they?" shot back Jim.

"President Coolidge, in the 1920s, I think," crisply replied Sophie, referencing this tidbit of American folklore.

"That's the bedrock legal principle every investor in bonds relies upon."

"When you're buying in at thirteen cents, I would think that bedrock principle becomes somewhat negotiable," said Sophie, and she again smiled thinly.

"For us, yes. We're transactional. But hey, there are always a couple holdout guys with hard-faced lawyers. They like to see some supreme court step up and say that rule of law is paramount, not political."

"Yes, the great Anglo-Saxon god—the sanctity of contracts."

"Hey, no contracts, no paper money. You wanna go back to gold coins?"

Sophie sighed. "Yes, paper money, the abstraction that builds all this." She waved her hand at the big buildings outside the window.

"You got it," said Jim. "But, hey, you're pretty good," he added with cool appreciation.

She dipped her head again at the compliment and murmured, "Thank you." She looked at Jim with genuine interest. She had not really ever met a speculator up close.

Édouard looked back and forth at the two of them; he could see a mutual regard developing before his eyes.

"We think," Sophie said to Jim, "each round of the overall buyback program will be priced so that banks will tender bonds without having to take big losses. That should guarantee a comfortable profit for investors who have bought shrewdly in the troughs." She looked at Jim. "I trust you are buying shrewdly?"

"Yes," replied Jim and laughed.

"If the price is twelve or thirteen cents, why aren't the American investors and the British speculators buying in?" asked Édouard as Sophie and Jim laughed at his pun.

"Great question," Jim replied. "Here's everyone's big worry. We're all afraid that if enough inflammatory stuff comes out about Greece—corruption and tax evasion and stuff—then the German public will revolt and the Germans will let the Greeks default. All those beautiful bond contracts would go up in smoke. Then we get the Grexit scenario," said Jim, mentioning the breezy buzzword "Grexit,"—a contraction of Greece and exit that newspapers used to describe Greece being booted out of the Eurozone currency union.

"Grexit?" said Sophie with disdain. "More Eurospeak. The media falls in love with the one-word simplification and fans the flames."

"You got it," said Jim. He looked at Sophie and held his palms out in a cupped fashion and said, "Boom." The palms again sprung apart as if cupping an explosion.

"The *Financial Times* notwithstanding, we do not see that for the foreseeable future. Defaulting on a bond contract is not just breaking a promise from the past but unleashing a series of dire consequences that will run far into the future."

"I agree with that. But do the Germans?"

"The Germans—all of Europe—face a more complex dilemma."

"Please explain," asked Jim.

"We have a simple strategic framework." Sophie tore out a sheet of paper and laid it on the desk. She made a little three-by-

25

two table. "I call this management by matrix, simple decision making."

"Yes," said Jim. "Clear away the underbrush. Focus on the make or break."

"Exactly," said Sophie. She wrote the names of three countries down on one side: Greece, Italy, and Spain. Next to each country, she filled in the two columns with the words good and bad. Then she explained, "As long as Italy and Spain have weak finances, Germany won't let Greece go. The risk of the contagion spreading to the other two countries is simply too great." She tapped the bad column with her pen next to the names Italy and Spain to make the point. "Italy and Spain stay weak; Greece stays safe."

"That word 'contagion' again?" said Jim.

"Yes, that's the overriding fear at the government level," said Sophie. "Higher even than Deutsche Bank's opinion of itself."

Jim laughed. "How much time does Greece have?"

"At least a year. Probably two or three," replied Sophie; the crispness of her reply was reassuring to Jim.

"What changes in two years that would allow the Germans to let the Greeks go down the toilet?"

"Italy and Spain would have to be pretty solid with world markets."

Jim snorted. "Pigs might fly. That means Greece looks pretty safe."

"So then it's nothing but price," said Édouard. "And the price looks pretty cheap today."

Jim and Sophie looked at him and silently nodded their agreement.

"Now that phase one of Strategic International's engagement is completed, to whom do we have the pleasure of sending our invoice?" asked Édouard, shifting the conversation.

Jim laughed and reached into his suit coat and pulled out a business card. "Our Monaco affiliate pays all our bills in France." Jim looked at Sophie and, with smiling eyes, added, "It also maintains a nice belle epoque apartment in Monaco and a spacious home in Antibes, plus a villa in Majorca."

"Monaco?" said Sophie skeptically. "You have not gone far to find your *paradis fiscal*," she said, using the French phrase for tax haven.

"We simply manage some European investor accounts at a Monaco bank; the few local investors are all on the up and up. We assume the French have perfect transparency into what goes on in Monaco," said Jim with a laugh.

"And your American investors?"

"We report all income and gains through Bermuda to New York. Bermuda is on the OECD's so-called white list for tax-reporting compliance. So they're on the up and up, too," he explained, mentioning the Organization for Economic Cooperation and Development, the advanced-country economic club based in Paris.

"Why go offshore then?" Sophie asked.

"We stay offshore to avoid registering with the SEC for compliance reporting." The SEC was Securities and Exchange Commission.

"And the Americans in the Cayman Islands?"

"There's a tax dodge out there somewhere," said Jim with a laugh. "All the money that comes out of the Caymans always seems to be fifteen percent money. Truly remarkable."

Sophie laughed and asked, "And your other investors?"

"You mean Dubai? We report everything to the bank that represents the investors. But, hey, do you read Arabic? We don't," said Jim, and he laughed.

"Monaco?" said Édouard. "It's different." He huffed and puffed and coughed into his hand.

"Édouard has only recently retired from the *brigade financière*," said Sophie, mentioning the financial police of the French national police force.

"You overestimate the French government's omniscience. In Monaco, it's only on a need-to-know basis," said Édouard. "Magistrates and paper work," he said with remembered disgust. "Procedure and, in the French way, lots of it."

"That's what all the governments say," said Jim. "Let's say we never underestimate a government's omniscience. We're in compliance in Monaco on reporting income for French nationals. Or we'd get booted out." Jim looked at Sophie and asked, "You worked at the finance ministry?"

"Yes."

"When Christine Lagarde was minister?"

"Yes."

"You knew her?"

"Yes."

"Well," said Jim, taking a long look at Sophie, "my partners and I have a sense that Lagarde's scolding of Greece last week over massive tax evasion by the country's elite is well informed. She knows something, must have some hard evidence of wrongdoing."

Sophie kept an even expression. Jim's eyes bored in on her. She responded, "Well, the International Monetary Fund is, undoubtedly, well informed on tax compliance among its member countries."

"So you don't have any inside dope into where Lagarde's stridency on the issue comes from?"

Sophie laughed. "The French government has its hands full keeping tabs on Monaco."

Édouard laughed. "Yes, Monaco."

Jim looked from one to the other; he could smell the falseness under their display of bonhomie.

Sophie looked at Jim and asked, "What are some of your other investment interests in Europe? Can we be of any help?"

Jim saw she wasn't interested in talking about Christine Lagarde. He wondered why. "We're long Portugal," replied Jim.

"Yes, that should work out," she said knowingly.

"If you're investing in sovereign government bonds, you must have some views on European banks?" said Édouard.

"Here's Bermuda Triangle's view," said Jack, leaning back in his chair. "Banks have a lot of incentives to push their risks. National governments stand behind their banks. Hedge funds have a profitable opportunity when we can call the big banks on their risks—by shorting the bank stocks. But we can only do that when the government standing behind the bank is all in. You have to nail 'em both or risk losing."

"I see," said Sophie. She had never thought about how hedge funds gauged targets and risks. "You're like wolves. You don't attack the prey until it staggers and that foreleg hits the ground."

"Both forelegs," said Jim with the hard edge of deep belief. "Both the bank and the government have to be going down. A healthy government can always back up a sick bank."

Édouard, obviously fascinated, leaned forward on both elbows and asked, "How would you summarize your strategy?"

"There's an old saying by stock traders—don't fight the tape. Another saying is don't fight the Fed. We've added a new one—don't fight the governments."

"Don't fight the big bazooka," said Sophie with a hearty laugh.

"Yeah," said Jim. "Bazookas beat wolves."

"So how do you play the banks?" asked Édouard.

"If you can't short them," answered Jim, "then you look for opportunities to go long. Buy them when they get oversold—chase the shorts."

"Chase the shorts, another wonderful phrase. Now it's wolf against wolf," said Sophie with good humor. "I'd like to see that."

"Maybe this summer you will," said Jim.

"What are you buying when you invest in a bank?" asked Édouard.

"A franchise, the opportunity to provide banking services, often with the support of the host government. Then the bazooka is protecting you."

"Do you have any bank investments in France?" asked Sophie. "Now it is us who are interested in what you are thinking."

"Well, I'll cut to the chase. We're long on BNP Paribas; it's selling at a real discount from book value. But that's it," said Jim, and he shrugged his shoulders. "As for SocGen, Crédit Agricole? Who knows?" He then looked blankly at Édouard and Sophie. They nodded in understanding.

"All the French banks are having a good year in the markets," said Sophie, hoping to get Jim to say something more about the French banks.

Jim made a quizzical look and said skeptically, "Assets?" He shrugged his shoulders in disbelief.

Édouard could see that lack of credibility in government assurances about bank safety was central to Jim's thinking. Bank assets tended to be worth what governments decreed, not what markets thought.

"Banks?" said Jim, the doubt in his voice again making clear his skepticism. He concluded simply, "We're solid BNP." He looked thoughtful for a moment then decided there was nothing further to say. "Oh, yes," he added, changing the subject. "We keep an eye on the big energy stocks. We've been short Gazprom on the London Exchange on a small scale—shorting Russian stocks in London is like trying to dance in a broom closet."

"You Americans, so colorful," said Sophie.

"Yes, but Gazprom has fallen like a rock the last three months. Pleasantly profitable." Gazprom was the big Russian natural-gas company.

"How did you decide to short Gazprom?" asked Sophie.

"Our computer geeks sniffed out the trade," said Jim. "A big pulse of insider information will rock the price, either up or down. The software said down."

"Moscow cheats?" asked Sophie impishly, her eyebrows laughing at Jim.

"They view the European Union as a bunch of sheep to be sheared."

"We are not without our own talents."

"We?" said Jim, arching a questioning eyebrow.

"She'll be back in government someday," said Édouard by way of explanation.

"We follow Moscow closely," said Sophie. "We believe we are well informed there. I think we would make two points—your position in Gazprom may have run its course, and we wouldn't oversubscribe to President Putin's belief that Russia is going to become the next energy superstate. Energy supplies are breaking out all over, and worldwide demand is sagging."

"I'll keep your opinion front and center." Jim looked at her evenly; she had insight, probably based on good information.

She looked at him to see if he was going to say anything else. Jim remained quiet. After a moment, he stood up and concluded, "This has been deeply informative. Bermuda Triangle would like to stay on regular retainer with Strategic International, so we can get continuous consultations from you."

Sophie and Édouard stood and came around the conference table and shook hands good-bye. They escorted Jim to the reception area.

As the door closed on Jim's departure, Sophie turned to Édouard and said, "Let's chat for a minute." They went back down the hall to the conference room.

"One thing bothers me," said Sophie, taking a seat.

"Just one?" said Édouard.

"Banks. He mentioned all the big French banks except for Crédit Générale. He's not tipping his hand about something," mused Sophie, "or about someone. He mentioned talking to other people in Paris."

"Yes, let me snoop around. See what I can find."

"Yes, please do," said Sophie. She sat quiet for a moment and then said, half to herself, "Possibly an interesting experience coming up?"

"Yes," said Édouard, and he looked at Sophie; he could see she was intrigued.

She smiled, stood up, and headed for the door, ready to return to her office.

Majorca Server Hub

Later that afternoon, back in his hotel room, Jim sent an encrypted e-mail through the Triangle server hub in Majorca: "Source is Sophie d'Auverne, former finance ministry official. Portugal validated; Greek strategy validated. She warns on Russian energy. Close out Gazprom. Source clever; she smells our interest in French banks. Do prelim backgrounder."

7. Le Bistro de la Banque

Édouard walked along the sidewalk of the esplanade and stopped at the top of the steps leading down to the terrace of Le Bistro de la Banque. It was quite vacant in the late afternoon. He walked down to the double glass doors and went inside. He looked over to the corner and saw the maître d' sitting in his accustomed booth, tallying up numbers on sheets of paper. Édouard watched for a moment, observing the black swept-back hair, the hawkish nose, and the dark eyes that darted around like those of an adder. He walked over.

"Hi, Pierre, can you spare me a few moments?"

"Of course, M. Édouard."

Édouard sat down and scooted around near Pierre and in a low voice said, "I have a few inquiries this afternoon."

"Of course. When else are you ever here?" They both laughed.

"Have you seen an American around? He's a banker from Geneva."

"Why, yes. Yesterday. Not New York, not London—he was not even close to Savile Row. I think Italian, possibly French, tailoring. So, yes, Geneva."

"That's him. Was he with anyone?"

"Why, yes. Sort of hush-hush. A rendezvous, perhaps?" Pierre smiled deliciously; bankers talked loudly about deals and whispered about women.

"Yes. That's it exactly. When two men are talking hush-hush at a meeting, there's almost always someone else involved—usually a woman," said Édouard, and he winked. "Who was the other guy?"

"French. Wore those funny little square glasses like an American graduate student. Sort of new to the…how should we say…the quarter," said Pierre, and he looked outside with a glance that took in all of La Défense.

"Do you know where he works?"

"He has come for lunch with people from Crédit Générale."

"*Voila.* A perfect fit," said Édouard. "Do you have any idea what they talked about?"

"No, *le français* wrote something on a cocktail napkin and handed it to the American."

"And?"

"The American wrote something on a napkin and handed it to *le français.*"

"And?"

"They stood up and left."

"Have you seen them since?"

"That's what's remarkable. Toward the end of lunch today, *le français* came up to me, wrote something on a cocktail napkin, put it in a stamped envelope, wrote down an address, sealed the envelope, and gave it to me and asked me to mail it."

"Yes?"

"I said—of course. He said there'd be more in the future, and he gave me a ten-euro tip."

"Where was the envelope going?"

Pierre looked around furtively and whispered, "Geneva."

"Let's keep this just between the two of us, Pierre. Let me know when he sends another one. An assignation," said Édouard knowingly with a wink. "They're sharing...*une femme.*" (One woman.)

Pierre leaned forward and said in a low voice, "Yes, so many...when the banks are making money...then the women...the hidden ones..." That was what Édouard liked about Pierre; he was so observant of life coming through the bistro.

Édouard pushed across an envelope with some euros in it. Then he reached into his pocket and pulled out another envelope and shoved it across. "Double for today."

"*Merci,*" said Pierre and dipped his head in appreciation.

Édouard stood and headed back to the office.

Back in Strategic Intelligence International's offices, Édouard walked down to Sophie's office and knocked.

"*Entrez.*"

Édouard opened the door and walked in and took a seat across from Sophie's desk.

"Discover anything?" she asked.

"The American was meeting a French guy, thinning brown hair, midthirties, little square glasses like an American grad student—"

"Alain Renier. He was an expert on bank regulation at the finance ministry. Almost like an ambassador to the Bundesbank and the ECB," she said, mentioning the European Central Bank, the true colossus of modern Europe.

"He's working at Crédit Générale."

"Yes, I'd heard. Director of policy planning. Right down the hall from the chairman." Sophie spun around on her chair and looked out the window at the skyscrapers across the esplanade, including the massive headquarters building of Crédit Générale. She thought for several moments and then turned back around and looked at Édouard. "But what does it mean?"

"Obviously, the American is getting information from him."

"But how does the American pay him?"

"An account in Switzerland?" suggested Édouard.

"Yes, but how do they communicate?"

"By cocktail napkins mailed in envelopes. The drop is the maître d' at a local restaurant." Édouard always kept his sources well hidden.

"How charming," said Sophie, a wry smile crossing her face as she soaked in the information.

"My source is going to keep me informed about the traffic."

"*Bon.*"

Édouard stood. So did Sophie. She looked at him and said, "We should learn something ourselves from this, something useful, possibly valuable."

Édouard dipped his head in acknowledgement. Yes, she was clever.

8. Monaco

The blue Mediterranean splashed at the base of the cliffs as Jack Hawkins, Bermuda Triangle's British partner, walked up the long, sloping walkway from the old residential quarter of Monaco, named La Condamine, which featured the principality's beautiful belle epoque apartment buildings. Triangle had a pleasant apartment for its use up one of the back streets of the old quarter. Jack liked to stay there. He was a Monaco tax resident. At the top of the walkway was the hilltop of Monte Carlo with its grand hotel and rococo gambling palace.

Reaching the heights, Jack walked around the front of the Hôtel de Paris and strolled through the parking area; here and there he saw a chauffeur polishing a piece of chrome while waiting for guests to descend the long steps of the hotel. Jack stood and admired a Porsche Carrera; Emile was right: quite complete, not an accessory missing. Jack turned and walked across the small plaza to the steps leading into the Monte Carlo Casino and the lobby of the luxurious gambling hall.

Emile had told him the American came in around nine o'clock in the evening. "Something to see," he'd said. A little bit of research revealed the American, named Giuseppe Smith, was running a hedge fund out of the Cayman Islands after having cashed in by massively shorting mortgage-backed securities in the 2008 financial crisis. He had learned half the lesson, probably too well, thought Jack. Not everything always went to zero.

Approaching the entrance to the gaming room, Jack flashed his Monaco identity card to the attendant, which showed his British nationality; Monacan citizens weren't allowed in the gambling rooms except to work. As a tax exile in Monaco, Jack lived here the appropriate number of days each year but was still an expatriate.

Jack spotted Emile over at the side of the room surveying his domain; the black tie, black tuxedo, brilliant white shirtfront, and the groomed, swept-back black hair showed the smooth manner of the professional host. Jack walked over and sidled up next to Emile and whispered, "Is he here yet?"

"No, *un moment*, my friend."

"What's his game?"

Roulette. Center table." Emile nodded to the center of the room, "*Là*." (There.)

Presently, a chorus of murmurs broke out among people standing around the roulette table, and heads turned toward a thirty-something man in a baby-blue sport coat and an open-necked, winged-collar dress shirt, with the inevitable gold chain around his neck and dark blue pants. Gold cuff links on French cuffs, with one cuff pulled back from the Rolex, completed the display. If this guy wasn't running a hedge fund in the Cayman Islands, he'd be running numbers in Brooklyn, thought Jack.

But the golden hardware aside, the jewels with Giuseppe Smith were the two statuesque blondes—bleached hair shining in the light of the chandeliers, exquisitely tight cocktail dresses with full décolletage turning heads, shining white smiles, long legs placing one well-spiked foot in front of the other, and rear ends…oh well.

"Unusual," whispered Jack to Emile. "He likes to be near the center of attention. Most of 'em want to be the center of attention."

Emile chuckled and said, "Ultimately, the money always is."

"Well, take the babes away, and you'd notice the watch."

"Keep an eye on the play. You'll see."

The two blondes came up to the roulette table, and people moved out of the way to give them room at what had become their accustomed places. Giuseppe Smith nodded to the croupier, who, with his rake, pushed across the table 50,000 euros in blue and red chips to one blonde and then another pile to the other blonde. Smith smiled and said, "We'll play table stakes tonight."

Emile leaned over to Jack and whispered, "The same every night. A hundred thousand to the two women, and when it runs out, they go across the plaza to the hotel for dinner."

"Then what?"

"*Tous ensemble*." (All together.) Emile flashed the briefest of smiles.

Jack laughed.

A waiter came into the room, a bottle of Dom Pérignon and three glasses on his tray, and looked at Emile, who nodded affirmatively. The waiter took the champagne over to Giuseppe Smith and the two women.

"You've never sent me Dom Pérignon when I'm at the tables, Emile," said Jack with a laugh.

"You've never lost money the way Giuseppe Smith loses money."

The two men stood and watched the play; the two blondes would push five- and ten-thousand-euro stacks of chips out on the numbers or sometimes just go red or black for a while to rack up a couple of wins. Each win would be met by clapped hands and glee across their beautiful faces. Smith stood behind and beamed at their good fortune. Slowly, the two piles of chips declined in size.

"We never seem to be able to win, do we?" said one of the blondes, a pout of disappointment on her face.

"Don't worry; there's plenty more where that came from," soothed Smith.

"Just where is this magical place named 'from'?" said a voice in the crowd.

"Oh, far, far away and out on our little island; we're shorting Greek bonds big time."

"Why?" asked another voice.

"Athens is the new Lehman Brothers," replied Smith flippantly. The bankruptcy of Lehman Brothers in 2008 had pushed the worldwide finance system over the cliff into crisis. Everyone who went short made a killing.

"Yeah?" said one of the voices, asking for more info.

"When the Greeks finish with the June election next week, default will be on the horizon. The Grexit will happen. Nobody can put Humpty Dumpty back together again. The German taxpayer won't stand for more," said Smith.

Jack and Emile stood and watched Smith pontificate with arrogant self-confidence for a couple of minutes.

"What do you think?" whispered Emile to Jack.

"It's what Angela Merkel thinks that counts. And she ain't saying."

Emile nodded sagely and said, "If it goes the other way, then it'll be the Americans from the Connecticut hedge funds at the tables."

"You may be right," said Jack. "I hear they're having a convention here later this month. You can ask them."

"Yes, if I see them. Do you think the hedge funds will be at the roulette tables?" asked Emile, and he looked at Jack for a clue.

"We think the Americans will be in the chips."

Now it was Emile's turn to smile. Easy income was coming his way.

The two men turned and walked into the lobby. Jack got ready to depart and turned to shake Emile's hand good night. Emile asked, "By the way, on which side are our accounts, the boobs or the hedge funds?"

"The hedgies," said Jack nonchalantly. "The boobs will be back on the beach in LA before Bastille Day."

Emile smiled broadly. Emile had a customer account, something for his retirement, with Bermuda Triangle at the local Monaco bank. It was all on the up and up. Jack liked to keep everyone's incentives going in the same direction.

"Thanks, Emile. I always like to see the chaps we're going against."

9. Île St-Louis

Jim picked up the phone and heard the bright voice of Sophie d'Auverne. "Hello, Jim?"

"Yes, so nice to hear from you, Sophie."

"I have a report prepared by our firm on Greece. Backs up our conclusions. I was wondering if I could fax or e-mail it to you...or possibly drop it off, if you are in Paris?"

"I'll be in Paris Saturday afternoon. We could meet near Île St-Louis late Saturday afternoon. I could get the report and...maybe we could have dinner together?"

"I'd love to. Where?"

"Do you know the bridge, the one behind Notre Dame, leading over to the island? I'm usually out there Saturday afternoons, listening to the jazz. We could meet there."

"Sounds fun. What time?"

"About five?"

"I'll take a cab. See you at five."

"And Sophie?"

"Yes?"

"I'll read the report Sunday."

She laughed. "I understand." She rang off.

Jim sat on the curb along the south side of Pont St-Louis and watched the two jazz musicians playing in the center of the bridge. The easy swing of a 1950s bebop jazz classic drifted across the late afternoon air. The roadway had long since been blocked off at either end of the bridge, making it a walkway connecting the two islands situated in the center of the River Seine. Over to the left, across a well-manicured park, was the Cathedral Notre Dame, its elegant flying buttresses sweeping away from the stone walls of the nave. Past the jazz musicians and beyond the balustrade was a channel of the river, flowing along the stone-walled side of Île de la Cité toward its junction with the main river coming around the far side of Île St-Louis.

Jim periodically looked over at the road in front of the park on Île de la Cité. Presently he saw a taxi pull to a stop; the driver quickly came around and opened the door. Sophie d'Auverne alighted from the backseat, smoothed her brushed-wool skirt with her hands, and opened the flap of her handbag with the interlocking, opposed Cs of a classic Chanel bag. A metallic golden-colored chain went over her shoulder and held the bag snugly against her side. She pulled out a small wallet and paid the cab driver. After putting the wallet away, she looked out to the bridge, saw Jim, and waved. She started walking across the bridge. Jim stood up and held his hand out to her as she approached.

"So nice you could join me this evening."

"Do you impress all your dates with your choice of entertainment?" she said with laughing eyes as she looked over at the two jazz musicians busking in the center of the bridge.

"Here, I've got the best seat in the house for you," said Jim as he pointed to a small cushion lying on the curb next to his own cushion. He held her hand and helped her ease down onto the cushion as she tucked her knees to one side. He sat down next to her.

"Jason runs little jazz groups all over France," said Jim, nodding toward the two musicians playing on the bridge. "Sometimes they are duos, like today, other times a trio or quartet, and now and again a larger band. The music—cool and sweet—is from the 1940s and '50s, the bebop era. It was a form of jazz big in New York and Paris and out on the West Coast. Still is pretty big in France. Guess that's why Jason can make a living in France. The music still lives here."

"Yes, I sometimes think nothing good in culture that shows up in Paris every really leaves. It stays in some corner of the city, its devotees dancing attendance forever," said Sophie, her face both positive and visionary.

"Yeah. Today, I wanted you to get a chance to listen to Isaac, the tenor-sax guy out there. You just don't hear someone this good very often anymore." Jim looked up just as the saxophonist started a solo. "Here he goes…"

Figure 5 Jason Kingsley and Isaac Narell busking on the bridge at Ile St-Louis, Paris.

Sophie sat and listened, taking in the melancholy notes as they wafted across the still afternoon air. "I see what you mean."

"Yes, the saxophone is almost like a human voice that sings the emotional harmonies to the bittersweet in life, to all the little might-have-beens of the modern journey, its losses, its joys..." said Jim wistfully as he watched the tenor-sax man glide through his solo.

"Yes, I can see. Jazz speaks to you," said Sophie.

The last notes died away in the hushed air. "Here, let me get you a glass of wine," said Jim. He pulled two plastic cups out of a knapsack and then reached further in and pulled a bottle out. He removed the once-opened cork and poured two half glasses. "Nothing's too good for my friends."

She took a sip. "The wine's almost as good as the music," she said, "but not quite."

"Then I got it just right."

Jason stepped forward to his 1940s-style mic, strumming the chords on his guitar and started his vocal. "Why not take all of me...your good-bye...how could I go on without you..." The words drifted across the vast space under the Paris sky, timeless and melancholy.

"The music does take you away to someplace far away in time," said Sophie.

"Yes, it has an authentic sound out here on the bridge. It is so real, not some overproduced, homogenized studio drivel," said Jim. "One of the drawbacks of the new age of mass affluence is everyone is paying top dollar for mass-produced stuff supposedly of 'quality.'"

"You're complaining?"

"No, it's a nice problem to have. But it's nice to get out on the bridge and hear something with the imperfection of originality and the perfection of naturalness."

"Yes, the sky…the openness…" added Sophie as she looked around the wide, open space surrounding the musicians.

"Yes, jazz…it was what I liked best about New York back in the 1990s…and that was decades after the bebop era ended. But there were keepers of the flame even then."

She reached out with her hand and squeezed Jim's left hand in hers. He smiled at her.

Out on the roadway, the music stopped, and Jason gave a little spiel about some CDs for sale. Jim stood up and walked over to the open guitar case and picked out four CDs and dropped forty euros in the open case.

Jason arched an eyebrow and smiled. "Thanks, man," he said in his best New York sideman style. He knew Jim well; he was something of a regular out on Pont St-Louis. Jason looked over at Sophie and said, "You got a new one with you today?"

"Yeah, I always like to bring 'em out here and see if they have the taste to go with their looks," said Jim with a laugh.

"Bet she passes," said Jason, giving Sophie another admiring glance.

"Think you're right," said Jim, and he walked back and gave the CDs to Sophie. "Put 'em in your handbag. Souvenirs from Pont St-Louis."

"Thank you."

"Now we'd better head for dinner. I have reservations down on the island." Jim nodded over at Île St-Louis. He held his hand out and helped Sophie to her feet. He stuffed the two cushions into his knapsack and pointed across the bridge toward the island. They started walking across together, chitchatting as they went.

They walked down rue St-Louis en Île, the long street running down the center of the island. Presently they came up to a restaurant with a gray stone facade and small, rectangular windows set in tall forest-green window frames. Jim opened the door and ushered Sophie in. A maître d' came up, and Jim gave him his name. "*Par ici, monsieur*," he said and turned and smiled at Sophie, "*et madame*." (This way, sir and madam.)

The maître d' held Sophie's chair as she sat down, and then Jim took his seat.

"Delightful," said Sophie, looking around the restaurant. She looked across the table at him, eyes sparkling, pleasure in her expression.

"*Monsieur*? *Du vin*?" asked a waiter as he came up and stood next to the table.

"A bottle of burgundy? Your recommendation?"

The waiter ran his finger down the *carte des vins* and said, "*Celui-ci*?"

"*D'accord*," agreed Jim.

The waiter returned with a bottle, and soon wineglasses were half full of dark red wine. Jim took a long sip. "Good." He looked across at Sophie as she took the tiniest of sips and set the glass down.

"So, have you always been in budgets?" he asked.

"Why, yes. I started as a budget analyst in the Public Works Department for the City of Paris."

"What did you do?"

"Oh, we monitored spending on public-works projects. Paris was undergoing its greatest renewal since the time of Haussmann."

"So, you were in a position to nudge a contract up for a favored contractor, someone connected to the top political guys? A little favor here, a reward there."

Sophie made a little pout and leaned back, sort of pushing her well-rounded bosom forward, and said, "I don't remember nudging any numbers up." She turned on a smoky smile, eyes dark with delight. "I mostly remember kicking them straight to the ceiling."

Instantly, an image formed in Jim's mind of a slender, pointed foot, toes tucked in, on a bare leg, kicking up past overturned bedcovers, satin sheets in disarray, toward a gilded ceiling. She watched with amusement as his expression changed to wonder.

"I had never really seen the joie de vivre in public works before," said Jim, his smile revealing his fascination. "In America,

I always associated public contracts with fat, greasy guys smoking big cigars."

"That's Marseilles," said Sophie, her eyes sparkling with merriment.

Jim laughed at the rejoinder and said, "Chirac was mayor then, wasn't he?"

"Why, yes. He was the great builder prince. Paris was brought forward toward the twenty-first century while maintaining its nineteenth-century charm. He is a man of great taste and excellent judgment."

"Seems to me I read recently that he got convicted after leaving the presidency for having phantom employees on the rolls while at the Hôtel de Ville," Jim said, mentioning the Paris city hall. "Was it that kind of place?"

"No, I thought possibly the judge was making an ironic statement. It was not the employees who were not there, these so-called phantoms," said Sophie with a wistful look, her eyes taking on a warm glow as she remembered back to those years, "but rather the magnificence of the men who were there...with all their pulsating masculinity. They were magnificent—*ils sont magnifiques.*"

"I can see you enjoyed your time at the City of Paris."

"Immensely," she said and smiled mischievously. "I learned a lot, too."

"When not kicking the covers...errh, I mean numbers up to the ceiling..."

She looked directly at Jim and then looked down to the side of the table. She brought her foot out from under the tablecloth; pulled the hem of her skirt up above her knee, revealing a well-shaped leg; and gave it a quick little kick. "Maybe someday," she said as she let the words float across the table toward Jim and followed the words up with a smile to die for.

Whatever *it* was—she had it, thought Jim. "Yes, my interest in government is going in new directions..."

"Someday, but not today," she said, closing off this verbal foray. Jim got a sense that she was truly the master of her own timetable.

A waiter came up and served the dinner dishes and provided a brief explanation. "*Merci, monsieur,*" said Jim. He looked at

Sophie as he picked up his knife and fork. "Well, that takes us back to budgets. So playing with budgets has carried you close to the top. Or did you just make a lot of powerful friends who helped you along the way?"

She took a long sip from her wineglass, set it down, and let the look of exasperation on her face give way to an ironic frown. "Oh, so easy to believe for you men, the playful young woman, with the eyes of a coquette, sleeping her way from one promotion to another."

"I didn't mean to imply—"

"Yes, you did." She looked sidewise at Jim with a playful look of reproach.

"OK..."

"In my now-rather-long career—over twenty years now—I have never, as you might say, 'made friends' with a superior official. *Jamais.* I have never dropped a handkerchief near a minister, as my *grand-mère* would say."

Jim's eyebrows shot up—possibly with disbelief, in astonishment for sure.

"You know so little."

"I do?"

"Over all these years, I have always made friends solely from my peer group, from my age cohort among all the delightful friends I have had inside and outside of government service. Friends from school." She looked at him mischievously. "In that sense, yes, I am a *grande horizontale*," she said, using the French slang term to describe the great coquettes of the past. "I have always chosen my friends from my own level."

Jim smiled at the double entendre and pointed across the table with his fork. "And left some older men frustrated?"

"I don't know about frustrated. There are so many others, women you know, for the older men. But, yes, you could see the consternation cloud their faces. And then I would walk off, hand in hand with some young man who had no sophistication or polish at all but had that great springing enthusiasm that young men have for young women—that desire to please and be pleased." Her face took on a wistful look. "Few ever bore me a grudge."

"OK, I get it. Your career has been the story of one great merit promotion after another in the Fifth Republic. Now tell me what makes a budget specialist so special?"

She took a sip of wine and looked across the table at Jim, her eyes laughing, and recounted, "Let me explain. Whether at the Hôtel de Ville or the Matignon, the dynamic is the same." She collected her thoughts.

Jim interjected, "I keep confusing government with endless spending. But it must have some limit, I suppose."

"Yes, government is the intersection of unlimited aspirations and limited revenues. Let's go forward fifteen years. I was at the Matignon, working for a small budget office in the prime minister's office." The Hôtel de Matignon was the residence and office of the prime minister, who was the head of the government.

"At the Matignon, the prime minster looks down the long conference table in the cabinet room at the assembled ministers; the walls along each side of the room are lined with deputy ministers and senior officials. These are the barons, princes of the political blood, with their own budgets, all with clamoring constituencies—"

"Who want more," added Jim.

"Exactly."

"Sounds medieval."

"It is," said Sophie. "But the prime minister is both appointed and elected to bring change. If he is of the same political party as *le président*, then he was selected to deliver on the change M. Président has promised to the French people."

"And it takes money," said Jim.

"And he doesn't have any, unless he raises taxes. And in France the tax orange has already been squeezed hard. Not a lot of juice left there. And the budget deficits have been way above the three percent allowed by the Maastricht Treaty that created the euro. So if you keep borrowing, you antagonize the Germans— more than they already are."

"So what does the prime minister do?"

"He looks at all the ministers solemnly and discusses the need for change. They all cluck sympathetically. Some will venture that if their departments were given more money, they could deliver some change."

"That doesn't solve his problem," said Jim.

"No. The prime minister has no friends. He needs new money, and none is to be had in the cabinet room. He goes across the river to the Élysée, and M. Président gets impatient with him. They need new money, new money—for the new priorities, the promised programs. The people demand change. The président raps his hand on his huge desk; the drapes quiver."

"So?"

"M. Prime Minister has just one friend, the budget analyst. Only the analyst can deliver new money to him. Only a budget analyst can work this magic."

"So how do you do it?"

"You have deep and detailed knowledge of every line item on the budget, how every program works, what every little department does. At the Matignon, when you are a top analyst you can come up with a billion euros."

"And?"

"You have real power. The prime minister needs you—a lot."

"He does?"

"You are now his trusted colleague."

Sophie looked off into the distance and made a little laugh to herself.

"An inside joke?"

"Sort of, she said. "As the women say—he's no longer looking up your dress."

"So what does the trusted adviser do," said Jim, laughing, "after she tucks her dress under her knees?"

"You give the prime minister a detailed list of areas that can be cut, sometimes entire programs or whole departments. This frees up money that can be redeployed to the new priorities."

"So you just walk in and take away the money from the ministers?"

"No. Again, the prime minister works with the budget analyst and his political aides. A lightning program is decided upon. The cuts are sprung on the ministers all at once. The cabinet room becomes an abattoir. "

"No prisoners?"

"No prisoners. No hostages. The people's interest comes first."

"The ministers have no choice?"

"We line the cabinet table with two binders in front of each cabinet minister. Plan *A* and Plan *B*—straight out of business school, *très Américain*. That way we give the ministers a sense that democratic choice is involved in the process, another American innovation."

"Nevertheless an illusion."

"There is little democracy in representative government."

"The bottom line is always the same?"

"Yes, new money for the new priorities. The ministers are thanked for their understanding."

"No appeal?"

"If explanation is required, the prime minister says in a low voice—he gets the tone just right; the slightest hint of menace is suggested—that the président insists. His displeasure cannot be risked. From that there is no appeal. De Gaulle's monarchal president turns a stony face to all such importuning. Few dare it."

Jim nodded sagely. He was getting it: a French Machiavelli with a Chanel handbag.

They drank coffee and continued chatting about Sophie's experiences in government. Coming to the end of the meal, Jim asked, "Maybe we could walk along the river?"

"Yes, I'd like that. Then I do have to go."

"I could drop you off…if I knew where you lived."

"Oh, I live on Avenue Victor Hugo out in the Sixteenth."

"Nice part of town."

"Oh, the apartment has been in the family since early in the Third Republic. The men have been bankers, for the most part, here in Paris."

"And the women?"

"Ah, now, there is where the tales are to be told," Sophie said brightly. "Some other day, I'm afraid." She batted her eyelashes at him.

River Seine

Later, they walked along the stone quay paralleling the river, past lonely fisherman and entwined lovers. They walked up to a surface street and saw a taxi, and Jim hailed it. In the taxi, Sophie said, *"Cent vingt-quatre, avenue Victor Hugo."*

"Oui, madame," replied the driver. The taxi sped off into the traffic. The taxi went up the boulevards of the Sixteenth, past the elegant nineteenth-century apartment buildings with their well-balconied stone facades and intricate ironwork. The taxi swung left onto Avenue Victor Hugo and came up toward a belle epoque apartment building on the right side of the street and swung into a parking lane.

Sophie craned her neck, looking up the facade of the building, and said, "Oh, good, the lights are on. Marie-Hélène is home."

"Who is Marie-Hélène?" asked Jim.

"My daughter. She's been staying at a girlfriend's this afternoon."

"I wasn't aware you were married?"

"Oh, yes. That's somewhat in the past—the marriage that is. He's a *préfet* in western France, near Nantes. He is on temporary exile from Paris."

"The marriage? An interlude on your journey between the City of Paris and the finance ministry?"

"Yes, but I would say more than an interlude," said Sophie with a smile. "A period of self-discovery, I might say. It was hard to settle into a marriage when my career at work was taking off. And I did not want to leave Paris; I never had much interest in going to the provinces, which my husband saw as his route to higher office." She paused and sat quietly for a moment and then continued. "Possibly he did not equally share my aspirations for advancement..." She let the words trail away.

"Yes..." mumbled Jim.

She grabbed his hand and held it in both of hers. "I so liked this evening. I would like to return the favor. Next Sunday I'm driving out to Auverne to see my grand-mère. You could come with me. We could make a day of it. If you're in Paris, that is."

"I'll plan on it. Auverne? It's a place, too?"

"Yes, that's the name of our little village. Our château is just outside. We've been there for centuries, since before the time of Louis Quatorze," she said, mentioning the seventeenth-century Sun King.

"That's a long time."

"We were Norman before we were French. The château is in Normandy. I'll have you back in Paris Sunday evening. You won't miss your Monday business appointments."

"Yes, I'd love to go."

"Good." The taxi driver had come around and opened the door. Sophie leaned over and kissed Jim on each cheek and then turned and got out. She walked over to the large double wooden doors, punched the key code, and pushed on the door at the faint sound of a buzzer. She turned and waved back at Jim. Then she was gone.

10. Nice

Jack Hawkins, Bermuda Triangle's British partner, walked along the treelined streets of Central Nice, past a five-star hotel, and up a street of tall apartment buildings in the Golden Triangle section of the fabled Riviera city. Coming to the doorway in front of an apartment house, he looked at the directory in the entranceway and pushed one of the buttons. The door lock buzzed, and he pushed the door open. He was expected.

He walked over and pushed the button for the elevator. He listened to the elevator descend, and the doors slid open. Stepping inside, he punched the button for the fifth floor and watched the door close and the elevator ascend toward the top. When it stopped, he exited and went over to a door and pushed the buzzer. The door opened, and a man in his late sixties opened it. He was dressed in nice slacks and a dress shirt.

"Marc Lanthier?" asked Jack.

"Yes, *c'est moi*," replied the man. "*Entrez*," he said as he stood aside and swept his arm into the hallway to usher Jim inside the apartment. "Here, let's go into the drawing room," he said, and he guided Jack toward a well-windowed room facing out over the street far below.

"So you want to know about Sophie d'Auverne," said the man named Marc.

"Yes, we're just doing some routine background work. We have retained her company, Strategic Intelligence International, to advise our investment partnership on the Greek debt restructuring and other European finance matters."

"I didn't know she was there. But she probably had to wind up somewhere after the election, the change in governments."

"Well, yes. That's sort of our difficulty. There's not a lot of background information on her, the kind you'd check into if she had been in the private sector. She's been in the French government up until just a few weeks ago."

"Fine, I really haven't seen much of her in years, except to say hello here and there. I knew her when she was a young woman, working for the City of Paris."

"Yes, could you tell me about that?" said Jack.

"She came in from Sciences Po—strong background."

"Yes, but hadn't she studied elsewhere?"

"Well, yes. She went abroad for languages and knew something about computers."

"What were her first assignments?"

"She was in budgeting, one way or another, the whole time she was with the city. She was quite good at it. She progressed up the ladder quickly."

"She is quite attractive. Did this...errh...help her in some ways?"

Marc laughed and said, "I can see how you might think that. But no, not in the way you think."

"In what way, then?"

"She was vivacious...had lots of friends...plenty of boyfriends, but they were all her own age and at her own level in the bureaucracy or out in the banks and professional firms...never any older men—not that many didn't try."

"Interesting. What do you think was behind that?"

"Like I said, she was talented. I think she wanted to advance on her own merits, and she made that clear through her behavior...so professionally accomplished, no doubt about it."

"Any other secrets to her success?"

"She was hardworking, the best prepared person in the room—always. Those older men came to rely on her—a lot—for her professional advice. Budgeting always involves painful choices, difficult trade-offs. She had answers and recommendations, imaginative recommendations in a world of gray, bureaucratic advice."

"Yes, that would do it. Her reports to us have been crisp, on point, and complete."

"Yes, I imagine they would be. Let me tell you a story. Our department was having a little dinner over at Le Polidor on the Left Bank. The department head was there and a lot of other people. There was plenty of wine and talk. And there was some banter, and the younger men were teasing Sophie about whether she wanted to go out to a château, to a soiree like the one in the *Story of O*." He was referring to the famous erotic novel about sex and bondage written by the mistress of one of France's great public intellectuals in the 1950s. "And this was all sort of playful."

"Playful?" said Jack, making a mental note.

"Yes, playful is a good word," said Marc, connecting with a pleasant memory. "Well, Sophie stood up, took the arm of that night's young man—the winner you might say—and started to leave. She turned back and said to the other young men, 'Fine. But for the soiree, I have my rules: no collars, no cuffs. I pick the toys.' Well, she just bowled those young men over, and the department head sat there, with his mouth agape, and had eyes like saucers." Marc laughed lightly in remembrance.

"Yes, I can imagine the vivacity, if not the electricity, in the room. She has a dazzling presence."

"Well, you asked me about her professionally. She was brilliant at budgeting," said Marc as he paused and guffawed, "but simply a genius at marketing. People spoke about her for weeks after that at the Hôtel de Ville."

"And the young men?"

"I spoke to several. They all liked her, even after she let them go. One told me that he went to a café to meet her and she explained that she was one her way to Auverne—her family has a château out there—and that for now maybe it was over between them. She said that she really enjoyed it, liked the good times, but she was not going to get serious, no matter how appealing the man was...you know the story."

"Yeah."

"She was really good at it, had a lot of practice. Each young man I spoke with was only a little bit sad about having been, as she said, 'set free.' I guess she always did these things in an afternoon, on her way to Auverne. It was sort of a ritual with her."

"Intriguing," said Jack. He stood up. "I better not take any more of your time."

"That's fine. My wife's out shopping. Retirement is a little slow, you know?"

"Actually, I can't wait to find out," said Jack. "A little place on the Riviera..."

Hotel Negresco

That night, Jack Hawkins sent an encrypted e-mail to Jim through Bermuda Triangle's server hub: "Prelim backgrounder OK...excellent at budgeting...string of merit promotions...vivacious career...all associations with young men her own age...avoided older men...let the young men down one-by-one...always at a meeting on her way to family château at Auverne...source said it was like a ritual to her...source full of affectionate admiration for her years later."

11. Auverne

A sleek white BMW pulled up in front of the hotel. A brightly smiling Sophie waved at Jim from behind the windscreen. A doorman hastened over to the car and opened the passenger door for Jim while Sophie popped the rear bonnet. The doorman went around to the back of the car and put Jim's bag in the trunk and pushed the bonnet down, making a loud click. The doorman walked back around, and Jim handed him a tip. Jim slid into the passenger seat. The doorman closed the door and then stood back and watched the car depart down the drive and merge into the traffic.

"So nice you could join me for a day at Auverne. We can lunch with Grand-mère."

"I'm sure I will be delighted," said Jim. "You said last time that your family has been at Auverne for a long time?"

"Yes, the château was built around the time of Henry IV, at a time when France truly became a modern nation, the most powerful in Europe. The château replaced a turreted Norman castle, really a fort. The family was, as we say in French, *noblesse d'epée*—nobility of the sword."

"And the estate?"

"Once, it was quite large and provided a princely income from rents. But that was centuries ago. It's much smaller today; just barely enough rents to maintain the château. For the past couple of centuries, the men—I call them *mes grand-péres*—have mostly been bankers in Paris. But the men still have a right to wear a sword," she said with a laugh.

"A sword? The past couple of centuries?" mumbled Jim, somewhat amazed at the sweep of time Sophie's statement covered. "So you went into finance?"

"Why yes—it was that or join my father in the bank."

"You did not want to work with your father?"

55

"No, it wasn't that. My mother was really his partner. As for the bank itself, there are a lot of cousins in the bank. They mostly run it. We've had the château; they've had the bank."

"And your father?"

"He died last year. Neither Grand-mère nor *Maman* have really gotten over it."

"So your family's no longer involved with the bank?"

"No, my mother continues on the board. Someday I will take her place."

"Your grand-mère was not involved in the bank?"

"Ah, no...she made her mark in Paris in other spheres—the salons and...how do I say it...social things. Yes, social things. She was stunningly attractive." She glanced over at Jim and smiled. "Still is."

"She must have been truly stunning, with that compliment coming from you."

"Why, thank you. How gallant."

They continued down the autoroute, skirting the outskirts of Caen, and continued west, just a half a dozen miles or so inland from the famous landing beaches at Normandy. Halfway to Bayeux, Sophie turned off the autoroute onto a country road heading toward the sea. After a couple miles, she turned down a small lane shaded by large plane trees, until they came to two stone pylons, on which were embedded weatherworn, cast-iron plaques inscribed with the name Auverne. Sophie turned into the gravel drive and headed a couple hundred yards up to the house, a beautiful stone two-story country château with a steeply pitched roof covered with gray slate tiles. Sophie parked the car to the side of the forecourt. They got out and walked over to the portico. There was another cast-iron plate, inscribed with Latin words, over the top of the door.

"It says 'fidelity and loyalty under this roof,' in Latin," said Sophie. "It's a family motto."

Presently an older woman in a housedress and apron opened the door and stood aside as Sophie and Jim entered.

"Joséphine, let me introduce my guest, Jim Schiller."

"*Enchantée*," said the woman.

"She's the housekeeper for Grand-mère.*"

56

The housekeeper hugged Sophie and said, "She's in the main hall waiting for you."

Jim and Sophie walked into the foyer, and Sophie guided Jim to the right, into a big, spacious room with massive open beams crossing the space. A large stone fireplace was at one end, with a small fire burning down to embers in it. A much-older lady stood up from a large chair and came forward.

Jim could see she was slender, but she stood quite erect, with square shoulders. She was wearing a nice black sweater, a gray skirt, and black pumps with dark stockings. Her gray hair was pulled back into a bun. She approached and stood before Sophie and Jim.

"May I present Inès d'Auverne, *ma* grand-mère," said Sophie.

"*Enchanté*," said Jim, and he reached out and shook her hand.

"*Enchantée*," replied Grand-mère with a welcoming smile. She swept her arm toward a chair and said, "*Asseyez-vous*." (Sit down.)

Jim sat down. Sophie took a chair next to him; Grand-mère sat in another chair across from them. She turned to Sophie and said, "Before we start, I wish you'd speak with Emile while you're here. He keeps nagging me to hire those Russian gardeners for daywork, and I tell him you said no."

"Don't worry, Grand-mère; I'll have a word with Emile and mention it to Joséphine. She knows how to keep Emile in line." Sophie turned to Jim. "Problems with the help. If I'm not here, things get a little off track."

"I understand," said Jim, knowingly. "It's worse in Geneva."

Sophie nodded in agreement and turned to her grandmother. "This is my business friend, Jim Schiller. We work together on projects in Paris."

"Were you in the government, too?"

"No, I'm an American. I run a little investment company in Geneva, bonds and things."

"As for the government, I remember...Paris...the Third Republic. I was old, and it was young..."

"No, Grand-mère, the Third Republic was old, and you were quite young."

"Oh, yes, these things get turned around as you get older," she said and smiled at Jim. "My time was the Fourth Republic...and then I had a brief renaissance during the Fifth...it's still the Fifth, isn't it, Sophie?"

"Yes, Grand-mère."

"I was close friends with Claude Pompidou, the wife of the prime minister, later le président. I went with her to fittings at Coco's little shop on rue Cambon. It was a grand life. We knew Pompidou when he was just a simple banker at Rothschild."

"Your family bank was close to the Rothschilds?" asked Jim.

"Well, we were close with everyone then," she said. "That counted." She smiled contentedly at her memories. She turned to Sophie and asked, "So you may go back into government? Why?"

"The UMP wants representation at the European Union level by someone who has detailed budgeting and fiscal knowledge. It looks like the European Union is going to implement a broad fiscal authority across the Eurozone to coordinate the spending levels of the member states. It's all quite German. They are implementing a Europe of rules."

"Oh, last time it was going to be a Europe of jackboots," said Grand-mère, and she looked at Jim and joked, "I can see it now. The Germans will line up all those rules in formation and then goose-step them past the reviewing stand in front of the new Iron Chancellor in Nuremberg."

"Frankfurt, Grand-mère, it will be in Frankfurt, home of the European Central Bank—"

"European Central Bank? Oh, that's just a front for the Bundesbank, the capital of the new Fourth Reich," Grand-mère said. She turned to Jim and whispered conspiratorially, "That's what the Greeks call it—the Fourth Reich. It must be true; I saw it on television, state TV. They only lie about politics in France, never Europe."

Jim laughed.

"Possibly we can speak about that at lunch, Grand-mère. For now, I thought I would show Jim the library. I want to get some things from there and take them back to Paris. Then we can have lunch."

"That would be fine. Let me go out to the kitchen and get Joséphine started on lunch. I'll meet you in the dining room later." Grand-mère stood up, as did Jim and Sophie. Grand-mère looked at Jim and said emphatically, "Then we'll talk."

"I look forward to it," replied Jim.

"This way, Jim," said Sophie, guiding him back to the foyer where a grand staircase led up to the second floor. They walked up the stairway together, Jim admiring the tapestries hanging on the wall.

"They're scenes copied from the famous Bayeux Tapestry; they're only three or four hundred years old."

"Great. I'm an admirer of modern art...and your grandmother's great wit. I'm sure Paris hasn't quite been the same since she left."

"Since they all left," said Sophie. "Hers was an age of elegant style and rapier-like wit."

At the top of the stairwell, Sophie pointed him toward the library, a large room at the back of the house. Jim entered and walked over to the tall windows overlooking a large garden, extending out to a park-like forest beyond.

"After lunch, we'll take a walk through the garden. It's done in the classic French style. Right now let me show you the library." She pointed to the floor-to-ceiling bookshelves lined with old and crusty books. "Some of these go back to the time of Louis Quatorze. The history of France is on these shelves."

Jim looked at a large leather-bound notebook over on a big wooden table. The table is not more than a couple hundred years old, Jim said to himself. The table sat next to another bookshelf full of volumes bound in deep purple cloth, all with similar gold-leaf titles but different years and volume numbers. Apparently it was a long-running series of books. He walked over and fingered the leather-bound notebook on the table.

"Those are Grand-mère's memoirs. They're awaiting publication."

"When will that be?"

"After she dies. They're published posthumously. It's the tradition."

Jim looked at the cover of the notebook, on which there was a beautifully affixed parchment, and he read aloud the title, *La Mémoire de la vicomtesse Inès d'Auverne*. Then, pointing to the volumes on the adjacent bookcase, Jim asked, "And those?"

"Those are the memoirs of all who have gone before her. After Grand-mère passes on, we will know the years of her life, and she will, of course, be the next volume." Sophie nodded, indicating where the volume would sit on the bookshelf.

"How many copies are published?"

"A limited number, usually a couple hundred. The family is now quite large, plus favored patrons of the bank and some for collectors and the libraries."

"You're not just the local landowners. Your family was the local aristocracy?"

"Well, yes. *Le vicomté*—the viscountcy, which, of course, encompasses *un vicomte et une vicomtesse*. The title goes back before the château."

Jim walked over and eyed the dozens of volumes of memoirs all written by *les vicomtesses* over the centuries; the books' physical presence opened up the imagination to the potentialities of centuries of history, causing him to wonder at what these women's lives might have been like.

"Let me leave you here for a moment while I get some things," said Sophie.

"Yes, fine," replied Jim, and he turned back to the bookshelf and looked slowly over the titles, all similar except for the beautiful parade of different women's first names in the titles—Mathilde, Diane, Catherine, Madeleine, Thérèse, and compound names featuring the ever-present Marie. They were all quite French.

He listened to Sophie rustle in the closet and open what sounded like a small wall safe. Presently she came out with a small jewelry case, and she walked over and put it in her handbag. She said to Jim, "It's a necklace. I don't want to leave it out here during a time when there might be many strangers in the house. I need to put it someplace secure."

"Yes, I understand," said Jim.

"Good," she said. "Time for lunch. Let's go down and join Grand-mère in the dining room."

The two of them walked side by side down the staircase, and Sophie guided him past the drawing room to a large dining room with a long, dark wooden table, the surface polished to a high gloss. At the head of the table sat Grand-mère. Sophie took a seat to her left, Jim to the right. Joséphine came around and poured an aperitif in small wineglasses set above each place setting.

"I was showing Jim the memoirs," said Sophie.

"Yes, good," replied Grand-mère. She turned to Jim. "The memoirs detail the lives of the Auverne women, mostly their times in Paris, over the centuries and their affairs and doings with some of the most distinguished and interesting men of the different eras."

"Sounds fascinating," said Jim with genuine interest.

"Yes," said Grand-mère somewhat dreamily, remembering back over the centuries and possibly from her own experiences. "You would drop a perfumed handkerchief in a salon and see which minister would spring to pick it up," she said, "so to speak." She smiled thinly at Jim.

"Ah, the eternal dance," said Jim.

"Yes, but one wearies of it after a time. I think in past centuries it might have been more passionate, the attractions stronger," reflected Grand-mère. "Everyone was younger in those times. In my own time, as I got older, by the time the men reached the heights of distinction, their handsomeness was often left far behind...if not their ardor. One's husband develops a new allure...his attentiveness to you rather than yours to some man..."

"So you returned with your husband to Auverne? To write your memoirs?" asked Jim.

Grand-mère frowned, and then she looked at him solemnly and, with a faint smile breaking on her face, said, "Yes, the tradition in the memoirs is to be frank. That's why they're published posthumously." She looked around the room contentedly; she spoke as the chatelaine of all she surveyed, commanding the deference of her age and position.

"Must be a fascinating commentary on how life was lived in Paris over the years," said Jim.

"Centuries," corrected Grand-mère. "Yes, each volume is full of instruction. Each generation of Auverne girls is carefully schooled in these lessons. They need to understand the role of flirtation and intrigue, the power of the dalliance, submission as a tool of dominance—in short the immense power of calculating women in a world of lustful men incapable of doing their sums while looking for their next fornication."

Jim laughed and said jocularly, "You must have met investment bankers during your long life?" He looked at her with an amused smile on his face. "Sounds like a Manhattan dinner party in a bull market?"

"All kinds of bankers, thank you," replied Grand-mère. "That's what the Auverne women have been mostly married to—after the rents could no longer support us out here in the grand style that we were accustomed to and we had to go into trade to maintain our station." This epochal event was said with an inherited distaste, obviously passed down from mother to daughter for a couple of centuries, or so Jim thought. Grand-mère turned to Sophie and inquired, "By the way, are you working with your mother on her memoirs?"

"Here and there, when I'm down in Aix for a visit."

"Shouldn't take much effort," said Grand-mère. Turning to Jim, she explained, "It should be a short book. Martine—Sophie's mother—only went to Paris in the company of her husband." She rolled her eyes at the naïveté of it all. She turned to Sophie. "I would think you could do your mother's memoirs in a long weekend."

Sophie came to her mother's defense, speaking directly across the table to Jim: "My mother was devoted to my father and he to her. Their stars never wandered. They did not wait for retirement to Auverne to begin their wedded bliss of fidelity and loyalty. They lived it together from the moment of their wedding vows."

"Remarkable," said Jim, truly astonished.

Sophie turned to Grand-mère. "I think my mother liberated herself from four centuries of tradition," she said, her eyes boring in on Grand-mère, "and expectation."

"Well, she wasn't of the blood," sniffed Grand-mère. "She married into it."

Jim looked at Sophie with a deeper sense of appreciation. Sophie looked across the table at him and continued, "Marie-Hélène adores my mother as she did my father. That's what she thinks married life should be. You can imagine that is a great comfort to me as a mother with a daughter about to become a teenager."

"Yes," said Jim in simple agreement.

"Speaking of your mother," Grand-mère continued. "How is life down at the farm?"

Sophie rolled her eyes and turned to Jim and explained, "What Grand-mère calls the farm is a beautiful, old stone country house. My father and mother bought it before I was born."

"Well, yes, it is *une belle maison*," admitted Grand-mère. "Some nice landscapes hang on the walls, too."

"The nice landscapes are Cézannes," said Sophie with a hint of wry exasperation.

"Yes, my son had an eye for value," said Grand-mère. "He got to them before all these collectors, the parvenus in London and New York." She brightened and asked, "Speaking of family, how is dear Marie-Hélène?"

"She is with her father down in Nantes for a couple of weeks."

Grand-mère turned to Jim and said, "She truly loves her father and really likes her stepmother and two little stepbrothers."

"Well, yes," said Sophie. "She really liked my parents—her grandparents. Going to visit her grandmother in Aix is one of her great delights. And my ex-husband and his family are just like them."

"Yes, my darling boy," said Grand-mère softly, and she looked off across the room, her eyes misty with remembered affection for her only son. She turned to Jim and confessed, "Martine captured a corner of his heart that I never could."

"How could you? You were always in Paris in those years when he was growing up," said Sophie somewhat waspishly. "Dropping handkerchiefs, I believe."

Jim sat silently for a few moments and let the family tempest pass. He turned and said to Sophie, "You seem to get on quite well with your ex-husband?"

"Well, yes, we simply came to a parting of the ways because I had little interest in supporting his political career and giving up mine to go to the provinces."

Grand-mère broke in. "He completely misunderstood Sophie. He saw her parents', in particular her mother's, unconditional support for her father's banking career. He thought he was marrying the daughter of Sophie's mother and that he would float along on a cloud of wifely support."

Sophie took on a look of resignation; she knew what was coming.

"Instead," said Grand-mère triumphantly, "he married the granddaughter of Grand-mère, a true Auverne."

"Well, yes, but things change. I'm coming up to a certain age myself, now. Time for Auverne."

"Well, you did motherhood with the first husband. You could try for happiness with the next one." Grand-mère smiled at Sophie and then turned to Jim and said, "Modern women these days are so lucky. They get two bites of the apple. I, and all the other Auverne women over these centuries, had to make one apple do two duties."

"Nevertheless, a magnificent journey," gallantly said Jim.

"And with that," said Sophie, and she turned to Grand-mère, "let me take Jim for a tour of the garden and park." She stood up and said to her grandmother, "We'll have a glass of port with you before returning to Paris."

She headed for the foyer, and Jim followed. Sophie led him through the foyer and up to two double doors opening out onto the garden. She opened one of the doors and stepped outside onto a broad stone porch on the same level as the floor of the manor house. From here a stone *allée* went straightaway out to a distant gate leading to the forested park beyond. The garden was terraced into three succeeding *parterres*, with steps leading up to each level in succession.

"It is within the classic tradition of a *jardin à la française*," said Sophie. "Not as ornate as an Italian garden but geometric within the French tradition."

"The stone walls have been here a long time?" asked Jim, looking at the ancient limestone blocks used to set off each *parterre*.

"Several centuries at least."

"The grounds are immaculate. Almost barbered," said Jim.

"Emile, Joséphine's husband, keeps the grounds. He is getting older, and I will eventually have to get him some more help. But I would prefer someone from the village, someone who would stay for decades. That has been our tradition."

"Yes, I'm sure that would be the best way. Has it always been so well kept?"

"No, it ran to seed during the war. *Grand-père* and Grand-mère were in Algiers then. Since the war, Grand-mère has seen to the garden's repair and improvement. Other than men, it has been her one true fascination."

Jim looked across the beautiful, sculpted space, the gray lines of the walls contrasting with the bright green of the lawns on the *parterres*.

"Let's walk out to the gate and look at the park," said Sophie.

"By all means."

They started to walk. As they crossed each terrace, they stopped and looked up and down the *parterre*, the green lawns neatly cut by gravel paths. Reaching the far gate, Sophie opened it, and they stepped through to the other side. She swept her arm across the wooded space, pointing toward the tall trees, the wild underbrush, and here and there grassy openings, too small to be called meadows.

"That is what is left of the once-wild woods that characterized the entire Normandy countryside."

Jim looked at the small forest and remarked, "It is a nice counterpoint to the manicure of the garden."

Sophie laughed and said, "Yes, I think you're right." She stayed still for a couple moments; then she noticed Emile out of the corner of her eye, standing and talking to two men—the Russian gardeners, she presumed. She turned to Jim and said, "Let me go have a word with Emile about the Russian gardeners. They are not needed, and I don't like strangers around the *maison* beyond our trusted help."

"I understand," said Jim.

She walked over toward Emile while Jim turned and swept his gaze over the entire landscape, the forest to one side, the beautiful symmetry of the garden on the other. Surveying the estate, he almost felt like an Auverne. He smiled to himself, his thoughts touching on a future with Sophie—he'd get all this and a marriage to an Auverne woman, too.

Presently, Sophie walked back, put her arm through Jim's, and said, "We better get back. Say good-bye to Grand-mère, and head back to Paris."

Jim nodded, and they turned and walked back to the château. Once inside the manor house, they went into the drawing room, and Grand-mère was sitting in a chair by a table, with three small wineglasses and a decanter of port. Sophie and Jim walked down and took seats on either side of Grand-mère. Sophie reached over to the coffee table and poured three glasses of port and handed one to her grandmother and one to Jim.

"*A votre santé*," said Grand-mère to Jim.

Jim raised his glass in salute and said, "The pleasure is all mine, madame."

"Inès," she replied, "*s'il vous plait.*"

"*Merci*," replied Jim.

Turning to Sophie, Grand-mère asked, "You're now working for a big consultancy? You could have gone to the bank?"

"I don't think now is the time for it. You might say I am active in a government in exile out at La Défense. There will be time for the bank later in life, I think."

"Do you plot your return to government service from this exile, my dear?"

"Yes, it is looking that way. The UMP has plans for me."

"Yes, with the European Union, you explained. That won't be in Paris, will it?" asked Grand-mère.

"No. Most of the time will be in Brussels, with the odd week in Strasbourg," Sophie answered. Strasbourg was home to the European Parliament one week a month; Brussels was home for the remainder of the month. Brussels was also the home of the European Union bureaucracy, the center of power in the supranational bureaucratic state.

"So, an Auverne will become a Eurocrat in Brussels rather than a woman of fashion in Paris," said Grand-mère with a sigh. She looked at Jim and asked, "Do you think that is a step up, Jim?"

"Undoubtedly. Sophie will conquer new fields of influence," said Jim.

"I hadn't thought of it that way. Times change and so must an Auverne woman."

"I'm so glad you're seeing it that way, Grand-mère," said Sophie. She looked at Jim with admiration for his reply.

Grand-mère said, a bright note in her voice, "Ah, if you're in Brussels, you can visit the money."

Jim looked perplexed by the statement. He looked at Sophie, thinking, what was that all about?

She looked back at Jim and explained, "My father set up a family foundation in Belgium. Favorable tax rules. He pioneered this strategy—now called expatriation of wealth—while at the bank. It is popular with his clients, but we try to keep it quiet. Or next you'll have movie actors and such moving to Belgium…attracting public attention to what is best left in the shadows."

"I understand," said Jim. "Public scrutiny is never a friend of well-heeled privilege."

"For an American, you are sort of wise," said Grand-mère.

Sophie nodded indulgently at her grandmother.

"Speaking of wisdom, Paris is different from Auverne," continued Grand-mère to Jim. "Here we live under our family motto." Her eyes turned lively, and she said, rather saucily, "But under other roofs there are other rules."

"So I am beginning to gather," said Jim.

Sophie made a deep sigh and said, "Maybe we'd better save 'other roofs and other rules' for another day; Jim and I need to get on the road to Paris. He'll find out about the other rules soon enough." She stood up.

Grand-mère stood up and shook Jim's hand. "Possibly I will get to see you again?"

"I hope so, Inès," replied Jim.

She turned to Sophie and said, "Possibly you might think about dropping a handkerchief, my dear." She winked at Jim.

Sophie laughed, and she took Jim's hand and said, "*Allons-y.*" (Let's go.) As they walked out to the car, Sophie whispered to Jim, "But not today."

Hidden Eyes

In a cheap, rented room behind an old farm couple's house, just outside of Caen, two Russians plugged in their laptop and sent off an encrypted e-mail to Moscow: "Subject visited château today. Had a well-dressed American with her. She came with her handbag and left with the handbag; possibly object is in handbag. Subject firmly told French gardener that he could not hire us to work on château. She looked at us with suspicion, seems unusually guarded. French gardener says she is out of character. Normally friendly and outgoing. Probably has object in her possession."

12. Dinner in the Bois

The sleek blue Jaguar glided along the Allée de Longchamp through the grassy urban forest of the Bois de Boulogne in the fading twilight of a golden summer day. The car pulled up to the entrance in front of the restaurant La Grande Cascade, a belle epoque jewel set in the forested splendor of the vast urban park to the northwest of Paris. The chauffeur got out and came around and opened the door, and Sophie d'Auverne alighted. Jim followed. He nodded thanks to his driver and escorted Sophie up the steps and into the reception area, with its regal aura of deep red carpeting and dark wood paneling. He gave his name to the maître d' in an undertone: "Schiller."

"This way," said the maître d', picking up two menus and a wine list. He led the couple across the chandeliered dining room to a small table next to tall windows looking out on a gardened terrace.

"Serene," said Sophie. "The light is perfect at this time of day," she said, remarking on the soft dove-gray light coming through the windows. "I love summer in Paris."

"Yes, a real romance to it," said Jim as he scanned the wine list. He asked, "Any preference?"

"I think it is for monsieur to choose."

"I doubt if I have the sophistication to make such a weighty decision."

"A Bordeaux will go with most dishes."

Jim raised a finger, and a waiter came over. *"Une bouteille de Bordeaux, sil vous plait."*

"Bien sûr, monsieur."

The waiter went away and brought back a bottle of wine; he swiftly uncorked it in one fluid motion and, like a ballet dancer, pirouetted through the wine ritual. Sophie watched with delight as Jim made a comical pantomime of sniffing and tasting his way to approval. With a flourish, the waiter filled Sophie's glass halfway and said, "Madame." He refilled Jim's glass and put the bottle into a small bucket at the side of the table.

Sophie looked over the top of the glass at Jim with inquisitive eyes, while she took a small sip, her expression inviting conversation.

"I enjoyed visiting your grandmother at Auverne last Sunday," he said.

"Yes, she liked you a lot..." said Sophie. "As do I." Sophie paused and looked thoughtful for a moment. "But I must say that I am not dropping any handkerchiefs...just yet."

"But there is hope?"

She smiled at him invitingly but said nothing.

"Yes, now," said Jim, clearing his throat. "I actually invited you to dinner to discuss some business things...among other hopes."

"We have a meeting of the minds."

"You have been a high-level budget specialist. If I may say, I sense you are marking time at Strategy International...just what is your next step?"

"We presume that the UMP will come back into political power, possibly sooner than many expect."

"You don't think the Socialists will sustain their support?"

"Stagnation—or worse—is the most likely short-term outcome. They don't have the money to maintain employment. They are unlikely to make the structural changes soon enough or deep enough to generate new changes. Sarkozy tried and was stymied."

"What do you think is the key to improving France's economic performance?"

"Structural change, particularly in the labor markets. But remember that new jobs from structural change are something of a mirage; it takes a lot of time for policy changes to have a positive impact."

"Structural change is not your specialty."

"True. But structural change requires that budget money be freed up from other uses to support the social costs of the dislocations created by structural change—people lose their jobs. Public costs go up. That is where the budget specialist plays a key role. A euro can only be at one place at a time."

"Is that where you see your future role?"

"Possibly. But an entirely new level is emerging in Europe, what is called a European-wide fiscal authority to coordinate the overall level of public spending across the European Union."

"I've been reading about that—the 'integrated budgetary framework' seems to be the buzzword."

"Yes, the framework would do two things: first, it would ensure sound budgets at both the national and European levels..."

"And second?"

"The second step is the good one...a process to identify unsustainable budget 'developments' at the national level. This step would provide never-before-seen scrutiny of national budgets by Brussels...and with scrutiny goes power."

"And the national-level politicians—the French deputies, the German bundestaggers—are going to just go along and approve this cut in their authority?"

"They will have much less say in this change than they—and you—think."

Jim laughed and asked, "What is the goal?"

"Eventually, a common Eurozone budget."

"That's a lot of power," said Jim softly.

"Yes, it is," replied Sophie.

"OK, in the world of money and banking, we have Draghi as the money czar at the top of the European Central Bank. So now we're also going to have a fiscal boss? Some high-level Dr. No?"

"No, I don't think so. No one person. One personality seems to work with monetary policy—Draghi and your Ben Bernanke. For monetary creation—a truly magical act in the modern world—one sorcerer seems best or the elf-like Alan Greenspan, who spoke in riddles. But spending is almost always rooted deep into the parliamentary process."

"Why?"

"Spending is just crucial to elected politicians. It is the center of their lives."

"The mother's milk of politics."

Sophie brightened. "Another great Americanism. But quite true. No sorcery here. The politicians will want a representative process, lots of participation, lots of negotiation. So some sort of commission is most likely."

"How will that work?"

"National budgets will be mediated at the European level. A new fiscal authority will be created that will have influence comparable to the monetary authority exercised by the European Central Bank."

"Centralized Eurozone budget controls?"

"Yes, precisely."

"And your role?"

"There will be two new areas where experienced fiscal experts can serve. One is to represent your country in negotiations with the European fiscal authority. The other, of course, is to work for the European fiscal authority—be part of the new Brussels bureaucracy."

"And the fiscal authority will consist of?"

"A cadre of elected officials—possibly from the European Parliament—with lots of staff experts—the process will involve continuous negotiation...detail after detail..."

"But no maestro?"

"No one is quite sure. There is talk about a big, new job in Brussels—lots of prestige."

"And with prestige goes authority."

"Exactly. Such an individual might head up the commission, provide a public face."

"Interesting. So you would be a staff expert for the commission?"

"Possibly. But there is talk by the UMP that I should move to the political side. There will be great demand for elected officials with deep expertise in budgeting and budget negotiations, both in the European Parliament and on the commission, which might be drawn from the Parliament."

"That would be exciting."

"Yes, it would—I would be in the center of a powerful, new institution crucial to the success of the new Europe. It would be good for both France and for women. No more dropping handkerchiefs in the salons," she said and laughed. "We'd be at the table."

"Possibly at the top of the table," said Jim.

"Soon," said Sophie, and she made an uncharacteristically demure smile.

The waiter brought up the dinner plates, smoothly laid them on the table, provided a brief explanation of the food offered, and asked if there was anything else they needed.

"Looks delicious," said Sophie. "So you can see that I'm not really much help about whether a speculator should go long or short some bond," she said as she took a bite.

"We see ourselves as investors," said Jim.

"So you said. But on the Continent there are just Anglo-Saxon speculators and, of course, the bond vigilantes."

"Bond vigilantes? I thought those guys were out in California…losing money on the wrong calls?" said Jim.

"Possibly they're just early. The threat of the vigilantes causes great nervousness within the highest echelons of government. If their thinking came to dominate…"

"Well, we at Bermuda Triangle try to stay on the speculator side of things. Dieter says there's no real signal on future interest rates, just a maze of crosscurrents—what he calls the data fog."

"Well, yes, you should stay on the speculator side of the street. The politicians can always buy off the speculators—that's what we think will happen this fall with the Greek bonds. The Europeans will pay a good price for a way out of the Greek bond imbroglio. That allows the politicians to solve the crisis for now, and the speculators make a lot of money."

"But we do put a lot of capital into those decrepit sovereign-bond markets."

"That is why you are tolerated, even welcomed."

"And the bond vigilantes?"

"Another kettle of fish," said Sophie. "They scare the governments. You can't buy them off. You have to cut the public budgets. Austerity is imposed by the great, worldwide money markets."

"Yes, the bond market has all the power, according to Bill Clinton's sidekick Jim Carville."

"Yes," said Sophie. "Carville is interesting to me—that a political hired gun could give voice to the great economic truth of our era. He has remarkable insight; he is another of the founding fathers of modern cowboy capitalism."

"Maybe that's why Clinton became president?"

"Agreed. Being on the right side of voters' minds about economics and jobs usually puts a politician at the top of the table," said Sophie. "That's what I've seen over the years—jobs, jobs, jobs."

The waiter came and cleared away the plates and asked if they wanted any coffee. Jim looked at Sophie.

"Why, yes. Café au lait."

"Deux, s'il vous plait."

Sophie reached across the table and took Jim's right hand in both of hers and said, "Strategy International feels your Greek position will pay off. We'll be by your side all the way. We do have sources high in German banking and finance."

"Thanks. Any other advice? You seemed to have an interest in French banks when I spoke to you in your offices."

"We think you might look at SocGen."

"It's selling way below book value."

"Well, yes, but then that is what I thought the game was all about—buy low and sell high."

"Well, you got the low part of it right."

"Strategy International feels that most of the bad news is out. There may be one more shoe to drop, but we think it will fall on a different bank. We're just not sure which one. Anyway, SocGen is rumored to be embarking on some restructuring and should converge back on the market average for big European banks."

"That's damning with faint praise."

Sophie laughed. Then she leaned forward and softly asked, "I was wondering if a personal favor might be possible?"

Jim's eyes brightened, and he leaned forward. "Just ask."

"If I came to Geneva, I was wondering if you could help me put my necklace in a safe-deposit box?"

"Well, that should be easy."

"Possibly in a name other than my own?"

"Ah, hah," said Jim, eyes twinkling. "I think I understand. Why, yes, I can put it under Bermuda Triangle's name."

"The necklace simply didn't get declared properly at the death of Grand-père. The lawyers recommend making the amendment after an inventory of property is made after Grand-mère's passing. All the other family jewelry is in safe-deposit boxes at our bank in Paris."

73

"For centuries?"

"No, I think just decades," Sophie said, laughing at the contrast. "This errand should be simple really."

"I will be in Geneva toward the end of the month. Could we meet then? I could introduce you to my partners and staff at Bermuda Triangle. They are dying to meet you."

"Yes, that will be fine. I will count on it."

Jim paid the bill, and they departed. Outside, Sophie asked, "Can you drop me at my apartment? I so did enjoy the dinner."

"Why, yes."

Hidden Eyes

A well-dressed Russian went to his office at the trade delegation, closed the door, and brought up the encrypted e-mail program. He typed out the message to Moscow: "Observed subject picked up at her flat for presumed dinner date by well-dressed man arriving in dark blue Jaguar coupe with chauffeur, presume same man as observed at Château d'Auverne by Team Minsk per description. Jaguar traced to Bermuda Triangle, Ltd., a hedge fund in Geneva. Presume man is managing partner James Schiller as descriptions all fit. Subject kissed Schiller warmly good night at end of evening but Schiller not invited in. Conversational manner seemed to indicate they are going to meet again. Schiller departed in chauffeur-driven Jaguar. Will monitor subject's movements closely. Alert Geneva team for possible pick up of surveillance."

13. A Visit to Geneva

The taxi crisscrossed the streets of Geneva, heading toward Banque Genève Crédit Suisse. Sitting in the rear seat, Jim turned to Sophie and said, "The bank is small and specialized. I think you will like it. Possibly, it is like your family bank."

"Yes, I'm sure it will be fine. This placement is really just a temporary arrangement."

The taxi pulled up in front of the bank, and the driver came around and opened the door, and Sophie alighted, followed by Jim. He asked the driver to stay while they were in the bank. Turning to Sophie, Jim said, "This way." He pointed toward the double glass front doors. She stepped around two men on scaffolds, washing the windows, and went up to the twin doors and pushed through, with Jim following. The bank manager came up and shook Jim's hand and asked, "Who do we have here?"

"May I present Sophie d'Auverne, a valued client of Bermuda Triangle," said Jim.

The bank manager shook Sophie's hand.

"As I explained on the phone," said Jim, "Mme d'Auverne has some personal objects of high value that she would like to keep in a safe-deposit box. I said that Bermuda Triangle would be pleased to allow her to use of one of ours."

"Of course," said the bank manager. "Let us go into the room where the boxes are. I have the one you requested open, and the box is on the table." The manager led them into the room, showed them the box, and said, "Let me leave you to your arrangements. When you're done, just close the lid, and one of my assistants will come and put the box away as you watch, then give you the key."

Sophie smiled warmly at the manager. He almost melted.

"I'll leave you alone," said Jim.

"Oh, no, please don't go. I won't take but a minute," said Sophie.

Jim stood there as she pulled a jewelry case out of her Longchamps handbag, her workaday companion. She opened the

75

case, pulled out a satin cloth and spread it on the table, and then laid the necklace out on the cloth.

"It's Second Empire. Been in the family for over a century." She pinched some Scotch tape tight around the hasp and said, "There. I need to get the hasp fixed when I take the necklace back to Paris."

"Yes, you wouldn't want it to fall off the next time you're at someone's grand ball," said Jim.

"Yes," she said and then smiled. "But I don't think it would fall far." She laughed. "It's only worn with a gown *très décolleté.*"

"Possibly something to look forward to," said Jim. "Watching the necklace, that is."

"Frankly, it's a dull boy that just watches the necklace."

"What can I say?"

She smiled beguilingly at him and then turned and folded the tops of the cloth over the necklace and put the package in the safe-deposit box. Jim stepped outside and motioned for an assistant. A young man in a black suit and tie came in, picked up the box, slid it into its place in the wall, turned the key, and came back and presented the key to Sophie. She took the key and held it out to Jim. "Possibly you could keep it at your offices?"

"Yes, our pleasure," said Jim. He turned and guided Sophie out of the room and walked out into the foyer of the bank, where the manager was standing, casting a critical eye over the work being done outside by the window washers.

"You would think they could wash windows," said the manager with mild exasperation. "Russians," said the manager to Jim with disdain. "Unfortunately, the last Polish plumber headed for Paris over half a dozen years ago."

Jim noticed that Sophie looked sharply at the two Russians, the same way she did at the Russian gardeners in Auverne. Interesting coincidence, thought Jim.

Then Sophie turned on the charm, looked at the bank manager, and laughed. "They did windows, too? The Polish plumbers?"

"Whatever needed doing," replied the manager. "In Geneva, getting casual labor is always difficult. Oh, well." He took on a look of resignation.

"Well, we must take our departure. I've promised Mme d'Auverne a tour of our offices."

The manager shook Sophie's hand and then Jim's. The couple headed out the door, past the window washers, to the waiting taxi.

14. The Alpha Dogs

At Bermuda Triangle's offices, Jim pointed Sophie over to the entrance of the Rubber Room. She glanced up at the hand-painted sign over the entrance, which read, "Home of the Alpha Dogs," and asked, eyes twinkling, "Are these the alpha males we read about in Anglo-Saxon psychology books? Are you the alpha dog?"

"No," Jim replied. "Alpha is the statistical buzzword for earning above-average market returns on capital. That is the Holy Grail for every fund manager. Achieve it, and the money flows in."

"And if you don't?"

"The money flows out."

"Then you wouldn't be the alpha dog anymore," she said with the pointed wit of a stiletto.

"No, I wouldn't," said Jim with a laugh. "Possibly a much more relaxed dog, though."

"We want him on a knife-edge," said Jack as he came up to greet her. "Let me introduce myself. I'm Jack Hawkins, the British part of the Bermuda Triangle triumvirate."

"*Enchantée*," said Sophie, and she held out her hand. Jack shook it and smiled warmly. With a playful toss of her hair, Sophie asked, "May I ask, if you're English, why aren't you over in the city of London?"

"When I was young, I decided to go abroad and make an honest living," replied Jack.

Sophie laughed and slyly added, "Yes, when it comes to money, London dodges rules as much as follows them. London is Brussels's bad little boy."

Jack smiled and said nothing, thinking, perceptive lady.

Jim pointed his hand through the door and said, "This way."

Sophie smiled and walked through the door, with Jim and Jack following.

"This is Jürgen. He's in charge of our computer operations," said Jim.

"And your ambassador to Frankfurt, I believe," added Sophie.

"Yes," said Jürgen, holding his hand out. "I have heard so much about you." He turned and pointed toward Dieter and said, "Let me introduce Dieter. He's our number-one computer geek."

"Such a charming job title," Sophie replied. She held her hand out to Dieter, who stood up and made a slight bow and shook the outstretched hand. Sophie looked around the room with wonder, while taking in the computer screens, the banks of disk drives, and other young men and women sitting in front of multidisplay workplaces, intently peering at the voluminous data flying across the screens. "Fascinating," she said, eyes wide open.

"Would you like a little demonstration?" asked Jürgen.

"Why, yes," replied Sophie. "Maybe Dieter could show me what he does?"

"Sure, no problem," said Jürgen, and he pushed a swivel chair up next to Dieter in front of a huge triple array of display screens.

Sophie sat down and leaned forward, her bosom pushing out tightly against her blouse, a pretty lace bra just visible below the first button. Jim watched with amusement as the Chanel Number 5 hit Dieter. He was captivated. Sophie isn't taking prisoners today, thought Jim.

"Would it be possible to see how you analyze the trading patterns? Jim and I have been talking so much about the Greek ten-years," Sophie asked. "I see them on TV, but I am not sure how analysts such as yourself pull the information out of what looks like sine waves racing across the screen."

"Here, let me put up the Greek ten-year. Here it is."

"So it's just one big wave?" asked Sophie, looking at the trading track snaking across the screen.

"Oh, no. Here, let me break it out." Dieter flashed his mouse around the screen, and the wave form broke into about a dozen smaller wave forms spread across the three display terminals.

"Yes, like in a physics class," said Sophie.

"Exactly," said Dieter, enthusiasm growing in his voice as he realized he was sitting with someone who sort of knew what he was doing.

"Do you analyze each wave train separately?"

"Yes," said Dieter, and he brought one of the wave trains up to full screen on the display right in front of them.

"When I was at the university in the computer lab," said Sophie, "we would run simple sine-wave patterns and then analyze them with fast Fourier transform functions. We had a multiple regression program that then analyzed the variables for the best fit. We were trying to filter the signal out of the noise. Do you do something like that?"

"That's exactly what we do! And then we have array programs that analyze all the variables across all the wave trains simultaneously. And we search out slight changes in the data terrain over time."

"So you apply physics to make investment decisions?"

"Exactly. We analyze all the data with sensitive pattern-recognition software. We can find a tiny dollop of signal in a hurricane of noise," said Dieter proudly.

"Oh, it's come so far since I was in school." Sophie turned and looked at Jürgen. "And you make money with all this computational finance?"

Jürgen, utter amazement spreading across his face at Sophie's grasp of what they were doing, said noncommittally, "Here and there."

Sophie turned back to Dieter. "Could you show me what's going on with the Greek tens today?"

Jürgen, anxiety spreading across his face, looked at Jim for his approval. Dieter was showing an outsider more than they had ever shown anyone else before.

"Sure, Dieter, go ahead. Show Sophie what's going on today. It's pretty interesting," said Jim.

Dieter flicked his mouse around the screen and brought the wave train back into one large graph showing the price track for the Greek 10s for the past two months. "See, you can see how the shorts drove the price down from around twenty at the beginning of May to about thirteen in the middle of June. If they covered, they made a lot of money."

"Did they cover?"

"That's what's interesting. A lot of them didn't."

"What happened to them?"

"We think they believed," said Jim. "Jack watched one of the biggest of the shorts play the roulette tables in Monaco while the bond was falling like a rock, didn't you, Jack?"

"Yes," said Jack. "Arrogant in a word."

"Well, I don't know; at the time I thought he might be right," said Jim. "There were headlines in the *Financial Times* screaming, 'Be afraid; be very afraid.' They made a compelling case—talk about a Greek exit from the euro exploded. There was a lot of talk about neo-Nazis goose-stepping into parliament or a Communist sweep in the May election."

"And the guy in Monaco?" asked Sophie.

"He was at the tables every night, losing a hundred grand a pop. He swooshed into the parking lot every evening in his Porsche Carrera and had these two hot babes with him—platinum-blond hairdos and silicon that would barely stay inside their dresses." Jack popped his elbows out in front of his chest to mimic the well-stacked bosoms. "Pure silicon, all California."

"Well-rounded high rollers," said Sophie with a laugh.

"Fun to watch—the losing that is," said Jack. He looked at Sophie and said with a grin, "Hey, you're kinda fun."

Jürgen looked at her like she was a modern-day Mata Hari.

She smiled fetchingly at Jack and turned and asked Jim, "What happened?"

"The May election was a loser for the investors," said Jim. "Greek exit looked like it was going to happen. Great for the shorts."

"The shorts were the speculators," explained Jürgen. "We're the investors here."

"Nothing got settled. Uncertainty was the winner," added Jim.

"So what kept the Parthenon from falling off its mountaintop?" asked Sophie.

"They called a new election for mid-June," said Jim.

"The call for a new election led to the bonds starting to rise in value," added Jack. "The election was a success. Greece was going to stay with the euro; the rest of Europe would continue the bailout one way or another." Jack chuckled, thinking back to Monaco. "The big short down on the Monaco tables was really starting to look worried. The fun was going out of the jiggle."

"The rise in Greek bond prices held until about two weeks ago. Then the tide of news broke in the other direction. First, Spanish bond yields approached new highs. That brought

81

everyone's attention back to the fact that not much had really been solved with regard to Europe's finances," said Jim.

"Then the European Central bank refused to accept Greek government debt in exchange for central bank funds. Slammed the window shut on their fingers, they did," said Jack.

Jim moved his palms apart and said, "Boom."

Sophie's eyes widened in astonishment.

"The bond price started to melt away from about seventeen to fourteen," said Jürgen.

"That's when Mr. Short in Monaco started to crow about a dead-cat bounce," added Jack. He held his hand flat out in front of him and gave it a short bump upward to mimic a dead-cat bounce.

"A dead-cat bounce? Wonderful phrase," exclaimed Sophie. She pulled a notebook out of her handbag and hurriedly wrote the phrase down. "I'm collecting all the great phrases from the colorful world of cowboy capitalism. We just have nothing like your color in French."

"Well, we've got the lingo in three languages," said Jim.

"And did the dead-cat bounce put the joie de vivre back in the silicon jiggle?" impishly asked Sophie.

"Exactly," said Jack. He turned to Jim. "She's a natural-born investor."

Sophie made a little bow with a smile. She looked at Jim and asked, "What happened next?"

Jim's face twisted in remembered disgust, and he said, "The dopes in the big bank in New York said there was a ninety percent chance Greece would exit the euro. Everyone called it 'the Grexit.'"

"Why didn't the bonds fall from fourteen to somewhere around zero?" asked Sophie. She was making a point, not asking a question.

"On August 2, Draghi said that the European Central Bank would do—quote—'all it takes,' to preserve the euro," said Jim, referring to Mario Draghi, the head of the European Central Bank and the most powerful man in European monetary affairs. "Draghi hadn't read what the dopes in New York had said."

"Or maybe he did and decided to answer," added Jack.

"But the computer screens know all," interjected Dieter with smug satisfaction. "The bond price turned up the week before Draghi's announcement."

"The software read the future?" asked Sophie.

"The efficient-markets hypothesis lives," exclaimed Dieter, pumping his fist in the air above his head.

"Yes, the power of math," said Sophie. She looked at Dieter impishly and asked, "So what canary ate the dead-cat bounce?"

"The Greenwich Whale," replied Dieter, a sense of satisfaction crossing his face as he threw out this unobvious piece of information.

"The Greenwich Whale?" asked Sophie, stupefied. "I heard about the London Whale. Who or what is the Greenwich Whale?"

"Watch this," said Dieter, and he moved the mouse over to last week's trading track and blew the track up so just a couple of days' trading was on display.

"Wow," said Sophie. "You have a lot of data up on the screen."

"Yes, we started to tease out the signal late last week. What we'd been waiting for," said Dieter.

"Waiting for?" said Sophie expectantly.

"Yes, the Greenwich Whale. The Whale had started to move. The price was moving up, bit by bit. The Whale was taking up whatever volume was offered—the big money was going long."

"Let's go back. Who or what is the Greenwich Whale?" asked Sophie incredulously.

"Those are the big American hedge funds in Greenwich, Connecticut," said Jim.

"And they will slowly squeeze out the shorts?" said Sophie, again making a question to state the conclusion that was dawning on her.

"Yes," said Jim. Jack was right; she was a natural.

Sophie pulled out her notebook and wrote the phrase about the Whale down.

"And there's more," said Dieter excitedly. Jürgen's pained expression went up a notch at all this disclosure of proprietary technique. Jim smiled at him by way of reassurance and whispered that she was one of them (*nous*).

"Yes," said Sophie, a hawklike interest in what she was seeing taking over as she put her notebook away.

"As more volume came into the market, the French banks started to slowly liquidate their inventories."

"How do you know that?"

"The traders have individual signatures; our software has identified these signatures, little characteristics in their patterns that give them away."

"Amazing. Like fingerprints," said Sophie.

"Exactly."

"So you know the French banks?"

"Intimately. But this time was different. The traders were mechanically and monotonously liquidating their positions. Each time the price went up a notch, a bunch of bonds were liquidated out of inventory—probably in a way so as not to show an accounting loss on the books. You know, appearances."

"Yes, appearances. The finance ministry would be concerned about any bank losses." Sophie turned to Jim and Jack and said, "Who wants more lectures from the Anglo-Saxons about bank capital?"

They chuckled appreciatively.

Dieter kept right on going. "But there was none of the flash and dance in the trading you would expect to see from traders doing the executing in their natural manner."

"Why?"

"The orders to sell were coming down from the top floor. There's none of the split-second agility you would expect from traders acting within their discretion."

Sophie leaned back in her chair and took stock. "Yes, orders from the top floor. And yes, there's no split-second agility up there." Again, she laughed—one got such a different perspective from a trading desk in Geneva. "You're really a bunch of renegades about as far from the groupthink of a big French bank as you can get." She paused, eyes sparkling, and concluded, "Yes, I can see the elite in their conference room in Paris—*les grands patrons*—the sleek blue suits, the groomed hair, a room brimming with pretension and self-regard." She turned and looked at the men. "Easy pickings for you cowboys."

Everyone laughed.

"And the dead-cat bounce?" she asked.

"A sucker play to get the shorts in deeper," answered Dieter. "A setup by the Greenwich Whale."

Sophie nodded in understanding. "Where does this go?"

"The Whale will start to gobble up the shorts—" said Dieter.

Jim broke in with his conclusion: "Hopefully the bond will go somewhere north of thirty by the time the European Union bails Greece out on its next debt payment in December."

"Yes," said Sophie thoughtfully. "And you want us at Strategy International to give you our best market assessment…and you are where?"

"We averaged in at about fourteen. So last week was something of a heartburn for us. But from now on, our average will go up as we keep buying."

"Would I be impolite to ask how much?"

"Hundreds of millions," answered Jim. "Billions in face value."

"And you're still buying?" asked Sophie.

"We're following along behind the Whale, slowly but surely. A swish of his tail and you can lose big money," said Jim, and he nodded at the screen. "Last week the Whale swished its tail."

"What do you think we should do, Sophie?" asked Jack.

"We think the final terms of the bailout will get sweeter the closer we get to December. Somewhere just shy of thirty-five."

"Well, talk is cheap," said Jack with a laugh.

"Our advice is not inexpensive," said Sophie. She batted her eyelashes. "Nothing about me ever is."

Dieter's jaw dropped. She was fascinating.

"We agree with thirty-five," said Jim, getting back to business. "We intend to keep buying right up to the close."

"You're going long," said Sophie. "All in?"

"Long," said Jack.

"Where will this end for the shorts?" asked Sophie. "A shootout on the streets of Laredo at high noon between the shorts and the Whale?"

"Better," said Jack.

"Jack says that a Porsche Carrera is going to go flying off the high corniche above Monaco," added Jim.

85

"Like Princess Grace?" said Sophie, a sense of that long-ago tragedy saddening her expression.

"Not exactly," said Jim. "Only figuratively."

Sophie's face softened.

Jürgen started laughing.

"An inside joke?" asked Sophie, breaking into a smile that asked for more.

"It'll be tits and silicon on the windscreen," said Jürgen. "That's what Jack says."

"I was right. How Hollywood!" exclaimed Sophie. She looked around at the men and said, "And boys will be boys." As she said this, she reached down a third time into her handbag and pulled out her notebook, started writing, and remarked, "More great quotes from the cowboy capitalists. Spice for my memoirs." She looked at Jim and said, "Although I will be hard put to outdo Grand-mère. She conquered men the old-fashioned way, not in the conference room…"

Dieter watched in open-mouthed amazement; he had never quite met a woman like Sophie. Suddenly he wished he were older—possibly even sophisticated and polished—instead of just smart.

"Your memoirs? When will they be published?" asked Jack.

"Many years from now. First, Grand-mère's memoirs must be published. Jim saw them. They were in the leather binders laid out on the table up in her study. That's where I will write mine someday." Sophie smiled warmly at Jim.

"And what will your grandmother's memoirs be entitled?" asked Jürgen.

"Oh, *La Memoir de la Quatrieme République par la vicomtesse Inès d'Auverne.*"

Jim nodded in understanding and said to his colleagues, "Yeah. I saw the memoirs laid out on the writing table in beautiful leather notebooks, ready to go to the printer for typesetting." Jim looked thoughtful for a moment. "Tell me again why they haven't been published yet, Sophie?"

"Oh, we publish posthumously."

"Why?"

"We—the Auverne women—write frankly and completely about our lives, the men in them, the triumphs and disappointments. It is our oldest tradition. It binds across the generations, through time—sisters in the adventures of love, so to speak."

Jim turned and spoke to his colleagues: "She's right. I saw the other memoirs in the bookshelves. Book after book, going back several centuries, I believe."

"Yes," said Sophie. "Centuries." She paused and looked thoughtful. "And, in turn, each daughter reads them. The wisdom passes down."

The men nodded in somewhat amazed understanding. It was so simple, so powerful.

"And what will you call your memoirs, Sophie?" asked Jack.

"Oh, I think something like *La Memoir de la Cinquieme République par la vicomtesse Sophie d'Auverne*."

The four men stopped and stared at her. That she would someday succeed to her grandmother's title had never really registered with them. It was like Marie Antoinette came back and sprinkled fairy dust around the computer room. They all nodded thoughtfully. Jack broke the reverie. "Does the château come with the title?"

"No," said Sophie. She raised one eyebrow with amused irony.

"Yes?" drawled Jack, sensing more to come.

"No, not with the title. I already own Château d'Auverne, from the time I was in the cradle. Grand-père put it in my name. Said that way it would not be necessary to bother the authorities with a bunch of inheritance transfers."

Jack roared. "The gold under the mattress and the property title in the granddaughter's cradle. Oh, so wonderfully French."

Jürgen laughed and then looked closely at Jim; he was starting to understand the depth of his colleague's fascination.

"Gentlemen," said Jim, "I've promised Sophie a lunch before taking her back to the airport...*tous les deux*...so to speak."

"Yes, let me not keep you from your work," added Sophie as she idly looked at a crowded corner of Dieter's desk, piled high with old magazines and paperbacks. She pulled a dog-eared paperback entitled *Kremlin Double Cross*, with a cover featuring a sexy young woman in a black bra holding a Kalashnikov assault rifle, out of the pile. "Oh, you like Philippe Lagrande, too?" Sophie remarked.

"He's one of my favorites," said Dieter. "The stories are full of true facts about international conspiracies and secret-service exploits."

"Yes, so I've heard," said Sophie rather noncommittally. She kept digging in the pile and pulled out *Kosovo Assassins* and *Moscow Center*, all featuring lurid covers with busty young women holding large pieces of ordnance.

"Supposedly the French secret service gives him all kinds of inside dope," said Dieter with adolescent enthusiasm. "Maybe you've heard about that, having been high up in the French government?"

"Oh, I don't know," she said in a rather dull and dreary voice as she turned the novels over in her hands. Then she turned and gave Dieter a high-wattage smile and an expression of intimate charm that said she was going to share a secret. "I used to keep a couple dozen of the novels in the bottom drawer of my desk at the ministry. I, and the other women in the office, would read them on break."

"You did?" said Dieter incredulously.

"Yes, we used to compare notes on the exciting sexual adventures in the novels—the back bedrooms in Damascus villas, pounding passions in Beirut apartments—just in case we might have missed some arousing experience in our own lives. You only live once..." Sophie smiled invitingly. "You know?"

Dieter's eyes opened like saucers. "Compare notes...adventures," he mumbled.

"There's something for everyone in a Lagrande novel," she said as she set the paperbacks down on the desk. "So, no, I don't know about the secret-service stuff. My friends and I were interested in the other things..."

Dieter was gaga. Jim stood there looking at her with open-eyed amazement. She was so full of surprises. Jack stood off to the side and watched appraisingly; she was good, a professional, lots of short-term charm for the long-term game. But what was the game? He wondered.

Jürgen stepped forward and took her hand and turned her toward the door and said, "By all means, go charm our managing partner at lunch, and I trust we will meet again."

"Yes, lunch. I've so enjoyed my visit. You have a fascinating operation here"—she looked at Dieter—"and such interesting personnel." She stepped over and wrapped herself on Jim's arm and looked up at him and said, "Yes, lunch."

15. Bookshop

Jim walked up the steps from the Metro station at Place St-Michel into the summer light of late morning. He walked over to Quai des Grands Augustins along the River Seine and past the bouquinistes, with their displays of used books and art prints. He looked out into the middle of the river to the Île de la Cité and the stone edifice of the Palais de Justice dominating the riverfront. Sticking out of the middle of the rectangular building complex was the spire of the cathedral of Sainte Chapelle, a medieval church built in a long-ago century and then surrounded in a later century by the palais of the state. Possibly Sophie would say, "*L'etat*," a somewhat grander concept than the utilitarian notion of government in the Anglo-Saxon world. There was no doubt in his mind; she had taken hold in his imagination.

He walked past the old stone bridge of Pont Neuf, like so many things in Paris, built to last. He crossed the riverfront boulevard, walked a few short steps, and turned left into a narrow lane crowded by four- and five-story buildings built centuries before. He continued through the warren of Left Bank streets, past galleries and antique shops, until he came to a small shop with a wood-paneled front painted a deep forest green with a little gold pigmented logo on the window: *Livres—vente et achete* (Books—bought and sold). He went through the door, and a bell tinkled, and a balding, bespectacled man came out from the back and stood behind a counter. The dormouse in front of his bailiwick, Jim thought. Jim looked around: beautifully bound books of some age were on every shelf. You could almost, but not quite, smell the mustiness of the books. They were excellently maintained. Jim was impressed.

"*Oui, monsieur?*"

"I spoke to you on the phone. My name is Schiller."

"Ah, yes. You are interested in the memoirs of *les vicomtesses* of d'Auverne. *N'est-ce pas?*"

"Yes, exactly."

"I have a small selection on hand back in the special-collections room. They are on consignment from the owners. If monsieur requests, I know where the other editions may be had. Only the most discerning of collectors purchase these memoirs."

"How many are there?" Jim asked, a little bit confused.

"Dozens. *Les vicomtesses* have been recording their memoirs from the time of Henry IV; that's more than five hundred years ago." The bookseller nodded in the direction of Pont Neuf. "Henry built the bridge. His statue is out there today, a reminder of his greatness."

"Yes, I just walked past the bridge." Jim made a note to go visit the statue.

"This way, monsieur."

The bookseller led Jim down the hallway, stopped at a door, got out a set of keys, and opened a series of locks.

"Excellent security," said Jim.

"Yes, the rare books are of considerable value. In a plebian age, such as we find ourselves, works of true patrician origin have great value."

"Yes," said Jim, walking through the door and into another small book room with more beautifully bound books on the shelves.

The bookseller walked over to about two dozen hand-bound books with gold embossed titles on the spines and said, "Here are some of the memoirs of *les vicomtesses*."

Jim walked over and looked at the volumes and pulled one out and thumbed through it gently. He said to the bookseller, "I think I am interested in some of the more recent memoirs. Can you tell me about them?"

"Why, yes, I am recognized by many as an expert on the entire series."

"Yes, that is what my acquaintance said."

"Well, in recent times, we have the Second Empire." The bookseller looked over the top of his glasses and explained to Jim, "That's Napoleon the Third and runs from about 1852 to 1870. It covers the Haussmann era, when Paris was rebuilt into the world's most beautiful and modern city."

"Yes…"

"And, of course, there are two memoirs from the late nineteenth century and prewar years; I'm speaking of the Great War of course."

"Of course."

"*Les vicomtesses* can be truly said to have put the belle into belle epoque."

Jim laughed. "And the current *vicomtesse*?"

"Well, of course, her memoir has not been published yet."

"Why?"

"They are only published late in life…"

"Yes?"

"*Les vicomtesses* have established a tradition of great candor in describing the men and amours in their lives."

"Frank?"

"Possibly beyond that. It would be a rare gentleman that might not learn something new and, shall we say, instructive from most of these memoirs."

"*Vraiment?*"

"Yes, and if I may say"—he made an abashed look like a naughty angel—"my wife has long encouraged me in this scholarship."

"*Alors*, obviously for people with a certain discernment," said Jim. The dormouse is now a tiger, laughed Jim to himself. The Auverne women had real power.

"*Mais oui*," said the bookseller, in complete and total agreement to the compliment paid him by the distinguished American gentleman.

"And the men in the Auverne family?" asked Jim.

"They have been successful in Paris in business, banking, and now and again politics."

"And the women?"

"In Paris…" The bookseller paused to let Paris sink in. "The women have had wide acquaintanceships with important and influential people for centuries, true ornaments of Parisian social life at its most fashionable."

A troubled look crossed Jim's brow. Something wasn't adding up. He looked searchingly at the bookseller, his expression framing the question.

"You must understand with the Auvernes there are two realms: Paris and the Château d'Auverne."

"Go on."

"All *les vicomtesses* write of walking through the garden hand in hand with their husbands, of the complete fidelity between them, the sanctity of the vows, devotion, and loyalty. They write of sitting in front of the great fireplace in their old age with their husbands. The Château d'Auverne was a temple to faithfulness, its citadel."

"But not their lives in Paris?"

"Yes, you understand. That dichotomy has fascinated scholars for several centuries—the two different realms orbiting around each other in harmony."

"Do you have any thoughts on the origin of this split morality? Where it came from?"

"Possibly it has its origin in chivalry...where a knight had great romantic devotion to a lady—a lady not necessarily his wife—the wife of another..."

"And how would this arrangement come down across the centuries?"

"Possibly handed down from mother to daughter or daughter-in-law, as the case may be."

"And the men?"

"All French children are well brought up, both boys and girls. It might be difficult for someone from the hurly-burly of the Anglo-Saxon world to completely comprehend." The bookseller smirked at him.

"So the boys would be well schooled in the tradition?" asked Jim.

"Yes, there is Paris...and there is Auverne," said the bookseller.

"It would be a dull boy that didn't see the wider horizons of adventure in this arrangement," said Jim.

"Yes, you half understand."

Jim looked at the bookseller again with a questioning expression.

"Importantly, the arrangement, as you call it, really brightens up the daughters, gives them a view of undreamed-of pastures not necessarily available to other women—at the proper time of course, after the births of the children, always few in number among the Auverne family."

"Yes, they were all eager to get on to Paris and the splendors of phase two."

The bookseller frowned. "People did not live so long in those years. So time was of a certain essence."

"Yes, time is the one element in life you cannot control. Possibly I am in need of some instruction from the Auverne women"—he winked at the bookseller—"and their mastery of life's mysteries...and pleasures. I would like to buy one of the memoirs from one of the *vicomtesses* of the belle epoque."

"May I suggest the memoir from Mathilde d'Auverne, who was something of a flame here in Paris in the years before the Great War."

"Fine. How much do they go for?"

"The minimum reserve is usually set at a hundred thousand euros for any of the memoirs. They are all equally almost priceless."

"Almost-priceless wisdom," remarked Jim under an arched eyebrow. "Or a very good time." He mentally drew a big breath: millions of euros in memoirs were sitting on those bookshelves in Auverne.

"To be a collector of these memoirs requires some means..."

"Bonds," said Jim.

"*Bien sûr.* A deposit of ten thousand euros will start the purchase process."

Jim pulled out his checkbook and wrote out a check and handed it to the bookseller.

"I will let you know when arrangements are complete."

"Before I go, do you have any insight into what might make the memoir of Inès d'Auverne so interesting?"

"*Mais oui.*" The bookseller looked furtively around his shop. Satisfied it was empty, he went to the front door and locked it. Then he went over to a rolltop desk, took out a key, and opened it. He then slid the top back, opened a drawer, and pulled out a large cardboard file full of yellowing news clippings. He brought them back to the counter, where Jim was standing.

"I heard they had been in Algiers during the war," Jim said tentatively.

"Yes, they—Thierry and Inès—made many friends among the top tier of the French settlers and elite there. Then they came back to Paris with the liberation. After the war, he prospered as a banker. She made many acquaintanceships, shall we say, among the political elite of the era—a favorite at the most fashionable salons. Then came Algeria..."

"What happened?" asked Jim.

"Thierry d'Auverne worked with great skill to get the settlers' money transferred first to Monaco and then to Switzerland. He had many contacts from the friendships he had made in Algiers during the war."

"Well, yes. That's what bankers do," said Jim.

"Yes, but the government in Paris really wanted the money repatriated to France. The settlers had caused de Gaulle much trouble. There was talk of settling scores."

"I see. So Thierry was acting against the government's wishes."

"Quite surreptitiously. But he was rumored to be well informed." The shopkeeper opened the file and pulled out yellowing newspaper clippings from the early 1960s. "There was an undercurrent of interest in how certain bankers were undercutting the government policy. People in the know said that Thierry had unusual access to information—one step ahead of the government—that powerful people were possibly protecting him."

"Yes, and Inès's role?"

"Many believe she was the key. She had these intimate friendships with a select few at the top. Many believe that possibly she received certain confidences, late in the afternoons..."

"Pillow talk?"

The shopkeeper looked askance at Jim. "Pillow talk?" said the shopkeeper incredulously. "No, her head was not on the pillow, monsieur. It was believed to be elsewhere. She understood what powerful men wanted late in the afternoon, the stresses of power..."

"I see," said Jim.

"Let me add, monsieur, all agree she was exquisitely beautiful, with a vivacity exceptional even for this city. To spend time with her was described as—"

"I see..."

"Let me say that the memoir you have ordered, the one by Mathilde d'Auverne, would have been of great instruction to Inès. There is little of amour she would not be schooled in after reading that volume, as you will see yourself."

"Thank you. You have answered many questions that I have had about this fascinating family." Jim reached out and shook the bookseller's hand and said by way of good-bye, "I look forward to hearing from you."

Jim walked out of the shop and headed back to the river. Reaching Pont Neuf, he walked out to the equestrian statue of Henry IV, a large bronze mounted on marble. He walked around the statue, stopped and looked at it, and then looked up the river past the Île de la Cité and the twin bell towers of Notre Dame Cathedral, already old when the statue was put in place in 1618. Today, the water was rippling down the channel, the sun sparkling on the wave tops as it had for centuries.

How could he put his mind around a story going back five hundred years? He took a breath. And just who would you be marrying? There, he'd said it to himself. He had marriage on his mind. So who are you marrying? The woman standing in front of you, the woman in your arms, or are you marrying all *les vicomtesses*—five or six dozen women? But wait, all women were descended from fifty or so women over the past five hundred years, nothing unique about that. What's so startling here?

Jim stared down the river, deep in contemplation, the centuries surrounding him. *Les vicomtesses* had a hold on his imagination. What did this line of matriarchs mean? Well, each *vicomtesse*-in-waiting would know who all her ancestors were by name. She could see their presence in the bookcase, book after book. She, like them, would succeed to a common title; they would be sisters across time. Most importantly, she would get to read the advice and warnings of the fifty women who came before her. All those wonderful little secrets. Isn't that what Sophie had really said: Grand-mère was tutoring her great-granddaughter in the eternal lessons, this careful schooling by the reigning *vicomtesse* to its youngest successor. It was not about how to hold a fork but how to be an Auverne lady.

Fascinating. Jim continued over to the Place Dauphine and had a glass of red wine at an outdoor café. Would he become part of this tradition? Did he want to? Should he ask? Or would they ask him? He thought about this as he waited for the next appointment of the day; he was meeting Jack Hawkins later in the afternoon to find out some more about Sophie d'Auverne.

16. Café le Rostand

Jim walked up from the River Seine in the afternoon sunshine toward the Luxembourg Gardens. He turned a corner and was on the sunlit terrasse of the Café le Rostand, its canvas awning sheltering the small round tables at the rear in shade. He scanned the tables, saw Jack reading a newspaper, and walked over and sat down.

"What's up?" asked Jim.

"Saw an old contact, a political troubleshooter for the UMP party here in Paris. He worked in both the Matignon and the Élysée."

"He knew our girl?"

"Yes, he did. Said she was brought over from the Hôtel de Ville to the ministry of public works during the Chirac years. Then she went to the ministry of the budget when Jean-François Copé was minister toward the end of the Chirac regime."

"Is he the guy that just announced that he would run for the presidency of the UMP against former prime minister Fillon?"

"One and the same. Our girl is well connected at the top of the UMP."

"Where'd she go after that?"

"She stayed in budgeting during the ministry of Éric Woerth."

"That's the guy that got caught taking all that cash from Liliane Bettencourt, the L'Oréal heiress?"

"Yeah, same guy. Bagman for Sarkozy. He's still being investigated."

"So Sophie knows where the bodies are buried?"

"No one knows what she knows. She developed a reputation for total discretion. A true confidant of powerful men and later women."

"Then what?"

"After that, she went to the Matignon and became a budget aide to François Fillon, Sarkozy's prime minister. Then she went over to the ministry of finance under Christine Lagarde. She was part of the economic-policy-making circle at the top of the government, a key go-between among ministers and the Matignon. She stayed in the ministry until May, when the UMP got booted out of power in the election."

"So she would know Lagarde well?"

"They were close, according to my source. Sophie handled confidential and sensitive matters for Christine."

"Anything about her personal life? What happened after she divorced her husband?"

Jack laughed. "My source said one minister complained that there was no room for a second husband in her bed."

Jim smirked and remarked, "A real girl about government."

"No, that's what's interesting. There were just a few men that she had known for years. The minister was just a sore loser. During her whole career, her relationships with superiors were always professional. The minister didn't get it."

"Thought she was like all the rest?"

"Maybe," laughed Jack. "But no, at that level, it's different. The women choose their companions from outside of government. By then, the dance is about power."

"So who'd she pick as a companion?"

"No one. Seems strange but after she went to the finance ministry, she went dark, as Dieter might say. No signal."

"She wasn't dropping any handkerchiefs?" mused Jim.

"Come again?" asked Jack.

"Oh, just something her grandmother told me about Paris in the old days."

"Well, Jim, you look interested in the lady. I would say be careful, but I don't know about what."

"Why?"

"Look across the street. That's the Luxembourg Gardens, created by Marie de Medicis, of the famously wealthy and devious House of Medici of Florence. Intrigue and scheming make up a dark undercurrent of the history of Paris. One should never forget that."

"You need to meet the grandmother," said Jim. "She knows all that to her fingertips—the women of this family have centuries of experience with intrigue in Paris."

"The men?"

"They simply made money."

"Well, sometimes it's not all about money," said Jack.

"Then I'm a babe in the woods," said Jim.

"I wouldn't disagree with that," said Jack with a chuckle.

17. Dinner at Antibes

The perky little BMW convertible with the ducktail rear end sped along the road bordering the beach on the east side of Cap d'Antibes. The two women and a girl had bright silk scarves tied around their heads, which held most of their hair in place; only the bangs and tresses flowing out from under the scarves were blown as the air rushed past. Big, black plastic sunglasses covered their eyes and much of their faces, providing a splash of Riviera glamour. Sophie looked over at her mother, Martine, and said, "Jim said go down to where the beach ends and follow the road around to the right, then across the peninsula, and take a right turn on his street."

Her mother shaded her iPhone with her hand and squinted at the moving blip on the little screen and replied, "You're going fine, dear." Sophie's mother, Martine, was in her late sixties and, like Sophie, was slender with chestnut-brown hair.

From the rear seat, Sophie's daughter, Marie-Hélène, ten years old going on eleven, asked, "*Maman*, what's so special about this man? We don't visit your clients in Paris when we're at home."

"I wanted to give you and *Maman* a chance to meet Jim. He's an American. And besides, we had a chance to all go shopping together." Sophie and her mother and daughter had spent the morning shopping for dresses along the broad sidewalk of Juan-les-Pins. Afterward, they had lunch in Antibes, its alleys and squares a favorite place for buying shoes and end-of-summer casual wear.

Sophie glanced across the beach at the turquoise blue of the Mediterranean, which contrasted with the washed-out blue of the summer sky. The road curved to the right, with well-gardened villas on one side of the road and forested hillsides on the other.

"An American?" said Sophie's mother. "That's never been something to attract you in the past." Her mother arched an eyebrow with deeply felt skepticism.

"He's an interesting American."

101

"Maybe he's a movie star," added Marie-Hélène, hopefully. "They're the only Americans you ever hear about down here."

"*Oui, nouveau riche...etrangère...toujours ici,*" mumbled Martine. (Yes, the newly rich and foreign are always here.)

"Well, he's all three," said Sophie. "He's an investor—a merchant banker really—and he has a firm in Geneva with several delightful partners: one's English and the other German. That's what caught my eye; you're not sure if you're with sophisticated investors or in a tree house with teenage boys."

"A tree house?" exclaimed Marie-Hélène, her interest piqued.

"Yes, they have a special computer room, all padded on the outside so none of the secret signals can get out," she said over her shoulder to her daughter in the rear seat. "A young German computer genius, who wears rainbow tie-dyed T-shirts and has long, frizzy blond hair and looks like something you would see walking along a beach in Tahiti works there, almost lives there, I think."

"Will he be there today?" asked Marie-Hélène expectantly.

"No, I'm afraid not. But even the adult is interesting. Jim Schiller will have some stories to tell."

"A banker? Is he a banker like Grand-père?" asked Marie-Hélène.

Sophie paused as her mind got comfortable with her daughter's question, which now seemed like an insight. "Yes, now that you mention it, I think he rather is like Grand-père," said Sophie, referring to her late father and Martine's husband. "Much more so I would think," Sophie said, mulling the words around in her mind. She had never really associated her father with Jim before.

"Oh good," said Marie-Hélène. Then her face fell. "I sure miss Grand-père."

"We all do," said Sophie with remembered feeling. She glanced at her mother.

Her mother looked back at her, her gaze making a steady appraisal of her sometimes-wayward, always-achieving daughter. Just what was this trip all about? Maybe this outing was more than just shopping in Antibes and having dinner and an overnight stay with an interesting new client. She pondered this and then said to Sophie, "Well, yes. I can understand you wanting to visit an interesting gentleman in Antibes, Sophie. But bringing your mother and daughter along…that's a new wrinkle for you." Now that eyebrow really arched.

Sophie laughed and said, "Oh, here's the street. Right turn. It's down on the left." She accelerated and drove almost a kilometer, her eyes searching the side of the road; then she saw the twin monuments marking the entrance to Jim's drive and turned in. She pulled over and stopped under the shade of a tree, next to a navy-blue Jaguar coupe. Sophie got out, followed by her mother and daughter. They walked to the rear of the car, popped the top to the rear compartment, and started to remove their bags.

The door to the house opened, and Jim Schiller stepped outside and walked over to the parked BMW, saying by way of welcome, "So nice to see you, Sophie. This must be your mother." He stuck out his hand in welcome.

"Yes, this is my mother, Martine d'Auverne."

Sophie's mother took Jim's hand and gave it a polite handshake and said, "We're delighted to be invited to such a charming house."

"And my daughter, Marie-Hélène d'Auverne."

"*Bonjour, monsieur,*" said the little girl with great politeness.

Jim bent his head down and said, "I'm pleased to meet you. Your mother has said so little about you."

Marie-Hélène looked at Jim with her head askance in perplexity.

"Undoubtedly, she was keeping you as a surprise," said Jim reassuringly as he dropped her hand. The little girl smiled suspiciously, as if the strange man were offering her an ice-cream cone.

"Let's go inside," said Jim. "Marie will show you to your rooms." He reached down and picked up some of the bags in both of his hands and carried them into the foyer of the spacious house. Marie, the housekeeper, was standing just inside the open door. As they trooped in, Marie closed the door, and Jim set the bags down.

"This way," said Marie, and she picked up several of the bags Jim had set on the cool red tiles of the anteroom's floor.

"I'll wait in the dining room while Marie gets you settled in," said Jim as he watched the women walk down the hallway to where the guest bedrooms were. He turned and walked through the

103

drawing room to the dining room. The dining room was separated from the drawing room by large head-high cabinets holding china table service on one side and an interesting collection of ceramics on the other. Large bay windows made up the far wall of the dining room; the windows looked down the slope and out to the sea, its wave tops glistening in the afternoon sunshine.

Presently the women came walking across the drawing room to the dining area, Sophie's mother glancing around the room with a soft look of approval on her face, Marie-Hélène with wide-eyed wonder.

"It's a delightful house, Jim," said Sophie. She walked over to the bay windows overlooking a series of terraces marching step-by-step down the side of the hill, each terrace thickly planted with local plants and shrubs. On each side of the terraced garden, along the property lines, stood single columns of pine trees, like picket fences, giving the garden a sense of being its own Eden, walled off from the outside world. A viewer's gaze was inevitably channeled toward the sea below. Sophie stopped and stared out at the blue sea and then let her eyes run along the beach to the forested point marking the start of the seaside city of Cannes. From Cannes, the rugged Riviera coastline ran far to the west. She turned around and faced Jim. "You bought the house for the view?"

"Mostly, I guess. It's a comfortable house. We—Bermuda Triangle—use it for meetings and gatherings while I use it to simply get away."

"What gave you the idea to acquire the house?" asked Martine.

"Oh, in the 1990s, when I was young, I was prowling around used bookstores in Manhattan one weekend and I came across a book entitled *Living Well is the Best Revenge*. I bought it and took it home and read it. It's about the Murphys—Gerald and Sara—who hobnobbed with the avant-garde in Paris in the 1920s. They came down here and bought a house in 1923, which they named "Villa America." They invited the writers F. Scott Fitzgerald and Hemingway and artists like Picasso down for long visits. What I enjoyed reading about were the delightful dinners by candlelight overlooking the garden and the sea beyond."

"So, this is the house?" asked Martine.

"No, it's actually right down the street a couple of hundred meters. It is on the same side of the street."

"You didn't try to buy it?"

"No. It was hardly necessary. I walked into this house, saw the veranda and the garden—the whole layout—and said to myself, 'This is it.' And so it has become."

"Well, I'm not sure we'll be able to sparkle at dinner like Hemingway and Picasso…but we'll try," said Sophie with a smile. "My mother and daughter have their moments."

Jim walked over to the adjacent side of the room, to the sliding-glass doors opening out on the veranda. "See, here's where we'll have dinner tonight. I really liked how the house makes a big *U* around the veranda. And as you've already seen, the guest rooms are over on the opposite wing, with a kitchen at the base. It's designed for entertaining."

"And the rest of the house?" asked Martine.

"My bedroom and a study and some other rooms are over on the other side of the drawing room." Jim turned and pointed down to another hall opening. "I can get away from the guests when I have to."

Martine laughed. "A well-designed house."

"Please sit down. Can I offer you something to drink, a glass of wine after your arduous morning of shopping?" said Jim, eyes sparkling. Looking at Marie-Hélène, he added, "And a lemonade for your?"

"*Oui, monsieur,*" she replied with childlike politeness.

Jim walked into the kitchen and gave some instructions to Marie and came back out and swept his arm across the sofa and some chairs. They all sat down.

"I gather you live outside of Aix, a home in the country?" Jim said to Martine. "Aix is a long way from Auverne."

"Yes, in fact, it is about as far away from Normandy as you can get and still be in France," replied Martine with laughing good humor.

"Why Aix?" asked Jim.

Marie-Hélène looked at her grandmother with intense interest, waiting for her answer.

"My husband and I bought this old, tumbledown stone farmhouse in the beautiful Provençal countryside just after our marriage. We scouted properties on our honeymoon. Then we restored and expanded it over the early years of our marriage. It was ours."

"Sounds romantic," said Jim.

"Terribly so. Then Sophie was born. We would come down for long weekends and on our vacations, leave Sophie in her nursery or put her in a playpen in the yard, and work on the house and yard; we would all come together for the meals. We were a family in a house of our own creation, refugees from a family history, the weight of which could be too unbearable."

"So you were never going to the château in Auverne," asked Jim. "I don't mean to pry."

Marie-Hélène looked daggers at Jim to silence such politeness; she wanted to pry into every detail.

"When Sophie was born, I suggested to my father-in-law—a great gentleman of the old school, all manners and understanding—that the château might better go directly to Sophie."

"And?" asked Jim.

"He looked at me a long time, a long, appraising look, and then he smiled broadly and nodded in approval."

Jim glanced at Sophie; she was looking at her mother with quiet affection, a pleased and relaxed look on her face.

"So you're different from the others, *les vicomtesses?*" said Jim.

Martine laughed and said, "I know Inès said my memoir would be short and that I could write it in a long weekend. Actually, it is going to be a beautiful story about love with a husband, the building of a house together, having a family together. I am going to write it with my granddaughter—I am not interested in 'lesson'"—Martine said this with mild contempt—"but rather as an example for those who come afterward, the example of a better way."

Marie-Hélène listened to her grandmother with rapt attention; Sophie beamed at her mother's explanation.

"When Marie-Hélène and I finish, then it will be published."

"Mother," interjected Sophie, "that's not the tradition."

"After Grand-mère dies, the memoirs of *la vicomtesse Martine d'Auverne* will be published, and the title to *le vicomté* will pass down to you immediately, my dear."

"Mother," said Sophie emphatically. "*La vicomtesse.* It's for life."

"I have a good lawyer in Paris, and he says it will go to you sooner than you think—and at my command." Martine had settled that.

Jim quietly listened and understood that these women put an iron will behind shaping life's flow of events. He mused to himself that you probably didn't even want to tangle with the ten-year-old.

In another chair, Marie-Hélène listened to the conversation with rapt attention and then a slow-dawning realization, and she said to her grandmother, "Then you will be free, won't you, Grand-mère?"

"Yes, *ma chérie, libre.*" (Yes, darling, free.)

Sophie nodded with accepting approval and sat quietly for a few moments. Then she moved to change the direction of the afternoon's activities. "Possibly your housekeeper could show my mother and Marie-Hélène around the grounds and you and I could briefly discuss our business—"

"And then we could have a coffee or tea before getting ready for dinner," said Jim, finishing off the sentence.

"A delightful plan," said Sophie.

Jim glanced at Martine and Marie-Hélène and said, "Here, let me take you over to the kitchen and hand you off to Marie. She'll know just what to do." Jim led Martine and Marie-Hélène over toward the kitchen, while Sophie picked up her briefcase and set it on the dining-room table. She opened it and took out some papers. Jim returned and sat down.

"Well, what do we have?" asked Jim.

"Strategic International continues to believe we are on track for the debt restructuring later this year, after the Troika makes its report and details are arranged," said Sophie, mentioning the big international report expected from the International Monetary Fund and its partners. She smiled and concluded, "You'll get above thirty cents on the dollar."

"Well that's good news. Any new facts to back up this rosy scenario?"

"Plenty. President Hollande and Chancellor Merkel are meeting with the Greek prime minister and reiterating their support for Greece's place in the euro. More importantly, they are solidly supporting Draghi's position that the European Central Bank will support government-bond markets. At the top of the European Union, the policy and the leadership are united."

Jim nodded. This was something Sophie would know.

"More importantly," Sophie emphasized, "Greece has done more than people think. They've cut labor costs, and their primary deficit is almost gone. So additional foreign money is not going into the proverbial black hole. Foreign money is going to foreign creditors, not Greek pensioners."

"Well, that will make some Germans happy."

"And a lot of French bankers," Sophie added. "Maybe you'll be one of the foreign creditors paid off?" Sophie's eyes twinkled with humor.

Jim turned thoughtful and said, "But there's still a big loan repayment coming up at the end of the year." Jim's voice betrayed his lingering pessimism on the issue.

"Yes, but a restructuring, even a technical default, can be accommodated. There's nothing to be gained by a disorderly default. The pieces are all coming together—more or less on plan."

"So we're not going to see the return of the drachma?" asked Jim, mentioning the old Greek currency unit now defunct.

"No drachmas in our future," said Sophie with clear-cut finality.

"May I interest you in a glass of tea?" asked Jim. He stood up. "On the veranda."

"Delighted," said Sophie, and she stood up and followed him outside. They took up big, comfortable padded chairs facing out toward the sea. Marie came out and handed each of them an iced tea.

"You mother and daughter have gone to their rooms to get ready for dinner," said Marie to Sophie.

"I'll join them in a little bit," said Sophie.

Marie turned and went back to the kitchen.

"So, you left New York. Why?" asked Sophie.

"Well, as you go up the success ladder, you become disconnected from the skills that initially led to your promotion."

"Just what was it you were good at?"

"Identifying specific investments that were undervalued."

"Simple, good financial analysis?" asked Sophie, her face sort of quizzical.

"That's half of it. The other half is identifying potential. A lot of times there is potential lying there unrecognized."

"The diamond in the rough?"

"Exactly."

"So after you find Cinderella, are you the handsome prince that puts the slipper on her foot?"

"Sometimes. Your bank might arrange a merger or acquisition, or you just might hand it off to the salesmen to peddle the stock to institutional investors."

"So what happens as you get promoted up the ladder?"

"More and more you're just a rainmaker, trolling for money to feed into the process."

"Rainmaker?"

"The guy who brings in the money."

"*Oui, la pluie.*" (Yes, the rain.) "And what is it you do now?"

"I shape the framework in which our investment decisions are made. All the partners share in the process, but at the end, I make the final call. I seem to have a small edge here—that final bit of confidence in my reading of the situation."

"Do you always win?"

"Of course not. But I win more than I lose. And so far I've done well on the big calls. My partners count on me not to capsize the boat."

"So in the storm-tossed sea of the future, what do you see?"

"I think we'll back away from macro plays like this Greek-debt gambit we're in now. As Dieter says, the data fog is getting too thick. Our computers aren't peering far enough into the future with enough confidence to make truly big plays."

"So do you play risk on, risk off, like all the experts on TV?"

"No, we prefer to think."

Sophie laughed and asked, "Then what will you do?"

"More stock picking, more special situations. Pick lots of smaller, good investments. Go for a steady game."

"So you're not going to do 'tits and silicon' off the high corniche?"

Jim laughed. "You nailed that one, Sophie. Where did this penchant for collecting the great quotes from cowboy capitalism come from?"

"Well, like you, I found my inspiration in a book. As you can see, I am expected to write a memoir someday. I wanted to do something different, get a broader perspective."

"How did you settle on cowboy capitalism?"

"I was browsing for used books on a Sunday afternoon back in the 1990s...in the bouquinistes down by the river. I pulled out a copy of Michael Lewis's *Liars Poker*—I had heard about it in school—and I started to thumb through some pages. I landed on the page where there is the great showdown between the two great bond traders, the august head of the firm and the savvy younger trader. I read and was fascinated, and then I was simply riveted by the quote: "One hand, one million dollars, no tears." To me, that is the iconic quote of cowboy capitalism, its defining moment, the beginning of an era. It is the first quote in my little notebook. All else flows from there."

"So you've been collecting ever since?"

"Yes, if French is the language of love, then English is the language of money. Making money is your most colorful cultural activity."

"But you're mostly in politics and government?"

"Money is always the coquette in the political theater, the winsome temptation that leads the politicians astray."

Jim laughed, took a long sip of tea, and said, "I'm not colorful; I'll be a disappointment there."

"Your friend Jack has the gift. Count your partnership lucky. The barbed quip is the lightning flash of insight."

"Yes, it is," said Jim. "Jack is crucial to our success."

She smiled and set her iced-tea glass down. "I better go get dressed for dinner," she said. "At what time?"

"Since your daughter's here, let's start early. How about half past seven?"

"Excellent," replied Sophie as she stood up. "Thanks for the tea." As she walked into the house, she mulled over his choice of words about a "steady game." Yes, he had good judgment. So rare in a man...her father...her grandfather...after that...

110

Paul A. Myers

Dinner

The two women and the young girl came out to the veranda, Sophie in a white sleeveless dress, her mother in a light blue dress. Sophie took her daughter's hand and twirled her around in front of Jim, the daughter's dark blue dress flaring, and asked, "Do you like her new dress? We bought it in Juan-les-Pins this morning."

"Yes, it's nice. Stylish like her mother's and grandmother's dresses."

"Yes, she's getting to be a big girl now." Sophie stepped back and said to her daughter, "See, the hem is just at the top of the knee, right where it's supposed to be." Sophie turned and said to Jim, "The love affair between the hemline and the knee is just the first of the intimate little dances a girl learns on her way to being a woman." She glanced at her mother. "Right?"

"Yes," said Martine, and she laughed. "But she's growing like a weed. That hemline won't stay there."

Sophie laughed. "The joys of youth, short dresses."

Jim found the women's banter charming, and he beamed.

"Where do you want us to sit?" asked Sophie.

"How about Martine at the head of the table," said Jim, pointing to the other end of the table from where he was standing, "and you and Marie-Hélène at the sides."

Martine stepped over to the head of the table, and Jim came around and held her chair as she seated herself. Sophie and Marie-Hélène seated themselves, and Jim went back to the other end of the table, his back to the garden and sea beyond.

"Oh, I love the lanterns, what are they?" asked Marie-Hélène.

"Oh, they're Japanese lanterns. We hang them in the garden to keep the bugs away while we're eating."

"Does it work?" asked Martine. "We eat out on our veranda in Aix often. We use the candles, but sometimes they get overwhelmed."

"Pretty much."

"I will try it."

Sophie looked over at her daughter, who was intently staring at Jim. "You shouldn't stare at people, Marie-Hélène."

"I was just trying to figure out why he's so special."

"Special?"

111

"Yes, you said he's been out to Auverne and saw Grand-mère. And now we're here. I don't remember you ever doing that with any of your other clients." She turned and looked at Jim and explained, "Boring old men in suits."

"That's because they're big corporations. Jim is sort of a small banker, like Grand-père," said Sophie, mentioning her father.

"Well, I was just wondering...I spoke with Valérie this morning and..."

"Oh, my," said Sophie. "And what did the wicked witch of Nantes have to say?"

"Now, Sophie," said Martine, cutting in. "Valérie is really a wonderful stepmother to Marie-Hélène."

"Valérie is my ex-husband's wife," said Sophie to Jim. "All the Auverne women love Etienne and Valérie."

"I love papa, too, *maman*," protested Marie-Hélène.

"You're supposed to. He's your father," said Sophie. "And once upon a time, I loved him, and with him, we had you," soothed Sophie. Marie-Hélène beamed. She was part of a divine plan.

Martine looked down the table and said, "Jim, when Sophie divorced Etienne—I have that right, don't I, Sophie?" Martine paused for a moment. "You divorced Etienne?" she said, making the question a statement.

"Yes, *maman*," said Sophie in her best little-girl voice, as Marie-Hélène writhed in her chair, delight dancing on her face at her mother's submissiveness to her mother.

Martine continued. "Etienne insisted that Marie-Hélène use the Auverne family name. He said it would be awkward at school if she had a name different from that of the parent she lived with. He sent a bouquet of flowers to Grand-mère insisting." Martine leaned back in her chair, a self-satisfied look spreading across her face. "Grand-mère hasn't said an ill word about Etienne since."

"Mother, he's a politician. They know how to do those things."

"Yes, I'm sure he does. He'll be in the cabinet someday."

"Yes, we all know that. The issue was whether I, too, could rise to that level," said Sophie with just a twinge of bitterness. Deciding to put that behind her, she turned to Marie-Hélène and asked, "So just what did Valérie have to say?"

"I told her we were coming down here...to see a man...your client."

"And?" said Sophie, not believing that was the extent of the conversation.

"Valérie told me to keep my eyes open and I'd really get to see my mother in action."

Jim laughed, Martine smiled broadly with affection at her granddaughter, and Sophie was momentarily embarrassed.

She looked at Jim. "See, all the Auverne women are quite interesting."

"So they are," said Jim, and he looked at Marie-Hélène. "And they start young."

"Jim, you have been in banking your entire career?" said Martine, changing the subject.

"Yes, investment banking in New York and now running a private investment partnership in Geneva. Before that we were in Bermuda."

"And the clients, if I may ask?"

"Sure. Wealthy Americans on the one hand and wealthy something-or-others in Dubai on the other. For the Americans, they're wealthy families and are looking for long-term capital appreciation, which is lightly taxed at fifteen percent—at least for now. And the people in Dubai, they just want to see their account balances go up."

"They don't worry about taxes?"

"Not that I can see."

"Very new money," pronounced Martine.

"And very far away," added Jim. Martine made a knowing laugh. Jim could see she had great sophistication in finance. "Sophie said you worked closely with your late husband on the bank's wealth-management business."

"Yes, I did. It turned out to be an experience rich in lesson," said Martine.

"What lessons did you draw?"

"My husband made it a cardinal rule to put the clients' interests first."

"Yes..." said Jim.

"So that involved finding good dividend-paying companies, where the ability to pay was firmly established over time and the resources were well grounded in sound business operations."

"Yes, quality stocks…" agreed Jim.

"The other surprising thing was finding bonds that would be good for the whole thirty-year term; bonds that would be able to repay the principal. Today's bond markets are surprisingly short term."

"An excellent insight," agreed Jim.

"I traveled with him out to the clients' homes in the country or to their town houses in Paris. Once, we were out at *une bonne maison* a half day's carriage ride from Paris, and the industrialist, who was an august presence of some years—his wife was somewhat younger, as is so often the case in these situations…"

"Yes, I understand," said Jim.

"He leaned over to me and said, 'Jean-Pierre always places the money in one good investment after another,' and plopped his hands in front of him, mimicking a horse plopping across a field. 'I will leave the money in safe hands,' he said."

Jim nodded in agreement with Martine's wisdom. "Sophie mentioned, when we were in Auverne, an entity in Belgium. I don't mean to pry…" said Jim, keeping the conversation going.

"No, by no means. My husband, Jean-Pierre, was one of the pioneers of putting liquid wealth in Belgian entities for income- and estate-tax purposes. This was a great concern the last time there was a Socialist president…even I was young then. But Mitterand proved to be more dark prince than egalitarian knight."

"Yes," said Jim, agreeing with the insight. "When I was in Paris at a lycée at the tail end of the Mitterand era, my host family was at once disdainful and uneasy of the Socialists. Everyone in Neuilly was."

"Yes, there's nothing like a Socialist in the Élysée or a foreign army at the gates to put the gold under the French mattress," said Martine.

Jim and Sophie laughed.

Martine continued, "My husband worked with a small law firm in Paris that did all of our family wealth matters for the bank. It has been successful."

"A small law firm?" asked Jim skeptically.

"Yes, my husband said the big firms always wanted to put the client money in something they called 'vehicles,' where everyone could participate in the investment's success. By this they meant skimming fees off the client's money. Jean-Pierre would never play that game."

Sophie smiled broadly and nodded sagely. Her father's integrity had been a great source of pride to her.

Martine looked at Jim with a sparkle in her eye and said, "I think my husband said it was being 'on both sides of the transaction.'"

Jim laughed and asked, "And he said something else?"

"Why, yes. He thought that was an import from the world of Anglo-Saxon finance, something from either New York or London. That was the era of the junk-bond kings in New York and Arab money in London."

"I think he was right," said Jim. "I can see where some of Sophie's attitudes come from."

"Well, in the political world, some of them say they are looking out for the people, but often they're looking out for whomever eases their way and helps them get elected."

"Organizing support is never easy, Mother," said Sophie.

"Yes, but Grand-mère says that the last prime minister who looked out for the people was Léon Blum," she replied, mentioning the great Socialist prime minister of the 1936–37 Popular Front.

"Yes, there's something to be said for that," said Sophie. Just then Marie came out with a tray laden with coffee and cups and prepared to set it down on the sideboard.

Martine glanced over and said, "And with that, let me take Marie-Hélène, and we'll go to our rooms and leave you two adults to your coffee." She stood up and beckoned for her granddaughter to follow.

Marie-Hélène stood up and turned toward Jim and said, "Monsieur, forgive me. I misspoke earlier; I think I got to see my grandmother in action tonight." She curtsied and followed her grandmother into the house.

Her mother watched her go into the house with an affectionate smile. She turned back to Jim and said, "So now you know the Auverne women."

"Well, I've met them. There's one I still don't think I know as well as I might like." Jim smiled and added, "Could I get you a small cognac to go with the coffee?"

"That will be fine. Can I just have it in a snifter? I think I'll let the coffee go."

Jim walked over to the sideboard and pulled two snifters out of a cabinet; he poured some of the golden-colored liquor into the glasses and walked back and handed one to Sophie. He sat down. "Where were we?"

"Well, I'm here," said Sophie, the insouciance and assurance radiating from her expression.

"You sounded like you were not going to let your husband's ambition overtrump your ambition. Am I right?"

"Frankly, yes."

"Why?"

"I started to see the path opening to me and that I could become an important person in a powerful ministry."

"So?"

"I didn't want to go to the provinces and be a *prefet*'s wife."

"Simple as that?"

"Oh, lord, no."

"Such as?"

"With a politician, it is always 'how does this look' and the calculation 'of the angle,' and private conversation is all about 'the scheme.'"

"Tedious?"

"Eventually, yes."

"But you are pursuing an ambitious career filled with politicians?" Jim let the question hang.

"Yes," she smiled. "Pursuing a career, not a partner."

"Is the position open?"

"*Peut-etre*." (Perhaps.)

Jim laughed and then turned earnest, asking, "Can I see you up in Paris?"

"Of course," she said with a winsome smile. "You're not a politician."

"When?"

"After *rentrée*," she said, referring to the traditional start of the French school year.

Jim got out his iPhone and wiggled his finger on the screen and brought up a calendar. "How about the Opéra Bastille and then dinner on the fifteenth?"

"Delighted. What's the opera?"

"*The Marriage of Figaro.*"

"One of my favorites. Sounds like an opening evening at the opera?"

"I believe you're right."

"A long dress, gloves, fun." She smiled and then took the final sip of cognac out of the snifter and set the glass down. She stood up, smiled glowingly, and said, "A long day. What time is breakfast?"

Jim stood up and replied, "Whenever you like."

"See you then. I have so much enjoyed the evening." She turned and walked into the darkened house, the candlelight playing on the gentle sway of her white dress, moving on those lovely hips.

Jim watched her leave, feeling like he was watching a faerie princess glide away in a twirling, swirling series of dance steps, just out of reach but with a heavenly smile beckoning him on. She turned around and waved good night. He smiled and then walked over to the sideboard and poured himself another cognac.

18. Bastille

The taxicab swung around the tall, needlelike obelisk rising out of the center of the square, named the July Column after the July Revolution of 1830, when an absolute monarchy—the only kind the centuries-long Bourbon dynasty understood—was deposed for a more constitutional monarchy under Louis-Philippe, or so it was hoped. The column sat in the center of Place de la Bastille, named after the revolutionary storming of the Bourbon monarchy's prison in 1789—a hated symbol of the ancien régime—which set off the French Revolution. The massive glass-and-metal edifice of the ultramodern Opéra Bastille sat overlooking this home to revolutionary fervor, its magnificence a temple to the modern world of bourgeois Paris. Undoubtedly the government hopes the opera house will act as a sedative to any future revolutionary fervor, thought Jim.

The taxi glided to a stop across the street from the opera house. Jim shoved some euro notes at the taxi driver and then opened the door and held Sophie's hand as she scooted across the seat and out. The taxi sped off.

"Well, we navigated the revolutions, though I'm not sure which one is which," said Jim. "Although I gather the Bourbon monarchs lacked the common touch."

"Yes, their fingers only touched velvet. The streets of Paris are famous for revolution. The July Revolution of 1830 was the one celebrated in Delacroix's famous painting *Liberty Leading the People*. Today, I think the spirit of the bare-breasted Miss Liberty is leading the charge in Athens."

"Against the Fourth Reich," said Jim, good-humored mischief in his voice.

"Those angry mobs are the force that is going to put you on easy street," said Sophie. "The Germans are only going to go so far as putting the bootheel down—at least this year." She pulled a white stole close around her shoulders in the chill fall air and held a small clutch to her chest, its color matching the sky-blue evening dress she was wearing. She looked at the busy street and said, "Hard to look ladylike doing the quick shuffle across a busy street in a long dress."

"Wish I could stand back and watch," said Jim. "But I guess second best is escorting the lady across the crosswalk."

She made a laughing frown at him. She had been bright-eyed and quick tongued since he picked her up a half hour ago; there was a certain expectation in her manner. Jim was sure it was the beginning of a delightful evening. Walking across the lobby, Jim reached inside his jacket and pulled out two pieces of paper passing as tickets. An usher pointed them toward an entrance to the orchestra seating.

"We're sort of halfway down and just off the center."

"Yes, I do like to be near the aisle."

A second usher led them down the aisle and pointed to their seats; they sidestepped past a couple of empty places and sat down.

"Well, I'm so pleased your iPhone picked *The Marriage of Figaro* for us to watch tonight," said Sophie.

"Well, that's what popped up on the screen when we were in Antibes."

"Oh, I thought you liked the story," said Sophie.

"Maybe the algorithm does. I presumed I wouldn't understand the story. I seem to have that problem when all the dialogue is in a language I don't understand. But I do like Mozart's music."

"Oh, the story recounts a single day of madness in the Spanish palace of a bullying, scheming count trying to gain the favor of his most beautiful servant girl."

"What stands in his way?"

"She is betrothed to his head of household, Figaro."

"Is the count two-timing the countess?"

"Of course. But she is scheming from another direction."

"So, lots of actors and actresses are running around on the stage?"

"Yes, and it keeps the music coming," added Sophie. "Oh, be sure to listen carefully for the sound of two horns playing together. That's Mozart's musical symbol for cuckoldry."

"I didn't know music did adultery. Any other symbolism to know about?"

"Symbols? That's too intellectual. Mostly music just moves emotions. Better than any other art form, I think."

"Yes, I understand. I rarely snap my fingers in an art gallery."

"Yes, it's the music that keeps people coming to these operas after two hundred years."

"Certainly."

"There, the curtain is going up," said Sophie, expectation framing her expression. In a few moments, the mighty overture swept across the concert hall, the strings seemingly emulating horses galloping across a meadow, the horns riffing against the tempo of the strings.

Jim watched the drama unfold on the stage but often just sat back and let the melody roll over him. Sophie watched intently, her head and eyes following the dialogue back and forth, the intricacies of the story catching her interest. She sat like an admiring songbird as the sopranos sang their beautiful tales of love and woe. Presently the curtain came down and the lights went up; members of the audience stood up and headed for the aisles toward the lobby for intermission.

"A glass of champagne for madame?" asked Jim.

"Delighted," said Sophie as she stood up, wrapped her stole around her shoulders, and followed Jim out toward the lobby.

Under the sparkling lights of the chandeliers, Jim walked Sophie over to the side of the carpeted space and, nodding in the direction of a table with champagne, said, "I'll just be a moment." He walked over and bought two flutes of the pale golden liquid and walked back and handed one to Sophie. "Well, I am enjoying the opera more than I thought I would. The music and the singing are of the first order."

"In Paris, the music is always of a high order or the audience starts throwing cabbages at the conductor."

Jim laughed. "Has that ever happened?"

"Yes, once, rather famously, to Stravinsky before the Great War."

"And people have been on their toes ever since?"

Sophie laughed again. "Yes, I suspect the incident has stuck in the collective memory. Sort of like the crash of '29 with the investing classes." She looked over the top of her glass of champagne with sparkling eyes and said, "It's been a charming

120

summer, full of fascinating new acquaintances. And you seem to truly live on your wits."

"It masks the churning unease of my many doubts."

"You don't have nerves of steel?"

"Hardly." Jim sighed. "I believe to be successful at investing, you have to keep—at a minimum—at least two opposed ideas in your mind at the same time. You may act on one idea, but the conflicting idea is right there behind you, day and night, while you're in the investment. You hear the footsteps."

Sophie turned thoughtful. "In government, I always feel that it is the creation of options, the setting forth of alternatives, which creates a sense of confidence. When leaders can't see alternatives, then the walls close in. After that comes the hypocrisy, the dissembling, the digging in, the appeals to orthodoxy and ideology. You start to hear the hoofbeats of the herd, the howl of the crowds in the street."

"Yes, but the governments are like frogs on a griddle—which way will they jump?" replied Jim. "Penetrating the maze of crosscurrents is at the heart of playing the sovereign-bond markets. You have to be able to imagine difficult-to-imagine outcomes, the ones no one wants to talk about; think about all those things not being said in the cabinet room; and hear the whispers out on the streets."

"Yes, that is quite true," agreed Sophie. "But this fall at least, I think events will unfold the way you see them. The cabinet room in Berlin in the final analysis will do what it has to do to keep the Greek government on its feet. But next year could be quite different. That seems to be the nature of the slow unwinding of this crisis—each year is different from the preceding one."

"I agree. We get past the next Greek bailout, and then I think a fresh *tour de horizon* is required."

"Yes, and, of course, that is Strategy International's business," she said. "But I'm not trying to make a sales pitch this evening." She took a final sip of champagne from her glass and set it on a nearby table. "The opera is about seduction, not finance."

"Well, possibly the music is a thrilling prelude..."

"Yes, maybe the melody will get more exciting..." She opened her purse and fished out a handkerchief and dabbed her lips. Holding the handkerchief between thumb and forefinger,

Sophie extended her hand toward Jim's chest, smiled seductively, opened her hand, and let the handkerchief drop.

Jim effortlessly moved his free hand in a swinging arc and caught the handkerchief, a smile broadening across his face. His expression changed to something completely new, something Sophie had not seen before, a look of complete assurance.

"Voilà…" she said and let the word hang.

"There," he replied with an air of finality.

"I think I have your mind down to just one thing…"

"I think you're right."

"I've seen this opera many times before, but you're new…"

"If we catch a taxi now, we'll avoid the rush…"

"Yes, let's." She liked the soft decisiveness in his manner.

He took a step back and set his glass down on a ledge. He turned and put his arm through hers and guided her across the lobby, under the lights of the sparkling chandeliers, and down the steps to the street. He hailed a cab and turned to Sophie. *"Chez toi?"* (Your place?)

"Oui."

Avenue Victor Hugo

The ancient wire-cage *ascenseur* creaked upward, the moving cables throwing eerie shadows on the stone walls of the circular stairwell in the middle of the nineteenth-century apartment house. There was a sense of traveling back in time to a long-ago era of Paris. The *ascenseur* came to a halt on the *deuxieme étage* (the third floor of a French building). Jim flipped the latch on the door and pushed it open and stepped out onto the landing; he held the door as Sophie came out, fumbling in her purse for the key.

Fishing the key out, she walked over to a large wooden door and opened it; she held the door open and ushered Jim in with her hand. He walked into the drawing room and over to the tall French windows and looked out on the busy street below. He turned around and faced Sophie, who was standing on a thick Persian carpet in the middle of the well-appointed belle-epoque room. Again, Jim felt a sense of being in a different century.

"Could I get you a cognac?" asked Sophie.

"Yes. Delighted in fact." He watched her walk over to the sideboard, simply enchanted with the sway of her body. "You have a way with words."

"You were watching my words?" she said, laughing, with complete assurance in her presence; she clearly had a sense of how her body played across men's minds.

Jim laughed.

At the sideboard, she pulled a bottle out of a cabinet and some snifters off a shelf and poured the golden liquid into each glass. She walked back to where Jim was standing and handed him a glass; she held the other in front of her chest with one hand.

Jim took a sip of his cognac and looked around the room, taking in the dark paneling, the minor Impressionist oil paintings on the wall, the chairs and divans from another century, and the embroidered upholstery, once richly colored and now slightly faded.

"It's charming," he said. "The Paris drawing room of *les vicomtesses*...I don't know quite what to say. All the charming soirees, the little dinner parties..."

"The gentlemen, the late afternoons, the assignations..."

"You said that, not me," said Jim.

"But you were thinking it..."

"Well, yes, to stand in this room...I bought one of the memoirs of *la vicomtesse*—Mathilde, I believe—from the belle époque just before the war."

"Yes, a vivacious woman and an exciting time...the grand-mère of Grand-mère," said Sophie, her eyes sparkling as they danced across Jim's face, alight with expectation.

"Yes, then I understand where those rumored talents came from," said Jim, fascinated at the allure of her darting dark eyes, the vibrancy of her manner.

"That is sort of why we are here tonight...together. It always comes down to this, and sometimes I really like that it always comes down to this."

Jim took her glass from her hand and set it on an end table. He enfolded her in his arms and gazed into her face, enjoying the feel of her breasts on his chest. He looked down at her upturned face, the intensity of the passion in her eyes absorbing his gaze. He murmured, "I was wondering if the handkerchief would ever drop. You enchant me."

"Love's rendezvous, possibly a destiny encountered..." She looked up at Jim and then glanced over to one side, looking around the room, her eyes fixing on the antique divan. She made a provocative wiggle of her shoulders. "I think the divan is too small, and possibly I'm too old...another room...*peut-être*."

"Lead the way. It's your cave."

She grabbed Jim's hand and led him down the hallway to the bedroom. Inside, she walked into a closet and came out holding two dressing robes. She handed one to Jim. "Possibly this one will fit...I'll be right back." She walked through a door into the bathroom, holding the other robe.

Jim undressed, picked up the robe, and held it up, looking at it skeptically. He threw it onto a chair next to the bed. Possibly of use later, he thought. He pulled back the bedcovers and slid in and rolled over onto his side and lifted himself up on his elbow, the better to watch the approach of the woman who had been in his mind's eye for some time. She did not disappoint.

She slipped off her robe and slid into bed next to him. She snuggled up and whispered, "Good, you're not overdressed for the rendezvous."

"A meeting of the minds," he said as he reached over and caressed her flank.

"A meeting of minds? I think not. Something else, *peut-être*?"

"With the memoirs of *la vicomtesse*?"

"Yes, so many enticing possibilities...where to start?"

"We have the rest of the weekend..."

"Yes, we can take turns, with our imaginations..."

"Work our way through the pages..."

"Yes, that way we won't miss anything, but who's going to get up and read?"

"Not me," murmured Jim as he pushed the sheet back, exposing her breasts in the dim light of the room. He leaned across and kissed the breast over her heart then set his ear to the soft skin just above and mumbled, "I hear it beating."

"Uhm, I feel you, and it is not beating. I think your current interest may be long for Sophie, soon," she said with a small laugh while she nibbled his ear.

He kissed her breast and worked his way down across her stomach, kissing her navel, nibbling with his tongue while he reached under her thigh with his arm and hoisted it up and away as he slid over her other leg and into the vee between her legs, his cheek feeling her damp moistness.

"You're skipping a few pages," she murmured, pure delight in her voice. "But I don't mind. A lover's inspired initiative is love's pleasures gained."

"I'm simply starting at the good part," he murmured.

"Yes, the lover who spoke of opening the fruit with his lips…"

Morning

Jim awoke in the morning to a flutter of fingers running over his body, a nibbling at his earlobe, and the sun streaming through the window, illuminating the smooth white skin of Sophie, putting a flash in her brown hair. "Uhmm," he moaned. He let his head sink back in the pillow.

"You were enthusiastic enough last night," she murmured, the sprightliness of her voice putting verve into the room.

"I loved the chapter we found ourselves in," he said.

"Bet I can rekindle the fire," she said, and the fingers started to flutter in the special places.

He rolled over and pulled her chest up to his face and put his lips around her nipple and played with it with his tongue. He pulled his face away. "No repeating," he said.

"Not even a little bit?"

"OK, just a little," he murmured and pushed his face back into her breast and dug his fingers into her buttocks.

Several hours later, coverlets on the floor, satin sheets in disarray at the foot of the bed, Sophie lay on her back, looking over the top of her breasts and holding one foot up for inspection, wiggling the toes, then the other foot. She let her head fall back, a smile of deep contentment spreading across her face, her mind playing with her memories. As the clock chimed noon, Sophie rolled out of bed and stood up. Jim leaned on his elbow and watched, admiring the well-shaped body, the white skin, and watching her slip into her robe. She turned to him and smiled. "I'll bring back some coffee."

"Yes, thank you."

"Do you want a newspaper?"

"Only if the Acropolis has slid down and crushed the Greek central bank," said Jim.

"Oh, we'll let the smaller wars slide by this morning?" she said with a smile.

"Yeah, today let's bore ourselves with domestic policy."

"I'm glad. It's been a long time since I felt this rush of happiness, the passion, the release…the enveloping sense of contentment."

19. Berlin

Berlin was having a beautiful fall day. The German energy minister stared out of the window of his large corner office at the bustling traffic on Scharnhorststrasse below. The energy minister was having a good year. New sources of supply, particularly natural gas, the arterial blood of the European economy, were being found and developed daily. World energy prices were in a long-term decline. This was like a big tax cut for the mighty German economy.

The minister leaned back in his chair, contentment spreading across his face as he reflected—why just last week at the cabinet meeting, the chancellor had not scowled at him for the first time in who knew how long. That was high praise from Angela Merkel, the Lutheran pastor's daughter and a leader gifted at demanding results while keeping all the little boys that passed as Germany's cabinet in the harness of cooperation.

Later in the cabinet meeting, he reported that Germany's best trade negotiator, Ulrich von Renke, had just negotiated another big natural-gas contract at near-record-low prices. He further told the cabinet he expected to work with other European countries this fall on energy-contract negotiations. He expected the negotiations would break the back of President Putin's plan to make Russia the next energy superstate. Looking up at the head of the table, the energy minister had detected a faint twinkle in the eye of the *machtfrau* (the power lady).

The line buzzed, and the reverie was broken. The minister swung around in his chair and picked up the handset and punched the button. His secretary said, "The Bulgarian prime minister is on line one."

"Put him on," bellowed the minister. The minister punched the button for the speakerphone and then leaned back in his chair.

"Hello, Herr Borisov, how are you?"

"Fine, Johann. Let's skip the formalities, shall we?"

"Sure, Boyko. What's up?"

"Russia, what else?"

"Give me a rundown," said the German.

"We've got three big energy projects with the Russians, and we want to cancel two."

"Well, how are you going to do it?"

"We're going to cancel the nuclear-power plant on environmental grounds. Can you get Siemens off our back? Cancel the contracts? We'll have enough trouble with the Russians."

"Consider it done. The other project?"

"That's the Russian oil pipeline to Greece. We're shelving it on environmental grounds, too."

"Well, when they're not being pests, those environmentalists have their use, don't they?"

"Yes, they do."

"And the third?"

"We're going to go ahead and complete the South Stream project; it's one of the Russian Grand Slam projects led by Gazprom. They really want it."

"Well, it might work out, but gas demand is flagging in Europe, and new sources of supply are popping up every day. Why even the French are going to have a lot of shale oil. We'd let Russia hump the money here."

"We agree. We're not putting any state money in."

"Smart. The Russkies are happily throwing their money at their so-called opportunities. Let them keep the fun for themselves." He let out a roaring laugh.

"I'm calling about the negotiations on our new ten-year natural-gas contract with Gazprom. Like you said, supply is breaking out all over. Why we even have new gas fields right off our own coast in the Black Sea. Bulgaria needs to step back from the Russians and their high-priced natural-gas schemes."

"Right you are, Boyko. Here's my recommendation: our lead trade negotiator, Ulrich von Renke, is leading a big negotiation in Vienna later this fall. After he's through there, I'll have him come down to Bulgaria and advise you. He's good. He's been negotiating with the Russians on energy since the Soviet era."

"Excellent. I'm sure he will be of great help. There's another question I have. It's sensitive."

"Go ahead."

"Have you heard about a secret list of over a hundred thousand names with accounts at a Swiss bank? Could be embarrassing, not for me of course."

"Yeah, we've heard about it. The French secret service got it from a disgruntled bank employee. Our government has seen part of the list with twenty-seven thousand names on it."

"We're concerned the Russians might try to use it to blackmail the negotiators in the upcoming trade talks."

"Yeah, that could happen. But first they'd have to get their hands on the list. The French are unlikely to leave it laying about."

"Are you concerned about your trade negotiator, Herr Renke?"

"Not at all. Renke is bulletproof. He follows the Bill Clinton rule."

"The Clinton rule? What's that?" asked the Bulgarian prime minister excitedly. Clinton was something of a political rock star in Eastern Europe.

"Renke never takes their money...but always takes their women."

The prime minister laughed. "A real skirt chaser? My favorite kind of diplomat. I look forward to meeting him."

"You're in safe hands; I'll make sure he brings his own playmate along," replied the German minister with a laugh. He rang off.

The minister leaned back in his chair, swung around, and looked out the window. Not only did Germany have the wind at its back on energy prices, President Putin of Russia's big geopolitical power play to be the next energy superstate—another Saudi Arabia—was crumbling with the fall of energy prices. As he'd told the supercilious German foreign minister—time and time again—real foreign policy was made in the energy ministry, not by some overmannered, sixth-generation aristocrat in the foreign service. He knew that; why even the *machtfrau* kept the dandies busy with diplomatic needlework while she did the heavy lifting herself—the state-to-state stuff.

20. A Small Bank Scandal

Jürgen came over to the conference table where Jim and Jack were drinking their morning coffee and discussing the news. Outside, beyond the windows, Geneva was gray and overcast, the fall weather settling in.

"Gentlemen, there are lots of rumblings coming out about Deutsche Bank...rumors everywhere about a giant misstatement of losses on derivatives during the financial crisis."

"I've been hearing the same thing," said Jack. He turned to Jim and explained, "A clutch of complex derivatives, so-called leveraged super-senior trades..."

"Those are the puppies," said Jürgen.

"How'd they do it?" asked Jim.

"Rumor is they booked the gains on the positive moves but not the losses."

"How clever," said Jim sarcastically. "And if there had not been a misstatement?"

"Twelve billion in paper losses...Deutsche Bank would have required a government bailout," said Jürgen, shaking his head in sorrow at the shame of a bank carrying Germany's name being engaged in such shenanigans.

"The stock price barely budged...it's old history," added Jack.

"So, that horse is out of the barn, and anyway, we don't short banks," said Jim. "Now what do we do?"

"Maybe we should look at the French banks. One of them could have done the same thing," said Jack.

"Same answer," said Jim, a trace of exasperation in his voice. "We don't short banks. You wind up going against the government printing press, or it drags out its big bazooka."

"But we could get in on the bounce," said Jack. "Take the upside for the long accounts."

"Yeah, I could go along with that," said Jim.

"Dieter has some news on this. Let me bring him in," said Jürgen.

"Yeah, of course," said Jim. Playing the bounce might be a good thing; next year was looking mighty murky on the investment radar, no big macro plays in sight.

Presently Dieter came in and sat down and said, "It's really simple. We picked up unusual volumes of message traffic out of the SEC's Paris office—some new handles, a visiting audit team, Target Bank B, which we think is Crédit Générale. There were a lot of derivative losses back in the financial crisis, but the French have an alternate way of valuing the derivatives that minimizes the losses. It makes the failure to disclose look small, and, of course, there is the safety of the bank system to think about, all that rot..."

"Yes, we can imagine the reasoning, can't we?" said Jim, looking around at the smirking faces of his partners as they digested more official bank speak.

"How'd it work?" asked Jack.

"That's what's fascinating," said Dieter. "The messages said this frog professor was really insistent on his valuation technique—a real wisenheimer—anyway, you value the derivatives that lose money the standard way, but the ones that make money are valued using an alternate method, one that brings the profits back to the valuation point. And those profits offset the paper losses, and you net the two together and have something much smaller to disclose...if at all."

Jack nodded thoughtfully. "Clever." He looked at Jürgen and said, "A lot more elegant than the Germans."

"Germans don't do elegance," said Jürgen with a scowl.

Jim glanced at him and said, "Jack's right. The French were clever." He stroked his chin and verbalized his understanding: "You move real profits back in time and offset paper losses. Give the regulators something to hang their hats on. You get a scolding, not a spanking."

Jürgen nodded in agreement, now seeing the cleverness behind the French banks' strategy. Then he turned to Jim. "I thought you had a good source high up in Crédit Générale?"

"We do," said Jim. "But he hasn't said a thing."

"Now we know why," laughed Jack. "He's been busy with the Americans."

"Yes," said Jim, and he again turned inward with his own thoughts, pondering. "Probably after the news comes out, the stock will fall, and we'll get a buy signal from the source"—Jim looked over at Jack and smiled—"to play the bounce."

"That's the smart play," said Jack.

"He's a smart guy," said Jim.

La Défense

Édouard Soisson rapped on the door of Sophie d'Auverne's office. He heard the softly spoken word, "*Entrez*," and opened the door and went over and took a seat across from Sophie.

"You have something interesting for me?" asked Sophie.

"Very. Our German friends at Deutsche Bank have stepped in it."

"Couldn't happen to a nicer crowd," said Sophie with a harrumph.

Édouard smiled and said, "Looks like the bank hid twelve billion in paper losses on its derivative portfolios, much of it in New York, and then kept it secret from the Americans at the Securities and Exchange Commission during the height of the financial crisis."

"What would disclosure have done?"

"The bank would have needed a government bailout."

"The hypocrites," said Sophie with scorn in her voice. "So they floated through the crisis on paper capital, a tissue of lies. Who knew about it?"

"Here's where it gets interesting. The German bank regulators sat in on many of the meetings; so did some members of the supervisory board and senior management."

"But the Americans were kept in the dark?"

"Yes."

"And our Bermuda Triangle clients in Geneva?"

"There's no unusual trading in either Geneva or Monaco. Deutsche Bank stock seems to just jump around in unpredictable ways—no big moves. There have been rumors about this stuff for quite a while."

"Unusual activity with any French banks?"

"None that we see."

132

"Looks like our Geneva clients are standing pat. I don't know whether that's unusual for them or not." Sophie speculated in her mind about what Bermuda Triangle might be up to.

"They're pretty tied up with Greece."

"True," said Sophie, and she leaned back in her chair and pondered, drumming her fingers on the desktop. "This sounds similar to the scandal last spring at JP Morgan, with the eight billion in losses on derivatives in London."

"Yeah, the London Whale scandal, eerily similar." He didn't believe in eerie similarities.

"It's hard to imagine that all of the French banks would be innocent on this matter," mused Sophie. She looked at Édouard. "Isn't it?"

He smiled broadly and said, "I see what you're driving at." She didn't believe in eerie similarities either.

"Yes, maybe the Americans are just waiting."

"I'll go look around."

"Yes, please do. Check up on our friend Alain Renier." Sophie swiveled around in her chair and looked across the esplanade to the hulking shape of the Crédit Générale bank building; she silently contemplated the possibilities.

Édouard stood up and departed.

Le Bistro de la Banque

Édouard walked through the chill fall air and descended the steps to the deserted terrace of Le Bistrot de la Banque. He pushed through the thick glass doors and saw Pierre sitting over in his corner, working on his papers. There were a few customers sitting about the tables in earnest conversation over steaming cups of coffee. Édouard strolled casually over to where Pierre was sitting, and Pierre waved him into a chair.

"What can I do for you today, M. Édouard?"

"Just a few questions."

"Good."

"Have you seen any auditor-type people around, people that might be looking at the books of some of the banks? Maybe Crédit Générale in particular?"

"*Inspecteurs?*"

"*Oui, exactement.*"

Pierre searched his memory, his face blank.

"Possibly Americans," said Édouard.

"*Mais oui*," exclaimed Pierre, the word "Americans" flashing a recollection in his memory. "Last week, right here. They came for lunch, often with Alain Renier and some other *français*, a professor—at least that's what the guy kept telling the Americans. Very important professor, you could tell, said so himself—often."

"Where was the professor from?"

"Sciences Po."

Édouard nodded and tucked the information away. "The Americans, what were they?"

"Oh, I should say government people," said Pierre.

"Like the FBI?" Édouard pantomimed shooting a tommy gun.

Pierre's eyes went wide with the delight of a child, and he laughed. "Oh, no. Not handsome or stylish at all, poor tailoring. Not at all like the FBI on television. These guys were drab."

"Drab?"

"Yes, you know. Gray off-the-rack suits—way down the rack…"

Édouard smiled and turned thoughtful and said to Pierre, "Not FBI, drab, gray…how about paper pushers?"

"Yes," said Pierre, his face lighting up in recognition, "paper pushers."

"Must be SEC from New York," he said, mentioning the Security and Exchange Commission office in New York, home of the compliance division.

"New York…Yes, that's where they said they were going back, taking a late-afternoon flight last Thursday."

"Good," said Édouard with finality. It was a good day's work. He pulled out two envelopes and pushed them across the table to Pierre. "I really appreciate your keen observation, Pierre. We'll stay in touch about the napkins."

Pierre put the two envelopes in his pocket and nodded in agreement.

Édouard stood up and walked out of the bistro and up to the sidewalk. As he walked back toward the office, he turned a question over in his mind: how do I get to the professor at Sciences Po?

Sciences Po

The following day, Édouard walked through the streets of the Left Bank, past the famous publishing house of Gallimard, and came up to two big wooden doors standing open. The doors opened onto a small stone courtyard of a building belonging to Sciences Po, the prestigious graduate university renowned for training the governing elite. He walked through a door and into a small conference room. It had only taken one phone call to set up the meeting, greased by mentioning the word "retainer." Inside sat a middle-aged man, reading some papers. Édouard asked, "Professor Vannier?"

"Yes," said the man, standing up.

"Édouard Soissons of Strategic Intelligence International."

"Luc Vannier, pleased to meet you. Please sit down."

"It's so nice you could talk to me on such short notice. We, of course, will pay the retainer we discussed."

"Yes, of course. Tell me; what is the nature of your inquiry? You mentioned valuing bank securities."

"Yes, we have a client in Geneva, an international hedge fund. They have a position in Deutsche Bank—whether large or small, we don't know. And there are a lot of rumors floating around that there may be some question as to how the Germans valued derivative securities during the financial crisis, which is history, and how they might be valuing these securities today—which is not."

"Well, I know little about the German banks."

"The client lost some money on JP Morgan earlier this year when there was a major misstatement of derivative securities in their London branch."

"Yes, the London Whale scandal."

"Exactly," said Édouard. "And the clients don't want to get beached by a second whale."

"Yes, I see. That would be wise."

"Do you know what happened at JP Morgan? Our experts are vague on the details. But we think it would help with understanding the current situation with Deutsche Bank."

135

"Yes, normally the banks should all value derivatives in a similar way. The simplest method is to simply value a derivative at the midpoint of the closing-bid ask-price spread."

"OK, that seems logical. What can go wrong?"

"First, in thinly traded securities, the spread might be skewed one way or the other or excessively wide or distorted in some form."

"Do you have an example?"

"Yes, if someone doesn't want to sell, they could put in a high ask price at the end of the day, or on the opposite side, if they really don't want to buy, they put in a low bid quote. Something like that."

"So, in thinly traded derivatives there's lots of room for manipulation?" said Édouard.

"Yes. Sometimes these trades are deep in the shadows."

"What happened at JP Morgan?"

"I gather—this is highly unofficial, and I do not want to be quoted on this—that in some cases, rather than using the midpoint, they used what they called an 'alternative-valuation point.'"

"What was the effect?"

"Apparently to understate the potential loss exposure. Remember, I said apparently."

"Yes, I've got that. I'm not taking any notes here. We're just looking for background," said Édouard.

"Yes, alternative-valuation techniques can be controversial."

"What do you think about alternative-valuation methods in general, Professor?"

Professor Vannier leaned forward across the table and said to Édouard, "I'm working on a paper on the subject. It hasn't been published yet."

"Can you share some of your insights?"

"Of course. If for disclosure of a bank's derivative position and that position includes some trades that later turn out to be unusually profitable..."

Édouard nodded to show he was following the argument.

"...then you could use a formula and go back and adjust the price using an alternate-valuation technique, which would use these unusual and excess profits to offset some of the paper losses on the books."

"I see," said Édouard. "That would lower the reported loss necessary for disclosure."

"I would say it would give a truer picture of where the net position really stood," said Professor Vannier with self-assured smugness. "Yes, a truer and more accurate picture." He folded his hands on the table. "Yes, it takes the transaction out of the shadows."

Édouard could see that the professor knew where his consulting fees came from. He smiled and said, "Yes, I see. Your expertise has been quite helpful, Professor."

The professor smiled and nodded agreeably.

"The retainer check will be in the mail next week," said Édouard. "Once again, thanks." He reached out and shook Professor Vannier's outstretched hand.

Café Les Deux Magots

Édouard pushed through the doors into the warmth of the café, which was just starting to overflow with the late-afternoon crush of patrons. He looked around and saw Sophie d'Auverne sitting at a small, round café table overlooking boulevard St-Michel. She was idly stirring a cup of coffee and gazing at the people hurriedly walking by. He walked over and said, "Hi, got some news for you." He sat down and waved to a waiter to bring him a cup of the same drink Sophie was having.

"So you've been busy?" said Sophie.

"Yes, I think I've got it wrapped up."

"Really? With no computers? You didn't crack their encryption?" exclaimed Sophie with a laugh.

Édouard smiled and continued: "Last week there were auditors from the New York office of the SEC at Crédit Générale. Alain Renier shepherded them around. Renier used a French professor from Sciences Po as a consultant, apparently to support an alternative-valuation technique for valuing the bank's derivative positions."

"How do you know they were Americans?"

"My source said they were all wearing gray off-the-rack suits. He follows tailoring closely—I've never known him to miss."

"So you did crack their encryption," said Sophie with a laugh.

"Shoe leather and human observation still work."

"Did the Americans buy it?" asked Sophie, getting back on track.

"Apparently so, but most likely the Americans will go back to New York, prepare their position, and spring it on Crédit Générale. We'll just wait and see."

"If it's back in the past, the Americans may go light on Crédit Générale, unless it impacts bank capital today."

"Well, you're the expert on that."

"Not really," said Sophie. "Who was the professor? Do I know him?"

"How about Luc Vannier?" said Édouard.

Sophie's eyebrows arched in amusement. "I had him as an instructor when I was at Sciences Po—money and banking. He had a detailed knowledge."

"Seen him since?"

"The finance ministry uses him. And, of course, Alain would consult with him a lot."

"Did you consult with him?" asked Édouard mischievously, eyebrows arched in expectation.

"If I did, do you really think I'd kiss and tell? What would my friends think?"

"That you're going down market."

Sophie leaned across the table and, in a conspiratorial whisper, said, "I will say that when I was a student, he did offer to get close to me, provide that special mentoring…"

"And…"

"I explained I was in love with budgeting," said Sophie. "I don't know what put him off more—that answer or the simple brush-off that followed."

"I didn't think the open collar, the gold chain, and the diamond pinkie would be a dazzle to you." Édouard looked up as the waiter put a cup of coffee down. He put some sugar in his coffee and stirred it.

"I think in France the path to renown as a public intellectual does not run through money and banking," said Sophie. "No matter how many gold chains, no matter how many fawning graduate students in black turtlenecks…" She looked off into the distance, remembering a long-ago thought, and said, "Besides, I don't think his hair is sleek enough to be a first-rank French public intellectual."

"Just stringy enough to be a hired gun for a bank?"

"Yes," said Sophie, smiling at her memory. She took a sip of coffee and composed her thoughts. She turned serious. "Well, Alain has had time to contact Geneva. Has there been any unusual stock trading?"

"None that we can see."

"Interesting. Bermuda Triangle is standing pat. Well, we'll just wait for the inevitable press conference from Crédit Générale and see what happens."

"I'll keep an eye on it," said Édouard.

"So will I. Jim and I are meeting this weekend. As you can guess, we're now best of friends."

"Yes, I saw the interest the first day."

"Yes, first some interest, then I discovered the boyish charm underneath the thin patina of sophistication…he is an American after all."

Édouard laughed and asked, "Mixing business and pleasure?"

"The women of my family have a long tradition of doing just that," she said.

"Yes, *les vicomtesses*," said Édouard.

"*La vicomtesse* is a long way off for me."

"But you know the title is coming."

"It's not so much the title, but you become the chatelaine of the Château d'Auverne. And that will be soon. My mother will never go to Normandy. She will stay in her country home in Aix; it's a temple to her marriage to my father—I should really say her husband. I was a daughter of the marriage, part of the family, but the marriage was the husband, the wife—and that was the diamond."

Édouard nodded in silent understanding; it was so rare to hear a marriage described that way nowadays. He looked at her. "And the Château d'Auverne has some special significance to you?"

"The motto above the door of the château is 'fidelity and loyalty.' That is what you come back to when you're through with Paris. For me, it is getting close to that time."

"So you want to bring back someone special?" said Édouard, his eyes keen with insight.

"Yes, but I think on the road to Auverne love needs to be tested, like in the time of the troubadours, tested for its trueness. If not, how can you be sure of its constancy?"

"A rather romantic vision for you, isn't it, Sophie?"

"We're playing for keeps here," she replied, her thoughts turning inward as she looked vacantly out the window, her resolve stiffening in her mind.

Édouard let the thought drift around the table and then said, "Yes, I see—a chatelaine who commands her household and estate, a woman who is not going to be someone else's ornament." He looked out the window deep in reflection, the gray afternoon outside almost like a magnet, thinking that for the right man, Sophie d'Auverne was the winning choice.

"Exactly, what if he mistakes making money for success?" she said.

"And misses the wider horizon," added Édouard.

"Yes," she said as she looked out the window. "Europe is coming into a time requiring a wide horizon." She looked into the distance and then turned back and took a sip from her coffee. "Yes, the vision must be shared, his commitment tested."

The two of them continued to chat and watch the people walk by on the busy sidewalk.

21. Weekend Rendezvous

The taxi pulled up in front of the terminal building of the commuter airport at Le Bourget outside of Paris. A porter stepped up and opened the door, and Sophie got out. The porter got her suitcase out of the trunk. Sophie paid the driver, took the handle of the wheeled suitcase, and headed inside the cavernous terminal building. She walked over to a counter and asked the receptionist a question. The receptionist waved to an attractive woman dressed as a flight attendant, who came over and asked, "Mme d'Auverne?"

"Yes," replied Sophie.

"This way; the plane is just outside the gate. Let me take your luggage." The attendant took the handle of Sophie's suitcase.

Sophie followed the attendant through the open doors and out onto the tarmac, moving toward a sleek executive jet. A small boarding ladder was slung down from the open door. On the side of the fuselage was a triangular symbol with an intertwined *B* in it, the logo of Bermuda Triangle. The attendant handed the suitcase up to a man wearing a well-pressed white shirt, pilot's wings, and a sharp blue cap. The attendant turned to Sophie and said, "Watch your head going up the boarding steps; then turn and go forward. Just follow the pilot. There's a large seat up on the right in the salon area that will be just right for you." The attendant followed Sophie up the steps, and the pilot pulled the door shut.

Over in the terminal building, a man in large sunglasses and a fedora looked out the open door and wrote down the tail number of the aircraft. He turned and departed.

In the executive jet, Sophie walked up the small aisle and sat down in a throne-like, padded seat with a large cocktail tray on the right.

"We recommend putting your handbag and briefcase under the seat during takeoff and landing," said the attendant as she took the items and placed them in a space under the seat. "We'll be taking off shortly." The attendant walked forward a couple of steps and took a seat directly across from Sophie.

"Aren't there any other passengers today?" asked Sophie.

"This morning? No. Just you for a flight to La Palma de Mallorca. It's a beautiful day. I'm sure you will enjoy the trip. I can get you some coffee or tea after we reach altitude. We have the *Herald Tribune* or *Le Monde*, if you like?"

"Yes, *Le Monde* will be fine."

The attendant stood up, reached into a shelf in the small galley, retrieved a copy of the French newspaper, and handed it to Sophie.

"Thank you," replied Sophie. "I trust I shall not be too demanding a passenger."

The attendant laughed and said, "No, business associates of Bermuda Triangle are always easy duty. Now the investors...that can be a different story. The ones from New York can be pretty boisterous, and, of course, the Arabs are a real challenge."

Sophie laughed and said, "Yes, capital is international these days, and new money is rarely well mannered."

The attendant smiled knowingly at Sophie and said, "Madame understands."

The aircraft started to move; the attendant snapped shut her seat belt. A couple minutes later, the aircraft stopped at the foot of the runway, released its brakes, accelerated down the concrete ribbon, and lifted off in a smooth, rising motion. Sophie was impressed with the sense of speed in the small aircraft; it was like she was riding on the back of swiftly flying eagle.

After the plane leveled off, the attendant brought Sophie a cup of coffee and then resumed her seat and opened up a paperback novel.

After a while, Sophie asked, "Does this happen often?"

"Madame?" replied the attendant.

"Well, just one passenger to Majorca?" asked Sophie.

"One passenger or one woman passenger on a Friday morning from Paris?" asked the attendant with a knowing smile.

"Well, how about both," said Sophie, cracking her own self-confident smile.

"Mr. Schiller said to take special care of a special passenger. That has never happened before. He's usually all business."

"Actually, we are going to discuss some business," said Sophie. "I'm a consultant at Strategic Intelligence International.

But, yes, it is mostly friendship." Sophie smiled with customary self-assurance.

The attendant was impressed: yes, this was someone special. "I did not think you were going to Majorca to brief an Arab investor," said the attendant with a wink.

Sophie laughed and said, "Does that happen often?"

"Briefings are usually in Geneva—over lunch. Then the investors are whisked off to London for their frolic. London understands, shall we say, their tastes."

"Yes, I can imagine. My name is Sophie."

"Mine is Anouk."

The two women chatted about this and that until the plane approached the airport at Palma de Mallorca.

Hidden Eyes

Later in the morning, at the Russian trade-delegation offices in Paris, an encrypted message went to Moscow. "Subject flew in Bermuda Triangle executive jet this morning; flight plan indicates destination is Majorca. Bermuda Triangle has secure computer center in a Majorcan villa that routes encrypted-message traffic. Believe object still in Geneva. Recommend alert Geneva team for next operation."

Moscow

The director of energy security services for Gazprom, the big Russian natural gas company, sat behind his desk and scowled at an underling. He threw the piece of paper down and said, "The energy minister wants that list. Where do you think the CD is?"

"In a safe deposit box at a bank in Geneva belonging to Bermuda Triangle, a hedge fund."

"Who says?"

"Team Geneva."

"We have to rely on those guys?"

"I'm afraid so."

"Tell them it's time to get the CD."

"And if things don't...well you know...don't go well...again..."

"Tell them it's the refinery."

The underling gulped, his voice quavering, and asked, "The refinery?"

"Yes, the refinery. Fear works."

22. Majorca

Sophie came through the portal into the arrival lounge at the airport just outside Palma de Mallorca. She was firmly holding a large Longchamps handbag and carrying a thin briefcase. Anouk followed, pulling the wheeled carry-on suitcase. Jim was standing right there and flashed a welcoming smile and cooed, "*Mon amour.*"

Jim smiled at Anouk and said, "Some of this weekend really is business, Anouk. Sophie's my window into how Paris thinks about the Greek bailout that you and Dieter are working so hard on."

Sophie's eyebrows shot up in amazement and then amusement; Anouk worked with Dieter? The Bermuda Triangle people were always full of interesting surprises.

Anouk gave Jim the handle to Sophie's luggage and smiled warmly at him. "I better get back to Geneva. I'll tell Dieter the research on Greek bonds is in caring hands." She turned and held out her hand to Sophie and said, "I so much enjoyed the opportunity to speak with you on the flight down. I think I'll be seeing you Monday morning for the flight back." She turned and walked out onto the tarmac, toward the waiting executive jet.

"I'm so glad you could come," said Jim. "It's even nicer here than on the Riviera at this time of year."

"I'm really looking forward to it. Anouk is an interesting person; I enjoyed chatting with her on the way down here."

"Yes, we lured her away from Air France with the promise of training in securities analysis, which she turned out to be quite good at. She speaks Arabic, so after we ply the Arab investors with wine at lunch and then pile them into the jet for the flight back to London, well, she hears all sorts of interesting stuff."

"Arab investors? You mean guys from the big sovereign-wealth funds run by the Gulf states?"

"Naw, nothing like that. Small fry, you know—the lower-tier billionaires. Guys who like to have a good time...with girls that like to get paid."

"Yes, life at the top, I suppose. And Anouk picks up valuable intelligence?"

"Yeah, about our investment program...and gossip about stuff going on down in the Gulf."

"And the other information?" Sophie arched a questioning eyebrow.

"Well, let's say those girls in London really earn their money for the work."

Sophie laughed and said, "Well, if you read Philippe Lagrande, you get a pretty graphic description of what you call 'the work.' It starts with the spanking and goes from there."

"That's London, but we're here on a beautiful, sunny day in Majorca, heading for a beautiful villa over on the east side of the island."

"A Mediterranean villa is about as far away from London as you can get. I look forward to our time together."

Walking across the parking lot, Jim pointed to a small car and said, "Here's our island car. Hop in." He opened the trunk and put Sophie's bag inside, adding, "You didn't bring much."

"I didn't think you planned on me needing a lot."

"Well, we'll have dinner tonight."

"There's a nice cocktail dress in there."

The Last Helicopter to Majorca

Jim wheeled the little Peugeot down the narrow one-way streets of Cala Bona, a village near the villa, in the late-afternoon twilight. He turned onto an alleyway, with the blue sea at the end of the street, and poked around for a parking place. Finding one, he backed and twisted the little coupe into the slot. They got out and walked down the street and turned onto the esplanade bordering the sea. They walked along, arm in arm, until they came to a small point with a little boat harbor in its lee. Jim held his arm out to Sophie, pointing across an open patio, with vacant tables and folded umbrellas, to steps leading up to a glassed-in porch underneath a circular awning with the name "Es Mollet" emblazoned across the crown. Jim opened the big wooden door and followed Sophie in while waving at the proprietor coming up from the long wooden bar. "Carlos, *buenos noches*."

"Ah, good evening, señor Schiller. So nice to see you again. Right over here," said Carlos, and he strode over and took Sophie's arm and guided her toward a table against a big plate-glass window overlooking the boat harbor, where small fishing boats lightly bobbed to their mooring lines. Jim followed, thinking that, yes, Sophie's white cocktail dress was both light and a delight.

The sun was just setting beyond the hills in the middle of the island, casting a soft, golden glow along the coast as the twilight shadow of the hills descended on the gunmetal-blue sea.

"It's beautiful," murmured Sophie.

Carlos brought Jim a wine list, and he opened it and handed it to Jim. Jim gave it a puzzled glance for a moment, then brightened and, with both hands, turned the list around and held it open under Sophie's gaze, saying, "You pick."

"*Avec plaisir, monsieur*," she said. She ran her finger down the list and said, "*Celui-ci.*"

"Good choice, a fine Chardonnay," said Carlos.

Carlos brought a bottle back and marched the bottle through the ritual with great aplomb as Jim sniffed and sipped and nodded gravely, his eyes alight with amusement. Sophie was greatly entertained by Jim's mocking savoir faire.

"*Bon Americain*," she said with a laugh. "My cowboy has been wine trained."

Carlos filled both glasses with a flourish and then turned to Jim and asked, "For dinner? Your favorite?"

"Yes," said Jim. "*La paraillada.*"

Carlos beamed and turned and headed for the kitchen.

"You'll love it," said Jim, leaning across the table to explain it to Sophie. "It's a big, heaping plate of all sorts of seafood. Three kinds of fish and *gumbas*—shrimp, crab, clams, and whatever else is lying about in the kitchen. Simply delicious."

"I'm sure I will. It will be all Mediterranean. Paris is almost always Atlantic, usually from Brittany."

Jim nodded, took a long sip from his wineglass, and shifted the conversation. "You were saying about Greece this afternoon…"

"You didn't seem much interested this afternoon, or were you—what did Mae West say, 'just pleased to see me'?"

"You distracted me."

147

"Do you say that to every woman you find unclothed?"

"No, I don't say it, but they are always distracting. But I really liked the surprise…"

"*Bien sûr,*" said Sophie with a naughty smile as she remembered the afternoon. She laughed. "Yes, one feels like an undraped goddess—the white sheets, the green trees, the blue sea beyond. An afternoon as Aphrodite…"

"Yes, I was with Aphrodite." He loved the metaphor; she seemed so goddess-like to him, the gift of her intimacy further enhancing her allure.

"The lovely pine trees, so billowy, rustling in the breeze…" she said.

"Yes, that's why we chose the villa as a computer-security center."

Sophie laughed and said, "What a clever disguise." She shifted her tone and asked a question. "When we drove in tonight, you pointed out the crossroads and said that was where the Guardia Civil could cordon off the entire Costa de los Pinos peninsula from the rest of the island. Does that have something to do with your computer-security center?" She nodded out the window in the direction of the crossroads at the base of the peninsula.

"Look out there, across the bay, at the peninsula," said Jim, pointing to the long black mass running across the far side of the window in the distance.

Figure 6 Dining along the esplanade at Cala Bona, Majorca. Costa de los Pinos is across the bay in the background.

Sophie turned her head and took the long peninsula in with a glance, the high ridge saw-toothed with the silhouettes of pine trees reaching into the night sky. Running along the peninsula, just above the darkened shoreline, were twinkling lights from villas hidden back in the trees, secluded and private. "Yes, your own little Cap Ferrat," she said, mentioning the exclusive peninsula along the French Riviera.

"Well, when civil unrest overwhelms Europe—"

"Civil unrest?" asked Sophie, her expression changing to one of shocked incredulousness.

"Yes, like in 1848, when revolution spread across Europe, sending kings flying—" *with the money from the treasury*

"Revolution?" she asked, her face betraying consternation. *of their countries*

"When the euro cracks up, when angry pensioners in France are screaming, '*Nein! Nein! Nein!*" as they burn buses on the Champs Élysées, while in Frankfurt frugal German housewives storm the European Central Bank…"

"Ah, yes," said Sophie, a dawn of recognition and a slow smile of amusement at the wild improbability of it all crossing her face.

"Well, the Spanish prime minister, many of the other ministers, and the king all have villas out on the peninsula." Jim swept his arm along the darkened expanse beyond the window. "And there's a heliport hidden in there, so when unrest overwhelms the mainland, the government goes into exile at Costa de los Pinos, and the Guardia Civil cordons off the peninsula from the prying eyes of democratic unrest, the raging accountability of the people."

"So Bermuda Triangle has a helicopter," said Sophie, getting the thread of the story.

"In Barcelona," replied Jim. "On standby."

"So it's the last helicopter to Majorca as European central banks melt into the ooze of insolvency," said Sophie.

"Yes, exactly. I'll save you a space on our helicopter," said Jim helpfully.

"And the prime minister is just going to let you fly into his helipad?"

"Dieter says not to worry. We'll have all the right recognition codes. 'Expect a royal welcome,' he said."

"No room for error?"

"Dieter says the king may have some explaining to do when he arrives but that we're home free. Plus we can offer to share some of our gold bars, buy supplies from the local villagers. The Spaniards will probably have to leave theirs in the vaults of the central bank in Madrid for political reasons."

"Yes, I see; I'll be flying with the black helicopter people," said Sophie as she gulped the last of her wine.

"Don't laugh. We'll be on the right side of the Guardia Civil cordon. That counts for something."

Jim reached over, picked up the wine bottle, filled Sophie's glass, and nonchalantly said, "In my world, you have to test your thinking at the end points, at the far end of the range of possibilities."

"Yes, I see; speculating in Greek bonds is just a walk in the park for you guys," Sophie said, "when you're not out walking with your black swans."

Jim smiled broadly. "I knew you'd understand."

Carlos brought up a large, steaming plate of seafood, with a big fork sticking out of the side of the plate. He put down a bowl of rice. Jim served rice onto each plate and then heaped piles of seafood on top. "Got enough?" he asked.

"Quite enough," she said with enthusiasm as she dug in.

They ate, chatted, drank the wine, and then drove back to the villa nestled among the billowy pine trees.

Shooting the Hostages

Late the following afternoon, Jim turned off the two-lane roadway leading in from Costa de los Pinos to Cala Bona and drove down a wide, divided avenue lined with trees. Coming to a traffic circle, he swung around the central island and pulled into a parking place in front of a low-slung, tile-roofed restaurant hidden behind a luxuriant growth of small trees and bougainvillea.

"Sa Punta," said Jim, naming the restaurant. "Hidden and exotic."

"A charming location," said Sophie as she looked at the lights twinkling along the coastline running to the north.

They walked in through an arched portico; past a small gift shop, now closed for the season; and into a reception area, where a jacketed maître d' met them.

"*Buenos noches*," he said with a wide smile. He led them out onto the terrace and over to a private spot under a low-lying thatched roof, behind a glass screen, which kept the autumn breeze away. A candle in a red glass lantern glowed in the center of the table.

The maître d' moved to hand Jim a wine list. Jim held his hand up as a sign to stop and said, "A good rioja will be just fine."

The maître d' smiled and said, "Of course." He turned and walked away and came back in a few minutes with a bottle of the fine Spanish red wine. He poured two full glasses, set the bottle down, and watched as the two guests took sips.

Sophie took a sip and murmured, "A good red. If I knew I would not be quoted, I would say better than most French reds."

"Your discretion is safe with me." He turned to the waiter and said, "*Muy bueno*."

The waiter beamed and took out his pad and held his pencil at the ready. Sophie said, "I'll try the seafood paella."

The waiter nodded enthusiastically in agreement with the choice. Jim added, "Me, too." The waiter wrote the orders down and turned and headed into the interior of the restaurant.

"I loved going to the seaside village today," said Sophie.

"Cala Ratjada."

"Yes, your own little Capri, tucked in down at the far end of the island."

"Yes, it's almost the end of the season, or there would have been more shops open."

"Oh, but what was there was delightful. Shopping in the village was a small adventure, and the holidays are coming. The consignment store was a great find."

"The saleslady saw you coming."

"Well, I saw the Chanel handbags in the window...I'm really shopping for three, not just myself. There's a daughter to think about and my mother..."

"I think you got the last three."

"Well, at five hundred euros apiece, they're a bargain. They're a thousand euros each at the consignment stores in Monaco, over three thousand new at the Bon Marché in Paris."

"Yes, the eternal lure of the bargain," said Jim, and he laughed. "Don't any of the consignment stores in Paris carry Chanel handbags?"

"Normally, yes, but my favorite, a little store in the Outer Sixth, was all out last week. Madame explained that a Chinese lady from California cleaned her out. She bought one—then all the rest, while her husband, an accountant, was doing the laundry down the street."

"Really?"

"*C'est vrai.*" (It's true.)

Jim laughed and said, "At least one of them knew value."

Sophie smiled and changed the subject: "The seaside esplanade with the outdoor restaurants was beautiful."

Jim remembered; Sophie had lovingly gone over each handbag, inspecting the certificate, checking the quality. Smiling at her triumph, she then looked across the top of her wineglass at Jim, with a mischievous smile, and said, "Maybe when we're in exile, we could take coffee with the king some morning on the esplanade?"

Jim laughed and turned thoughtful and said, "More likely, Jack will simply confer with the finance minister."

"On the loan of the gold bars?"

"You laugh, but gold bars are going to be the new derivatives. Everyone will want some."

Sophie laughed and added, "Yes, a return to first principles."

"Fiat money was always a little suspect."

"Now on the drive over, you were asking about Greece, modern Greece..." said Sophie, changing the subject.

"Yeah, there are no gold bars there," retorted Jim.

"My recollection is that you're betting on pieces of paper."

"Yeah, and if they pay off, we can always convert the paper profits into gold bars later, after the little people are sold out..."

"Good thinking," said Sophie, amused with all this talk about gold bars. She looked across at Jim, her face asking Jim to proceed.

"What do you think?" Jim asked. "Is Bermuda Triangle's position going to pay off?"

"Right now, the Greek ten-year is trading above thirty cents to the euro. A lot of the American funds got in over the summer at seventeen cents. We—Strategic International—think your position is safe."

"Yeah, the December play looks almost locked-in."

"We think the December buyback will come in at thirty-three cents," said Sophie. "The Germans balk at anything above thirty-five cents. But remember, a lot of European banks make a capital gain at this price. No losses have to be reported. Bank capital is strengthened. The finance ministers really like that."

"It's the sweet spot."

"Another great Americanism."

"Yeah," said Jim, and he scowled. "But I hear that those jerks at Deutsche Bank want to invoke the collective-action clauses and force the price down below thirty." Jim's face clouded over with disgust.

Sophie laughed and leaned back in her chair. "No way. Deutsche Bank is blowing in the wind. Italy and Spain are the hostages in this drama; they're too big. If they started to wobble, Europe would be on the edge of a colossal financial crisis. Europe's leaders would be standing on the precipice—a financial 1914 before them."

"Hostages?" said Jim.

"Yes, Spain and Italy," replied Sophie. She held her right hand out to the side, making it into a toy pistol and aiming it at the olive oil. She continued, "The top hedge-fund lobbyist—that's your lobbyist, cowboy—called all the capitals of Europe, spoke to the top people at the highest levels, and said that if there were any collective-action clauses invoked in Greece, then the hedge funds would sell Italy and Spain into mega-crisis territory—shoot the hostages so to speak." Sophie popped her thumb down twice, shooting the bejeezus out of the olive oil. She looked at Jim with laughing eyes and said, "The hostages are too big. We have tapes of several of the conversations. Your lobbyist is quite good."

"Gets lots of practice in Washington."

"What do you Americans call that? The big leagues?" said Sophie.

Jim relaxed and laughed. "You're right. But I'm paid to worry."

"You do it well," Sophie soothed.

"What about next year?" asked Jim. "We see that Société Générale agrees with you that when Spain gets back on its feet, Greece probably goes back on its butt."

"Yes, I would say that Greece will be out of play. Too difficult to call." She turned thoughtful and mused, "The northern European voters will, at some point, demand a blood sacrifice."

"An interesting way to phrase it," said Jim. "Jack will like that phrase."

They continued chatting through their dinner, enjoyed a dessert, and then went back to Jim's villa and a sumptuous feeling of togetherness in the large and warm bed, with the soft murmur of billowing pine boughs rustling in the breeze outside the windows.

The Wine-Dark Sea

Early Sunday evening, the last evening of the sojourn, Sophie came out onto the wide veranda at the rear of the villa. The veranda overlooked a long, slopping hill down to the rocky shore bordering the sea. It had been a day of leisurely lying about the villa. Beyond the rocky shoreline was the blue sea, stretching away to the horizon in the late-evening twilight.

"We'll eat inside," said Jim, nodding at a table just beyond the large bay window. There was a small fire in an ancient stone hearth at the side of the dining area, giving a sense of warmth to the room. "It's getting a little late in the season for the veranda."

Sophie pulled her sweater close to her and nodded in agreement. Jim's cook came out with a small tray with two champagne cocktails in wide, long-stemmed glasses. Sophie picked one up and took a sip. "Umm, good. It's been a delightful day, reading and listening to classical music without a care in the world."

Jim nodded in agreement and then held his hand out and pointed inside toward the table. "We better start. I told Ismelda— she's our cook—she could go after she served the dinner."

"Fine," said Sophie, and she walked through the door and over toward the table. "Where am I?" she asked.

"Here," replied Jim and held the chair. Then he walked over to the sideboard and opened a bottle of wine and brought it back to the table. He poured a nice, dry Riesling into two wineglasses. "Fish tonight. Oysters to start."

"Lovely."

Ismelda came and put a plate of oysters, sitting in ice, in the middle of the table. A lemon sauce, creamy and smooth, sat in a well in the middle of the plate.

Jim looked up at Ismelda and then turned to Sophie and said, "The lemon sauce is one of Ismelda's specials." Ismelda beamed at the recognition.

Sophie picked up one of the oysters, dipped it in the sauce, put it in her mouth, and chewed. "Delicious."

Ismelda beamed again and turned and went back to the kitchen.

Sophie looked at Jim inquisitively and said, "I have been meaning to ask, since that first meeting in Paris, about the division of profits between New York and Dubai. Then when I was in Geneva, you pointed out the Max Ernst painting and called it *The Sausage Cooker*. Do you have some secret process, or is it like Ismelda's lemon sauce, some sort of exotic concoction?" She dipped an oyster into the sauce and held it up between her and Jim for inspection before popping it in her mouth.

"It's simple. A couple of years ago, I flew into New York for a weekend. I met with our tax attorney at the Four Seasons for Sunday brunch. He is tall and thin, real starchy, with thinning, swept-back gray hair; long, bony fingers; and a haughtiness about him that would make a duke deferential."

"Arrogant?"

"Not at all. Way past that."

Sophie laughed and asked, "What was his background?"

"Simple he said, 'Harvard and Harvard,'" cracked Jim. "Then he turned his head toward Washington and nodded and added, 'Of course a little midcareer work as a deputy treasury secretary...'"

"Working for the people?" asked Sophie, eyes twinkling with mischief.

"I don't think he said that," answered Jim. "I doubt if it even came to his mind."

"What was his advice?"

"He said we should just structure the investments in common with distribution agreements saying that certain partners, say the investors in Dubai, should get certain types of income and other investors, say the American investors, should get other types of income by equitable division by preference...or something like that."

"Sounds simple," said Sophie.

"That's what he said. Busy work for the accountants."

"And?"

"You run the American share through what's called a white-listed offshore entity in Bermuda and send it happily on its way to New York for distribution by a bank—one correct piece of paper after another correct piece of paper in one long daisy chain of correctness." Jim beamed a smile at Sophie. "It's all posted electronically by the bank to the IRS..."

"And because it comes from a computer, it must be correct," said Sophie, completing the sentence, her eyes flashing with amused pleasure.

"You forgot. Getting that white listing OK'd by the Paris international economic organization, the OECD, was a stroke of genius by the international tax bar."

"The home of the truly dark designs," said Sophie with a sigh. "You're saying the system is crooked?"

"No, just greased."

Sophie laughed and said, "By lawyers like him?"

"Yeah, I told him it was really neat that the top lawyers in New York had the tax code all figured out, because all the legal mumbo jumbo mostly just confused me."

"You confused?"

"Yeah, I just black box it in my mind."

"And the lawyer?"

"He said, 'Well, that's the way it's supposed to work.'"

"But he understood?" asked Sophie.

"Yeah. He really understood. Then he turned thoughtful and nodded toward Washington and stretched his eyes hard right, almost as if he could see the Capitol dome. He asked the central question, 'But do they?'"

"And?"

"I asked him: 'You mean the senator from Montana, the guy that wipes the manure off his cowboy boots after walking across the rug?'"

"Manure? *Qu'est-ce que c'est?*"

"*La merde.*" (The shit.)

"Oh, yes. We're talking about politics. And what did the lawyer say?"

"He said, 'You understand.'"

"What is his explanation of why politicians act the way they do?"

"He explained it to me. Said the elected representatives never know more than the people. Beyond that, they know what they're paid to know. Simple."

"Yes," said Sophie with a moment's reflection. "Until you're sitting somewhere like the Élysée with *le president*, trying to figure out just what the people will actually know at the time of the next election, where they will come down—an impossible enigma to unravel. Then it's just le président straining an ear to hear the distant voice of the people. Not knowing drives many elected leaders deep into indecision."

"Sort of lonely at the top?" said Jim.

"Yes, there's also a large irony. Le président is at the top. He rides in his limousine and looks out the window at the people walking on the sidewalk, hurrying into the Metro, honking the horns of their cars—but they have the power. The contradiction is psychologically unsettling. You can see it when he erupts in a sudden flash of anger, like lightning across a gray sky."

Jim raised his wineglass and clinked glasses with Sophie. "To the lightning."

Ismelda came and set down before each of them a plate with a steaming sea bass laid down the center of the plate—the fish split down the middle from head to tail, with the light white meat lying above the skin and the thin white bones of the skeleton below—and creamy potatoes and long green beans arranged along the either side of the plate. Ismelda stood back and said, *"Bon appetite."*

Sophie took her fork and carefully carved a piece of the sea bass away from the skin below, the light white meat perfectly flaking on the fork. She lifted it up to her mouth and savored the dry taste of the fish. She looked at Ismelda and said, *"Très bien."*

Ismelda beamed and looked at Jim for approval.

"Thank you, Ismelda. You've done it again."

Ismelda turned and headed back for the kitchen.

As Sophie worked away at her fish, she asked Jim, "So, the Greek bond deal coming up is at a price of thirty-three cents, with payment in short-term notes from the ECB—payable in six months. What do you think?"

"The lawyer from New York emailed me this morning. Said take the notes, since it rolls the tax date of the transaction over to next year and converts it from ordinary income to a beautiful, low-tax long-term capital gain."

"Why did the Europeans do the investors the favor?"

"All the American funds will take the deal. It's sweet. The Europeans don't want any holdouts."

"So the Troika knew that," said Sophie, carefully chewing her fish.

"Yeah, they knew how to bait the hook."

"Before joining Sarkozy's government, Christine was chairman of the big American law firm McKenzie and Baker. She knows Americans. She once told me to always understand the other side's bottom-line position in a negotiation. Then she told me about Americans. Said that if you knew their hole cards—that's a poker term from cowboy capitalism—"

"Yes, I know that," said Jim.

"Then you would know when they're bluffing."

"Well, in this situation, for the investors, it's just a question of scooping up the money on the table. No bluffing. It's the governments that are bluffing, guessing that the European Union won't let 'em go down the drain and default on their bonds."

"Yes, but the governments in southern Europe—the Club Med—are playing weak hands, no hole cards. Christine would know that," said Sophie with the thoughtful air that came with grasping a new insight.

"She's always the toughest voice at the table," said Jim. "Never wobbly. As Dieter would say, always a strong signal."

"Yes," said Sophie. "She always extracts that final provision, makes some parliament pass the unthinkable; let the most venal of special interests know that Christine is in town."

Jim laughed and said, "That would make a great 1960s rock 'n' roll song—'Christine is back in town.'"

Sophie laughed and took a sip from her wineglass. They continued chatting and finished the meal.

Jim stood up and walked over to the sideboard and looked back at Sophie and said, "I have some decaf here…and cognac." Jim poured coffee in cups and cognac in big, globular snifters and put them on a tray and brought them back and set the cups and snifters on the table.

Sophie smiled and said with a touch of dreamy sweetness, "I like you—you wear your success so matter-of-factly that it provides a veneer of humility."

Jim swished the cognac in the glass and looked at it, his mind deep in reflection. "Well, there is always the well-founded fear that the efficient-markets hypothesis is vengefully correct." He took a sip and set the glass down and said, "It could all go poof."

"Well, if life is going to be short, there is only one thing to do."

"What's that?"

"Go to bed early."

"And?"

"Fall to sleep late," said Sophie with an edgy provocativeness. Turning reflective, she said, "You really make me feel like a girl."

She sipped her coffee and murmured, "And I really liked being a girl."

Jim looked through the candlelight and stared into those gray-brown eyes, enchanted, the efficient-market hypothesis left far behind.

23. Russians in Geneva

Jim sat in the coffeehouse a couple blocks away from Bermuda Triangle's Geneva office, sipping his coffee. He'd been floating on a cloud ever since getting back from Majorca, his thoughts constantly turning to Sophie d'Auverne and the possibility of having a future with her. The Greek bonds just seemed like a distraction.

Turning to business, he started reading the *Financial Times* on his iPhone, catching up with the fast-moving events of Europe. The bailout of Greece seemed to be on track, but the German public was angry as hell and didn't want to take it anymore—whatever "it" was. The self-righteousness of the German politicians was comical. The German banks had recklessly lent hundreds of billions of euros to the southern European countries—the so-called Club Med countries so disliked by the German public, except on the holidays, when they were vacationing there.

Two burly, working-class guys in their early sixties ambled up. They were vaguely familiar and, in thick Russian accents, asked if they could sit down. Taking no for an answer didn't seem to be on their minds.

"Sure," said Jim a little nervously.

"You're Jim Schiller of Bermuda Triangle, right?" one of them asked, a heavyset man with a brush-cut flattop coming down to a brutish forehead.

"Maybe. Why?" replied Jim, somewhat startled that they knew who he was.

"You're in thick with the French babe?" the other one said, making the statement sort of a question. He, too, was heavyset but with a completely bald head, making him look like a Slavic version of Goldfinger.

"Well, I know many French ladies," replied Jim.

"You know which one we mean," said the brutish Russian, a menacing insistence to his voice, that big forehead furrowed in determination.

161

"No, I don't," replied Jim rather indignantly.

"Don't play stupid with us," warned the Russian Goldfinger. "We're pros. You're not."

"Now back to Sophie d'Auverne, your sweetheart."

"Well, yes, I know her, but I would hardly call her a sweetheart."

"That's not what Paris says," said Goldfinger.

"Mistress," said the brute, with an unsettling relish of expectation.

"Just a little fling, I would say," replied Jim in a voice straining to sound nonchalant.

"We hear she's a good fuck," said Goldfinger.

"We have friends who might like to find out," said the brute. "In Syria."

"Syria?" gasped Jim. "What's all this about?"

"Don't play dumb with us. We want the CD," said Goldfinger.

"The CD?" asked Jim, perplexed.

"You some sort of slow learner?" asked the brute, cracking the knuckles of his right hand with his left.

"No, it's just that I don't have any CD," said Jim nervously. He was confused.

"It's in the safe-deposit box at the bank," said Goldfinger. The brute cracked the knuckles of his left with his right. Goldfinger continued, "Let me refresh your memory, golden boy; it was at the local branch of Banque Genève Crédit Suisse—right around the corner—and here's the date and time you and French *poule* opened the safety-deposit box." He slid a piece of paper across the table with the details written on it.

"Oh," said Jim, a realization coming over him. "Yes, I was there with Mme d'Auverne. No CD, just a necklace—avoiding a wealth tax in France. I lent her the use of a safe-deposit box." He looked at the two Russians and said in a tentative voice, "Harmless enough, I would think."

"Let me give you a little background on the CD, bright boy," said the brute. "It's a computerized list of over a hundred and thirty thousand secret Swiss bank accounts at the Swiss branch of HSBC bank," he explained, mentioning the big, worldwide British bank. "The French secret service got the list. Then the French finance ministry was given a copy. The finance minister, Christine

Lagarde, then sent a CD with over two thousand names of Greek account holders to Athens for investigation for tax evasion. Lagarde is now the big wheel at the International Monetary Fund—"

"Yes, I know," said Jim, trying to regain his composure.

"Gee," the brute said to Goldfinger, "pretty boy knows something."

Goldfinger nodded at the brute to continue.

"So some of our friends at a big Russian arms manufacturer sold a TOR-M1 missile system to Greece. Nice deal. Some of our Greek friends got nice commissions on the deal. You understand?"

"Yes, I think so," said Jim. "Bribes."

"Slow learner," said the brute. "I thought I clearly said commissions."

"Yes, commissions," repeated Jim. "Sorry."

"Well, these Greek guys seemed to do their family banking at HSBC—"

"They're on the list?" asked Jim.

"Pretty boy is catching on," said the brute to Goldfinger.

"Yeah, but something happened to one of the Greek guys. So sad," said Goldfinger, and he gazed directly at Jim. "One of these guys got depressed when the news came out that he was part of the defense-ministry scandal."

"Yes, embarrassing," said Jim. "For him and his family."

"Yes," said Goldfinger, and he looked at Jim and added, "He got so depressed that apparently he committed suicide in a Jakarta hotel room."

"Jakarta?" said Jim with some perplexity.

The brute broke in. "Then another Greek on the list, one of our good friends who got a nice commission on the missile system, was exposed as being on the list."

"Apparently in Greece depression is contagious," added Goldfinger.

"Sadly, the second Greek apparently committed suicide in Athens."

"Is there a pattern in here?" asked Jim in a quavering voice.

"Yeah, the Lagarde list is turning lethal to people associated with it. So we want to take it off your hands…keep you nice and healthy. Understand?" said Goldfinger.

"Yeah," said Jim. "I follow the healthy part."

"We're the good cops here," added the brute. "We want you to understand. Some of the other agents aren't so nice, the ones in Jakarta and Athens. They like to vacation in Syria—with French women."

"I see," said Jim. "So you guys aren't going to take my word that there's no CD in the safety-deposit box."

"Easy to check out. We'll just all go over to the bank and look at the safe-deposit box," said Goldfinger. "Clear this all up in half an hour."

"Well, I don't have the key. Mme d'Auverne has it, and she's in Paris."

"You better get her and that key up here really quick or..."

"Let me text her."

"You do that, pretty boy."

Jim picked up his iPhone and quickly sent a text message to Sophie: "Come to Geneva with box key ASAP."

Goldfinger reached over and snatched the phone out of Jim's hands and read the message. "Good. We'll wait and see what she says."

The brute looked at Jim and said, "Let me tell you about Syria. Our service is the backbone to the Assad regime."

"Yes, I understand Russia is a big supporter of Syria," said Jim, trying to be conversational. "A lot of aid."

"We get the CD, or she goes to Syria. Understand?"

"I think so."

"The director of state security likes French women. He says he enjoys them before they talk...and after they talk."

"What happens then?" asked Jim in a tremulous voice.

"A trip to Beirut, with the director, on the road high up above the Bekaa Valley. They stop, bend 'em over the hood of the car, and spread their legs—their last orgasm..."

"The climax of the trip," laughed Goldfinger.

"That last ecstasy, and then...the woman never gets to Beirut." The brute looked at Jim with an expression of great finality.

"I see," said Jim.

"No, you don't, smart boy. You won't be making the trip." He whisked his fingertips across his throat.

Jim gulped and sat silent. The two Russians watched him. They were good at this; Jim could tell. A couple minutes later, the phone beeped with the sound of an incoming message: "Returning to Paris. Will be in Geneva Monday, noon flight, with key."

Goldfinger carefully read it. He handed the phone back to Jim. "We'll see you at the bank, half past noon on Monday. Mess up, mister…"

"Syria for the lady," said the brute.

"You'll never leave Geneva," said Goldfinger. "Yeah, like I said, two of our senior agents are flying in Monday night. One from Jakarta, one from Athens—to pick up the CD or find out why—before they start their vacation in Syria…"

The two Russians stood up, and Goldfinger said, "Have a nice day. I wouldn't talk to anyone about this."

Jim nodded in agreement. The two Russians left. Jim stood up unsteadily. He looked over at the proprietor behind the counter, who was giving him some sort of signal. He walked over and said, "Yes?"

"Another envelope from Paris," he said as he handed Jim an envelope.

"Thanks, Johann," said Jim. He stuffed the envelope in his suit coat and headed back to the Bermuda Triangle office, thoroughly rattled, not shaken.

24. Hackers at the Gate

Jim walked into the office, face ashen, and went up to Jack and looked over at Jürgen and said to his two partners, "We need to meet in the conference room—something really troubling."

"About an investment?" asked Jürgen.

"Worse, about me and Sophie d'Auverne."

Jack smiled inwardly: somehow he thought there was always something else going on with the vivacious Mme d'Auverne, the all-too-charming *fonctionnaire*.

The three men sat down at the conference table. Jim filled them in about the conversation with the Russians.

"That's interesting," said Jürgen. "Dieter had Russian hackers trying to break into our computer files yesterday. He said they were looking for a simple computer list."

"A computer list?" asked Jack, a suspicion growing in his mind.

"Yes, let's get Dieter in here," said Jürgen. He stepped outside the conference area and spoke with a secretary.

"By all means," said Jim.

In a few minutes, Dieter came in and sat down and opened a laptop in front of him. "Easier to explain by demonstration."

Jim jumped right in. "When did this happen?"

"Yesterday."

"How do you know they were Russians?"

"They had a characteristic signature. Comes from the quasi-official security agency that supports the Russian energy companies. They're always nosing around."

"With us?"

"No, with everyone."

"They were nosing around, looking for a list of names and possibly account numbers?" asked Jim.

Jack interrupted. "There are lots of rumors out there that the two thousand names that Christine Lagarde sent to the Greek finance ministry in 2010 came from a much-larger list."

"A larger list?" The Russians knew, thought Jim.

"Yes, it's rumored to be about a hundred and thirty thousand names. French intelligence got the list from a disgruntled employee of the HSBC branch here in Geneva."

"Here in Geneva?" exclaimed Jim.

"Yes, Lagarde sent the Greek finance ministry a spreadsheet on a CD—really primitive technology," said Jürgen.

"A CD, that's a pretty good size...not so easy to hide..." said Jack.

"Anyway, spreadsheet files have a computer-file suffix of '.xls,'" explained Dieter. "Easy to identify."

"That's what the Russians were looking for?" asked Jim.

"They didn't know what they were looking for," said Dieter a little disdainfully. "But they were looking for something from the old file technologies."

"OK, so who were these guys?" asked Jim.

"I researched them."

"Yes?" asked Jim expectantly.

"This security service is full of old KGB agents—retreads—and they do background work for the big Russian energy companies...get background information on the Europeans that they will be negotiating with, try to find some dirt, stuff like that. Material they can use for blackmail if possible."

"And?"

"Well, everyone sort of plays along. They're nicknamed 'The Leaf Rakers,' and so if these old duffers could find some secret Swiss bank accounts...well, they'd earn their pay, they think."

"If you heard what they plan to do to Sophie this morning—and me—you would be more respectful of these 'old duffers,'" said Jim.

Dieter shrugged his shoulders. He hadn't heard the threats. "They sent a worm," said Dieter.

"A what?"

"A worm," said Dieter. "Let me show you on the laptop." He turned the laptop around, and a vast matrix of hexadecimal lines flashed on the screen. "That's the worm."

"How would I know?" said Jim plaintively.

"Let me put it on animation for you—easier to understand." Dieter hit a couple of keys, and an animation screen came up with a perky, little worm on it. "That's the worm."

"So what does a worm do?" asked Jim.

"It noses around in the disk drives and the main memory, looking for something—either to steal or to infect."

"So what did you do?"

"Oh, I have a special disk drive—I call it 'the Garden'—with a bunch of old files in it that I use to test things. I let the Russkies' worm roam around the Garden for a while, sniffing at all the files." Dieter hit a couple keys, and the animated worm slithered around a garden, looking at bushes and flowers with an increasingly discouraged look on its little animated face.

"What was it looking for?"

"Oh, something simple, either a spreadsheet or something else. You sort of knew it was Eastern European, because it was also looking for all the really old technologies; you know, comma-delimited files, dBASE files, COBOL, Fortran—all the usual suspects from back when the Rolling Stones were young. Then I had a flash…"

"Yes?" pumped Jim.

"I thought just possibly, in all those ancient technologies, maybe someone had encrypted a new message, hidden a modern stash of information deep in the ancient file formats…"

"Did you find anything?"

"No," said Dieter, but his expression brightened. "But it's a great idea."

"So what did you do?"

"I sent the worm on its way, empty-handed."

"Well, the Russians are looking for a CD, a CD just like the one Christine Lagarde sent to the Greek finance ministry but with a hundred and thirty thousand names on it." Jim slammed his fist down on the table and shouted in frustration, "And I have no idea where such a CD might be."

"I thought you opened a safe-deposit box for Sophie at Banque Genève Crédit Suisse?" said Jack.

"I did. But there's only a big diamond necklace in the box. I was there. There's no CD in that safe-deposit box. Maybe she's dodging the French wealth tax, though she says she isn't."

"A CD?" said Dieter, a little perplexed. "So primitive."

"Primitive?" said Jim, exasperated. "You should see the Russians—one looks like a Neanderthal man and the other like Goldfinger without the polish. A CD is what they want...using pliers on fingernails is their idea of data extraction."

"Well, except for maybe the Greek finance ministry, no one uses CDs anymore," said Dieter.

"They don't?" said Jim, with a perplexed look on his face.

"No," explained Dieter. "Here, let me show you."

"Please do."

Dieter reached across the desk and pulled Jim's iPhone over. He expertly flipped it open and pulled out a little chip, with a beautiful mother-of-pearl luster to its surface. He laid the chip down on the table and put his little pinkie next to it. The chip was smaller than his fingernail. "You could keep half the French national archives on that chip," said Dieter. "A hundred and thirty thousand names and numbers—child's play."

"I see," said Jim.

"What do you see?" asked Jack.

"A small chip. It could fit in the hasp of a necklace—a broken hasp with Scotch tape wrapped around it, a hasp that needs to be taken to a jeweler for repair when it goes back to Paris, or so the owner said."

"I think you see the light, buddy boy," said Jack.

"Yes," said Jim, disappointment spreading across his face as the realization that he had been used settled in.

Jack watched and said nothing.

Jürgen said, "We have until Monday at noon to get that chip out of the necklace. What do we do with it?"

Just then Jim's iPhone rang. He pulled it back from Dieter and saw it was Sophie. He put his finger up to his lips to silence his partners. He answered the phone and put it on speakerphone. "Yes, Sophie?"

"I got your text. I think I understand."

"I had visitors."

"Like the Russian gardeners at Château d'Auverne," she said, making a statement not a question.

"Yes."

"Fine. I need to spend a few minutes with the necklace before we meet the visitors. Can we do this?"

Jack waved his hand and wrote something down on a paper. "We can meet the bank manager Sunday evening at nine," he replied.

"That will be perfect."

"I would like to meet with you at Antibes tomorrow night. Is that possible?" asked Jim.

"Of course. I will take the TGV and arrive early Saturday night," she said, mentioning the high-speed train from Paris.

"Yes, I'd like to talk. Someone owes me an explanation," said Jim plaintively.

"When I gave you the necklace, I told you everything would be explained, and it will. You have not been deceived, possibly just delayed in your understanding a little." She laughed over the phone.

"You haven't met the Russians."

"If we need French secret service help, I can arrange that…they do Russians rather well. See you tomorrow night." Sophie rang off.

Jim stared at the phone with a look of perplexity.

"She's a cool one," said Jack.

Jim explained to his partners. "I'll meet her at Antibes tomorrow night and get to the bottom of this. Then we can come up to Geneva Sunday afternoon and meet the bank manager Sunday night."

"One other thing, Jim," said Jack. "You and Sophie better be at the bank at half past noon on Monday. We want the Russians to see everything they expect to see…then will come the surprises. I'll have some acquaintances there that would like to meet our Russian friends, if Sophie's French friends don't get to 'em first."

"Got ya," said Jim, and he leaned back in his chair, relaxing for the first time in hours. He felt the letter in his pocket and reached in and pulled it out. "Oh, a communication from Renier in Paris." He threw it on the table, and Jack reached out and pulled the napkin out of the envelope.

"Let's see," said Jack. "'DB *mal*,' is the first line.

Jürgen chimed in: "Something bad is happening at Deutsche Bank. That's on everyone's grapevine. We've already discussed that. What's next?"

"'*Attends*,'" read Jack, and he translated, "Wait. 'Crédit Générale' is the next line, followed by '*attends*' again," said Jack.

"OK," said Jürgen. "Something similar will happen to Crédit Générale."

"'*La-bas*' followed by '*achetez*,'" read Jack.

"I would say that means to wait for the lows and then buy Crédit Générale," said Jürgen. "In any language."

Jim leaned back in his chair and stroked his chin and reflected: "Yes, who could ever fault a French bank official, one heading back to the government someday, of patriotically buying the stock of his bank when it was in trouble, when it was on the bottom?"

"And we can make a nice long-term capital gain," said Jack. "Our favorite investment."

Jim nodded to go ahead.

Jürgen turned to Dieter and said, "You got it? We'll execute as the events unfold."

"*Ja*," said Dieter. His mind was off on Sophie d'Auverne. He sensed she knew more than she had let on. Maybe she really was out of a Lagrande novel—and not the sex part either. He could see it all so clearly now—Jim was hot; she was cool, opposites.

Jack turned to Jim and said, "Let me walk you to the elevator." The meeting broke up, and the two men walked into the corridor and down toward the elevator.

"I know you're disappointed," said Jack to Jim. "You think you were used."

"Maybe, but somehow I don't think so."

"I'm sure she has been a real romance for you, but—" said Jack.

"That night after the opera, and the other nights, well…she'd have to be a great actress, but I think she loves me."

The two men walked down to the elevator in silence. Jim pushed the button; the elevator came up, and the doors opened.

Jack put his arm around Jim's shoulder and said in an avuncular manner, "Jim, I want you to understand one thing…" He spun Jim around and shoved him playfully into the elevator. As the doors closed, Jack shouted after him, "She *is* a great actress."

25. Antibes

The taxi pulled into the drive at the spacious house on Cap Antibes. Two large cars were parked in the drive. Sophie recognized Jim's Jaguar; the other car looked vaguely official. She got out, paid the cab driver, picked up her valise, and walked over to the front door, which swung open as she approached. Jim's driver was holding it open. "He's in the dining room," he said perfunctorily. "So are the others," he said enigmatically.

"Hmm. Thank you," replied Sophie. She handed him her valise and started walking back to the dining room. As she approached, she saw Jim standing, talking to two men. They turned and faced her.

"Let me introduce myself," said one of the men. "I'm from Direction Générale de la Sécurité Extérieure." He flipped open his identification and flashed a badge.

Sophie had seen the badges before. She nodded.

"My colleague is from the financial police." The other man flipped open his identity wallet and showed his *Police Nationale* badge.

Sophie had seen these before, too; she nodded. She looked at the two men and slowly said, "*Alors?*"

"There is a question that you may have property belonging to the French government."

"Just what property, may I ask?"

"A computerized list of a hundred and thirty thousand names of individuals with accounts at a Swiss branch of HSBC bank. The list is the property of Direction Générale."

"Yes, I see. Just where might this property be?"

"We believe the list may be contained on a small computer chip in a safe-deposit box rented by Bermuda Triangle at Banque Genève Crédit Suisse."

"And?"

"If it were to be returned to us, there would be no further investigation. We understand you possibly secured this information at the behest of an individual now prominent in international financial circles…at, shall we say, the highest level."

"Yes, that is true," said Sophie.

"Sophie," Jim broke in, his voice pleading. "It's much more serious than that. Two high Greek government officials are dead as a result of the list. Another's in jail. They were involved in a billion-dollar weapons-bribery and money-laundering scandal involving a Russian arms exporter. They were on the Lagarde list."

"Yes, Édouard informed me. I don't see how that has anything to do with me."

The security flic broke in and said, "*Le directeur* would like to speak with you, Mme d'Auverne. He is in Paris. Here, let me connect you to him through my cell phone." He indicated for Sophie to take a seat on the couch. He sat down next to her and put his cell phone on the coffee table. He punched a number and then turned to Sophie. "You are familiar with our headquarters, *la piscine*—the fishbowl—in Paris?"

"Yes, I was there several times for budget meetings…years ago."

"Well, here you can see *le directeur* on Google Maps…from where he's talking."

A little light blinked on the map on the phone screen, flashing out from a little, drab colored square labeled DGSE. A voice came out of the speakerphone. "Good evening, Mme d'Auverne. I believe we have met before…at an interministerial meeting when you were working in the Matignon."

"Perhaps…there were so many meetings," said Sophie.

She isn't giving much away, thought Jim. Maybe she knows a lot more about this game than I do.

"We have information from a source inside the finance ministry that you may have had a second copy of the HSBC list…"

"And if I have?" asked Sophie.

"No 'if,' Mme d'Auverne," said the voice coming out of the speakerphone with a real ring of authority.

Sophie quickly composed herself and answered with insistence, "I was only following instructions from a higher authority, an individual who was afraid that if there were only one copy, then it might go missing…or some names might get misplaced…as happens in Greece all the time."

"Yes, a good concern. But the source inside the ministry, it is not our source. It's an informer in the pay of the Russians for many years, nicknamed 'the Mouse.'"

"Incredible," said Sophie; a smile flashed across her face. "I can imagine who she is. We always guessed she was spying for someone but made light of it. We heard more about her boyfriends than we cared to know. Someone really paid to show her a good time."

"Yes," said *le directeur*, and he laughed. "Standard Soviet practice carried over to the new regime. In some ways we, too, treated it lightly here in the DGSE. However, our surveillance revealed she told security agents working for a semiofficial agency supporting the Russian energy companies all about the HSBC list."

"The Leaf Rakers," exclaimed Jim.

"What's that?" said the voice in the speakerphone.

"The Leaf Rakers is what my computer geek calls them," said Jim.

"He's unusually well informed."

"He's unusually well paid," said Jim.

The French security flic turned to Jim and held his hand up as a signal to let *le directeur* continue.

"Sorry," said Jim sheepishly.

Sophie turned to Jim and asked, "Is this what you were trying to tell me on the phone yesterday?"

"Yes, first we treated the Russians as sort of a joke. Dieter ran a backgrounder on them when they tried a primitive hack job on our computers. They were looking for some simple computer file with a list of names and numbers. About a hundred and thirty thousand names, according to Dieter's parameter check. Dieter let 'em sniff around in our disk drives and then sent them on their way empty-handed."

"Who's Dieter?" asked the French security flic sharply.

"He's our computer geek," replied Jim.

"That's the computer expert who runs Bermuda Triangle's computers," explained the finance flic to the security agent.

"Of course, I know that," sniffed the security flic. He turned to Jim and said, "So you, a civilian, thought you knew better than trained security professionals?"

"Well, yes. I guess we were wrong."

"Then what happened?" asked the finance flic, getting the discussion back on track.

"Two Russian agents tried to bribe me to let them into the safe-deposit box yesterday. I texted Sophie, and she said she'd be in Geneva Monday morning on the flight from Paris. She said she'd meet me at the bank at half past noon."

"What did the Russians want?"

"They wanted the list. They thought it was on a CD, like the list sent to Athens. The two Russians said they were working with the Russian network that sold the TOR-M1 missile system to Greece. These guys said they were the 'good cops' and that some truly rough characters were on their way to Geneva to get the HSBC list. Nothing would stop them. They were flying in from Jakarta and Athens."

"Jakarta?" said the security flic skeptically.

"Yeah, Jakarta. I told my partner Jack that, and he really got discomfited. He whispered to me that a Greek businessman that was part of the defense-ministry bribery scandal had been found dead in a Jakarta hotel room."

"That's true," said the finance flic. "I've seen the Interpol report."

"Who else?" asked the security flic, taking charge of the discussion again.

"The Russians said another guy was coming in from Athens and that he had just silenced another Greek on the Lagarde list. The Russians said the list was turning lethal to anyone who knew about it."

"That's also true about Athens," said the finance flic. "The guy's dead."

"Why were they asking you about the Lagarde list?" asked the security flic as he bore in.

"They said they knew all about my girlfriend, Sophie. They knew that she had visited Geneva and gone to the bank with me. They knew the branch, the date, and that I opened a safe-deposit box."

"Possibly a loose end," broke in the finance flic. "We need to find the leak at the bank. The Swiss are getting sloppy."

The security flic turned thoughtful and mumbled, "Maybe not a leak, possibly outside the bank. Surveillance is penetrating many secrets today with the new technologies." Turning back to the conversation, he said, "So, the Russians guessed right that you had the HSBC list. And you didn't accept their bribe, obviously. Then what did they do?"

"They said my girlfriend, Sophie, might have a rendezvous with the director of Syrian state security—dark things were suggested..."

"Syria?" asked Sophie, raising her eyebrows with a look of skepticism.

"Yes, they said they'd arrange for your kidnapping and delivery to Syria. They said your last conscious thought, after interrogation, would be the Bekaa Valley at sunset. They said French women were a favorite with the security director and that he enjoyed them both before and after they talked."

The security flic watched with an amused look on his face. Was the woman biting on this?

The finance flic also watched Sophie, his face a simple deadpan. Sometimes this stuff worked.

Sophie broke in: "And so Jack called Édouard?" There was not a trace of alarm in her voice.

The security flic looked at the financial flic and shrugged his shoulders. She was a cool one.

"As soon as we got back to the office," said Jim. "Someone really wants that list, Sophie."

"And did Jack know that Édouard is retired from the finance police?" She nodded over at the finance flic.

Jim's eyes followed Sophie's glance over to the finance flic, who was smiling like a Cheshire cat. "Maybe."

"Mme d'Auverne," broke in the security flic, "we have been following you almost from the time the HSBC file left the ministry in your cell phone. The Mouse squeaked as you went down the elevator. The phone call from Geneva just confirmed that it was now time to return the list to its rightful and secure place."

"They weren't going to kidnap her and take her to the Bekaa Valley?" asked Jim incredulously.

"No."

"We were set up?" asked Jim plaintively.

Sophie gave Jim a big frown, like he was an errant schoolboy; she tapped her foot with impatience. "You were set up, not we, *mon chéri,*" she said as she reached into her handbag and pulled out a paperback novel with the lurid cover of a busty babe holding a big assassin's handgun.

"Philippe Lagrande," exclaimed the security flic, his face coming alive. "Are you a fan? Do you read him, too?"

"Of course, in the middle of a long afternoon of budgeting, it helps to take a break with something that gets the blood moving. With Philippe, everything is big," said Sophie, "and fast moving." She batted her eyelashes at the security flic. "Please call me Sophie."

"*D'accord,*" said the security flic. "Lagrande is best. I am something of a liaison to him for the agency. I keep him well briefed instead of fed with all that self-glorifying CIA propaganda the Americans give him."

Jim looked at Sophie, a dimension of her was revealing itself that he had never suspected. After Sophie had mentioned reading the Lagrande novels while at Dieter's desk, Jim had followed up on the French writer. Jim knew that Lagrande was the best-selling French author of the *Deuxième Bureau* series of novels, featuring the freelance spy Mec Duclos. The old *Deuxième Bureau* was long gone, but it was now the code name of a walled country estate in Provence, where the resourceful spy lived with a bevy of young "assistants" between assignments, doing what he called "deep research."

Dieter was virtually addicted to the hundred and fifty novels written by the prolific Frenchmen. Duclos was always bailing out the hapless American CIA in countless foreign imbroglios with the schlock formula of guns blazing in twisting, violent plots where the women were lurid, the sex torrid. But most interestingly, the novels were strewn with authentic details from the world of foreign espionage, provided by the French secret service and other spy services. Dieter knew the real-life details by heart.

Sophie looked at Jim, batted her eyelashes, and asked, "Did you know Lagrande is a best seller in Germany and Russia? Quite popular. Possibly your Russian agents were reading from a script?" She looked at the two Frenchmen and then back at Jim; she shrugged. Then, with a seductively inviting smile, she held up the paperback and read the title, "*Le Chemin à Beyrouth*" (*The Road to Beirut*). She explained, "The book opens with the director of

Syrian security picking up his girlfriend in Damascus to take her to Beirut." She looked at Jim. "Sound familiar?"

She flipped the book open to the first pages of the novel and began to read. "He walked into the darkened bedroom in Damascus. Jamilah was there, modest in a flowing robe. He pulled the robe up and pulled her panties down and stuffed them in her handbag. He whispered in her ear, 'You won't need them when I show you the Bekaa Valley.' She dug her fingernails into his back and whispered, 'I can't wait to see…to feel…'"

Sophie flipped forward a dozen pages and began reading again. "From the road overlooking the Bekaa Valley, the scenery was grand: mountains snowcapped…no villages…'Habibi,' she cooed, 'it's lovely. We'll do it in the car.' Instead he took her outside the parked Mercedes and pushed her against the hood of the sedan and pulled her robe up and jammed himself against her body. Jamilah felt his hands grab her breasts. She opened her legs further. Jamilah moaned with pleasure, ever more excited, moaning 'Yo, Habibi…Yo, Habibi…'"

Sophie flashed a smile at the listening men and turned the page and continued reading. "The enraptured couple didn't hear the little Fiat come along the highway, the Kalashnikov barking as it let loose a fusillade of bullets…the expression on Jamilah's face forever frozen between ecstasy and the little death…the blood frothing out of Bahir's mouth and running down Jamilah's shoulder and across her limp breast and congealing in a puddle on the surface of the car."

Sophie set the book down and looked at Jim. "So, no, I don't think I had a rendezvous with the Syrian security service in the Bekaa Valley in my future…for the ecstasies of interrogation."

Jim stammered, "I didn't know."

Sophie half turned toward Jim and went into full John Wayne mode and purred, "No tears, Jim."

Jim rolled his eyes and said, "Great cowboy—"

Sophie batted her eyelashes at him. "Lagrande is French cowboy."

"Yes, for the notebook…"

"For a truly great memoir," said Sophie.

"What's all that about?" asked the security flic, puzzled.

"Someday Jim and I have a rendezvous in a library with a book," said Sophie.

"A library?" asked the security flic incredulously. "He's going to take you to a library?" He looked at Jim with cross-eyed wonder. "I've heard of the backseat...but the library?"

"We're going to compare great quotes from capitalism," said Jim.

The security flic gave Jim a completely blank stare as he mumbled the word "Capitalism,"—the French viewing the very word as some distasteful import from across the Channel or, worse, from east of the Rhine.

Sophie turned and, tapping the cover of the novel, said to the two Frenchmen, "Besides, when I imagine myself in a Lagrande novel, I see myself as the mistress of a monstrous African warlord. We're riding in a four-by-four at the head of a column of legionnaires, heading into Timbuktu to liberate the desert women from the terrors of Shari'a law, the crowds cheering."

The security flic gaped at her with lascivious wonder. "An African warlord?"

Sophie turned sultry. "Remember, for a Lagrande heroine, too much is never enough. I imagine I won him in a catfight in a disco in Bamako with a *pute morocaine*, because, how should I say, I proved to be better." She wetted her lips with her tongue and batted her eyelashes.

The security flic's jaw dropped. A couple more minutes of this, and he'll be tearing her panty hose off—with his teeth—thought Jim.

"*Mon Dieu*," exclaimed the finance flic. "It's all right here." He pulled another paperback out of his bag. The cover of this novel featured a scantily clad young woman, armed to the teeth with a pistol and assault rifle, and was entitled *Disco À Bamako*. Bamako was the capital of the West African country of Mali, bordering the Sahara Desert. "The warlords, the disco, Bamako, the Islamist terror of the desert people—it's all right here."

"But not the legionnaires, not the liberation of Timbuktu, the cheering crowds," said the security flic. "That's all in the next novel, *Mali Libre*, and it hasn't even been written yet."

The finance flic flipped through some more pages and said, "Yeah, you're right." He looked at Sophie. "How'd you know? You read the future?"

Now Sophie smiled like the Cheshire cat, but she said nothing.

"Mali," the security flic said emphatically, slamming his right fist into his left hand. "Top secret. In Paris, we're working on the plan day and night. It's going to be better than Iraq, than Afghanistan…"

"Dien Bien Phu," interjected Jim, smiling, recalling that long-ago defeat of the legion in the highlands of Vietnam in 1954.

The security flic scowled at Jim. "How American."

"No, it was French," bantered Jim.

The Frenchman rolled his eyes and looked at Sophie. "He's with you?"

"He has his charms," she cooed.

"In a library?" The security flic nodded sadly then looked at Jim and said disdainfully, "Not much of a warlord? Looks more like a poodle."

"With money," murmured Sophie.

"Yes, that always explains it, at least in Paris." Then he perked up and looked directly at Sophie. "Mali. How do you know? We haven't even shared the details of that operation with Philippe yet."

"It's Strategic Intelligence International's business to know," Sophie answered. "We're a government in exile. Besides, we have lunch with Philippe, too. He's often ahead of the game, way in front of the official briefings."

"Yes, he is. You have lunch with Philippe?"

"I haven't, but one of my associates does. They go way back. Our clients demand the best."

"When this is over, we must all have drinks with Philippe in Paris—compare notes."

Now the finance flic rolled his eyes. "Let's get back on the mission." He looked at Jim and asked, "How do we get the computer chip back?"

Jim looked at Sophie for approval of what he was going to say, and she nodded affirmatively. "Jack has arranged for the bank manager to open the bank Sunday night at nine in the evening. We could meet you there Sunday night and give you the chip."

"That's fine with me," added Sophie, "with a proviso. Have one of your men meet Édouard at our offices in Paris at the same time and sign a release that we do not have any property belonging to the French government. We don't want any future political repercussions while we're all on the road to Timbuktu, heading for final victory, do we?"

"*D'accord*," said the security flic. "Do we have some champagne here? We need a toast to Timbuktu, to final victory. Show the Anglo-Saxons how it's done."

"I'm ready to collaborate. Let me get the champagne," said Jim.

26. Banque Genève Crédit Suisse

It was dark and cold in Geneva Sunday night; winter was closing in. Dim reflections from the lamps of the streetlights reflected off mirrorlike puddles on the rain-wetted street, now empty of cars. Jim and Sophie sat in the backseat of a sedan, the two French secret-service *flics* sat in the front. Across the street was the Banque Genève Crédit Suisse. One flic said to the other, "There he is." He looked back over his shoulder at Jim and asked for confirmation, "Is that the branch manager?"

"Yes," said Jim.

"Good," said the security flic, and he opened the door to the car and got out. He looked up and down the street to see that it was empty. Then he said, "*Alors, allons-y.*" (Let's go.)

The other flic opened his door and got out and, in one fluid motion, opened the rear door; Sophie got out. Jim opened his door and stood next to the security flic. They all crossed the street just as the bank manager finished opening the door.

"Highly unusual," said the bank manager.

"Unusual situation," said the security flic.

"Yes, withdrawals at this hour," said the bank manager.

"We're not taking anything. Something is just going to become inoperative," said the security flic.

"You don't want it?" asked Jim, a plaintive tone of perplexity in his voice.

"Why?" said the security flic. "We've already got it. We just don't want others to have it."

"Oh," said Jim.

The bank manager swung the door open, and they walked in. The bank manager walked down the hallway and punched the code into a keypad lock. The door swung open. The manager walked over to another keypad and punched in another code. He turned the lights on and slid back a metal screen, exposing the safe-deposit boxes.

"And the key?" asked the security flic.

Sophie reached into her handbag and pulled out a key on the end of chain. "Voilà."

The security flic took the key, opened the safe-deposit box, pulled the box out, and carried it over and set it on the table. He lifted the lid and looked inside. There was just a large necklace with a hasp held shut with Scotch tape.

"That's it," said Sophie.

"Get me a large ashtray," said the security flic. The finance flic went out into the main office and brought back a large, ceramic ashtray.

"*Parfait*," said the security flic.

"Don't damage the necklace," cautioned Jim.

"Don't worry about it," said Sophie. "It's costume jewelry, all glass. It's been years since we've worn real jewelry to a public event. The real one is in the family bank in Paris—where it's been for decades."

Jim laughed. "So you weren't dodging the wealth tax?"

"No," said Sophie. "But I presumed that would sound credible to an American hedge-fund manager."

"Touché," said Jim.

The security flic looked at Sophie and remarked, "I liked him better after the fourth magnum of champagne."

"I liked him better after we put the champagne away," said Sophie, and she arched an eyebrow provocatively.

The security flic ground his teeth.

The finance flic smoothly intervened. "Here." He handed a long fountain-pen-shaped tube to the security flic.

The security flic opened the hasp of the necklace and, with his fingernail, flipped a small computer chip out into the ashtray—a chip just like the one Dieter had pulled out of Jim's iPhone. "Voilà."

"Boy, Dieter had this one nailed," marveled Jim in an aside to Sophie.

"You're lucky to be surrounded with so much talent," said Sophie.

The security flic opened up the narrow metal tube and pumped a small button, igniting a small butane torch. He applied the torch to the surface of the chip, and it curled and blackened and melted into a small glob on the bottom of the ashtray. After a thorough smelting, the security flic extinguished the torch and handed it back to the finance flic. After a few moments, the security flic took out a business card and scooped up the melted chip and put it back in the safe-deposit box. He put the business card in next to the chip.

Jim looked down into the safe-deposit box and read the business card, "Philippe Lagrande, *auteur de romans*." (A novelist.) On the card, there were images of a big Kalashnikov assault rifle and a busty young woman, images big enough to fill any adolescent imagination.

"Let our Russian friends know the French were here. They might wonder."

"What if your Russian friends get angry with me tomorrow afternoon?" said Jim, testiness in his voice.

"Our Swiss colleagues will be nearby. They want to chat with the Russians. Possible violations of Swiss banking law have been mentioned."

"Oh, I see," said Jim.

"Is that it, gentlemen?" asked the bank manager.

"Yes," said the security flic. He started walking to the door. The finance flic followed then Sophie and Jim. The bank manager punched codes into the keypad and walked out into the hallway. The group headed for the front door.

In the lobby, the finance flic tapped a text into his smartphone, pushed send, and watched for a reply. The phone beeped; he nodded and put the phone in his pocket.

Sophie held her iPhone in front of her and watched the screen. It beeped, and a message flashed on the screen. "It's Édouard. *Ca va*."

The security flic nodded. "*Ca va*."

Out on the sidewalk, the security flic said, "We're heading back to Paris. Can we drop you someplace?"

"Yes, thank you," said Jim. "I have a flat a couple blocks over. You can drop us there."

"Yes, that will be fine," said Sophie. She gave the security flic her business card and said, "Call my secretary. We can arrange an after-work drink with Philippe back in Paris and go over our adventures together. I've never met him."

"He will be charmed, Mme d'Auverne," said the security flic with great seriousness.

The group walked across the street and got in the sedan and took off, the two French security flics dropping Jim and Sophie off at Jim's flat.

High Noon at the Banque

Jim and Sophie stood in the bank lobby with the bank manager, watching the clock approach half past noon. Outside, sort of following the Monday morning routine, were two window washers, polishing the glass to a bright clarity. The bank manager nervously looked at his watch. The lobby doors swung open, and the two Russians walked in. Sophie was somewhat startled—yes, they were as large and threatening, in a crude way, as Jim had said.

"I hope this goes OK," she whispered to Jim, anxiety in her voice. The bank manager had assured her that the Swiss finance police would intervene before anything got out of hand.

"We'll just do what they say," whispered Jim, looking at the two approaching Russians. A gnawing, little thought rattled around in his head about the two Russians; some little, unexplained thing that he seemed to have forgotten was further stoking his anxiety.

"Well, Mme d'Auverne, we've heard so much about you from our colleagues," said the Russian with the billiard-ball head, the Goldfinger among the two. The brute sort of just chortled and rubbed his hands together in delight at the thought of some future fun.

"Yes, well a lot of people seem to be interested in what I might have these days," she replied, her characteristic coolness returning.

"You were going to give"—the bank manager paused and drew the words out sarcastically—"these *gentlemen* something from your safe-deposit box, Mme d'Auverne."

The brute scowled at him for his impertinence. The bank manager seemed unfazed, crude foreigners being something Swiss bankers took in stride.

"Yes, it's right where we left it last August," said Jim. "Unless the tooth fairy came and whisked it away."

Goldfinger bore in on him and said with low menace, "Our tooth fairies are coming in by plane tonight from Jakarta. We wouldn't want them to rough up your tooth fairies, now would we?"

The bank manager sighed at the childishness of it all and turned and walked back to the room holding the safe deposit boxes. He punched a key code into the pad and pushed the door open. He walked inside and punched another code into another keypad. "This way," he said.

The four of them entered the room. Sophie got her key out and handed it to the bank manager, who walked over and pulled the safe-deposit box out of its place in the wall and carried it back and put it on the conference-room table. He flipped the top of the box open and said, "Gentlemen."

The brute quickly stepped over to the open tray and looked inside and saw the necklace and picked it up in his hands, almost lovingly, and then let his eyes search the inside of the box. Crestfallen, he said, "No CD."

Goldfinger impatiently pushed him aside and looked inside the tray—there was no CD, just an old business card. He turned and looked at the necklace and reached out and snatched it out of the brute's hands.

"Let me look at this." He turned the necklace over in his hands, and then his gaze fixed on the hasp. "Ah, hah," he said in recognition. He opened the hasp, and the small, burned-out silicon chip fell out.

He looked back at the tray and reached in and picked out the business card. He read aloud, "Philippe Lagrande." He looked at the busty young woman on the card and the assault weapon portrayed across the top of the card. "Who is this?"

A troubled look furrowed the brow of the brute. "That's the frog that wrote the book I'm reading. Remember, the one about Syria?"

Jim was sort of surprised that the brute could read.

"Oh, yeah," said Goldfinger, with the dawning realization that something was beginning to unravel.

"He's a writer associated with the French secret service," said Jim smugly.

"Smartass," spat out Goldfinger. Deciding on one last gambit, Goldfinger turned to Sophie and waved the card in front of her face and shouted, "This is your ticket to Syria!"

A calm voice from the doorway spoke out, "Messieurs, Swiss finance police."

The other Swiss finance policeman stepped forward and took the necklace out of Goldfinger's hands. "You won't need this."

"Finance police?" said the brute, looking at the two men dressed as window washers and standing in the conference room, flashing badges.

"Oh, now I understand," said Jim with the shock of recognition. He turned to Sophie and explained, "These two guys"—Jim pointed to the Russians—"were outside washing the windows that day you and I came here to put the necklace in the safe-deposit box the first time."

"Yes, I remember them now," said Sophie. "Like the gardeners at Auverne."

"Exactly," said Jim.

The Swiss finance policeman silenced Jim with a glance and turned and addressed the two Russians: "There appears to be a serious violation of the Swiss bank secrecy law."

"A serious violation of the Swiss bank secrecy law?" said the brute. He leaned over and whispered to Goldfinger, "Is that serious?"

"Could be capital," said Goldfinger nervously. "The Swiss are serious about this sort of thing."

The Swiss finance policeman nodded gravely and murmured, "Capital."

The brute gulped.

"A high crime," said the other Swiss finance detective.

"High?" said the brute in a sinking voice.

The other Swiss finance policeman stepped forward and said in a conversational manner, "Of course, it might just be window washing without a work permit, a civil infraction. We go to the station, you pay the fine, and then we escort you to the *bannhof*— the night train to Vienna."

"Yes, that's it exactly," said Goldfinger. "Window washing without a work permit, we are completely guilty."

"Yes, yes," said the brute, relief flooding across his face. "We were already planning on taking the night train to Vienna," he said. "It's right where we want to go. The next assignment."

"Yes, we know," said one of the finance policemen. "We already printed out the tickets you reserved." He reached into his pocket and pulled out the two train tickets and handed them over. "You saved us the cost," said the always-thrifty Swiss policeman.

"*Alors, allez*," said the other finance policeman, and he pointed with his hand toward the door. The two Russians started walking out.

The other finance policeman turned and made a small bow to Sophie. "Mme d'Auverne, our friends in the fishbowl said to take exceptionally good care of you. We trust we can release you in the company of your gentlemen friend. Our French friends said he was quite harmless." He smirked at Jim and smiled broadly at Sophie.

"Yes, I think this whole episode has been one of high finance meeting low farce," said Sophie, and she smiled at the finance policeman.

She took Jim's arm and looked at him and smiled fetchingly. "Time to walk my poodle."

Jim rolled his eyes and sighed. "Maybe I'll go back to New York and chase secretaries around the desk. They're easier to catch."

The bank manager laughed. They all turned and walked back to the lobby of the bank, where Jim and Sophie took leave of the finance policeman and bank manager. Across the street, the other finance policeman was putting the two Russians in the back of a small sedan, for transport to the police station.

Outside Jim turned to Sophie. "Let's go have lunch. Can you stay until tomorrow? The final terms of the Greek bailout will be announced tomorrow morning."

"Love to. I want to curl up with my poodle tonight in front of the fireplace."

"Bowwow."

'Meow," she purred, but the look was all fox.

27. The Rubber Room

The next morning at Bermuda Triangle's office, Jim escorted Sophie into the Rubber Room. They walked over to where Jack and Jürgen were standing to one side of the vast computer console, at which Dieter was sitting like the pilot of a huge airliner. Over to one side stood Anouk, in a stylish sweater, with a soft cream blouse underneath and denim jeans—beautifully fitted to rapier-like legs narrowing down to black heels, observed Sophie as she smiled at Anouk.

"*Bonjour, Madame d'Auverne.*"

"*Sophie, s'il vous plait,*" replied Sophie.

"Final victory is at hand," boomed Jack, and he looked playfully at Jürgen.

"Never would have happened with the deutsch mark, only with the weakling currency," snorted Jürgen. He spat out the words, "The euro." He looked at Sophie and smiled sarcastically. "The French ransom for allowing the reunification of the fatherland."

"And a cheap price it was," said Sophie, smiling as she broke into a soft hum of "*Deutschland über alles,*" the stirringly martial German national anthem.

"You hum that so sweetly," said Jack. "You can barely hear the sound of the tank tracks."

Jürgen rolled his eyes.

"Speaking of the antimilitarists, how is our übergeek this morning?" asked Sophie as she turned and walked up behind Dieter. She stood and read off the silk-screened logo on the back of his T-shirt. "Private Manning, the last hero?" Manning was the renegade intelligence specialist who put the diplomats' secrets on the Internet, to the horror of officialdom everywhere. She patted Dieter on the shoulder. "Yes, the information wants to be free, doesn't it?"

"It's almost like a law of physics," said Dieter. "Markets can't do their magic without information, and truly free information is

190

the greatest enemy of the security state—we must free ourselves from the shackles of closeted information. My generation's calling."

"Well, we're on the broad, open plain of a great, free market this morning," said Jack. "What do you think the price will be, Sophie?"

"Thirty-three cents," she crisply replied.

"Dieter?" asked Jack.

"I'm with the lady—thirty-three cents," replied Dieter. "That's what our algorithm says."

"Who'd question the algorithm?" said Jack with a grin.

"Not thirty-five?" asked Jürgen. "Why not?"

"It's where the average will settle, according to our experts, about four cents above last Friday's closing price," said Sophie. "Experts from some of the big French banks."

"That's what Frankfurt thinks also," said Jürgen with a sigh.

"No reason to sigh, Jürgen," said Sophie. "Thirty-four is just a way station on the road to zero, the finance ministers' real goal."

Jürgen and Jack looked at her with perplexity, their faces begging explanation.

"Sophie says eventually the bonds will be taken out by zero-coupon perpetuities," explained Jim.

"Zero-coupon perpetuities!" exclaimed Jack, rolling the words around on his tongue, truly excited. "There's true genius behind this scheme."

"And we get to collect a toll along the highway," said Jim with a broad smile.

"Then we better get out of town," said Jürgen darkly. "Or the sheriff will arrest us for vagrancy."

Everyone laughed but nodded about getting out of town.

"Quiet everyone," said Dieter. "Here comes the news flash."

The letters flashed across the screen, forming words, then paragraphs...and then the number thirty-four. Everyone in the Rubber Room cheered.

"Oh, the number wiggled up," said Sophie, wiggling her hips with glee. Standing behind her, Jack took a deep breath while watching Sophie's derriere and thinking to himself, Greek bonds, French ladies—life at its best.

"The big money," said Jim thoughtfully, a sense of relief flooding his expression.

"A good call last summer, Jim," said Jack in a tone of sincere congratulations. "Once again, we're on the profitable side of a hard truth."

"A little over a billion," murmured Jürgen.

"A little?" said Sophie, with wonder in her voice. "Little seems hardly the right word." She turned the number over in her mind and mumbled, "A billion for playing with symbols on a computer screen...truly the modern alchemy." She turned and smiled at Jim. "You are a sorcerer?"

Jim sighed with resignation and said, "Nothing to it but six months of über anxiety."

Sophie turned to Anouk and said with heartfelt feeling, "You're flying with the right crowd."

"Yes," replied Anouk softly.

Dieter turned around and smiled at Anouk and then stood up and went over to her. He guided her over to the far corner of the Rubber Room, engaging in earnest conversation, the words, "just like we talked about," floating across the room. Anouk's eyes were bright, her smile a glittering white as she nodded in agreement. The two of them started walking around at the far end of the room and then turned toward the computer console, Dieter in earnest conversation.

"It's not at all like Geneva," said Dieter. "There's intelligent life all over town. We can start at one end of the avenue and work our way up, coffeehouse to coffeehouse, Internet café to Internet café, tweeting our way to the center of the data flow. We'll be exploring on the frontier, not in this backwater...truly talented minds from Berlin, London, and Amsterdam are coming."

"But I don't have anything to wear," said Anouk plaintively.

"No problem. We'll hit the vintage stores in Amsterdam before catching the plane," soothed Dieter.

"Oh, that sounds fun...go camp," said Anouk with enthusiasm.

"Yeah, we'll ride in the back of the plane with the hacker elite...Berlin, London, and Stockholm will all be converging on Amsterdam for the overseas odyssey," explained Dieter. His face beaming, Dieter turned to Jim. "Boss, it's still on, right? That bonus?"

"Of course."

"Anouk is going to go with me, OK?"

"Sure," said Jim. "In fact, it's a great idea." He turned and winked at Jack. He looked back and spoke to Anouk, "You'll make sure he gets back, won't you?"

A flicker of doubt crossed Anouk's face—what was she getting into? she wondered.

Jim turned his gaze directly at Dieter and took a stern Dutch uncle tone. "Now that idea you shared with me last week...I don't want to see anything come of it, understand?"

Dieter nodded slowly in agreement, like an errant teenager.

"We all know you could do it," said Jim. "But if you routed all the hacker elite's contributions through the Pentagon's checking accounts to the WikiLeaks Foundation, you would surely antagonize the Americans if you got caught."

"It would be child's play to execute," said Dieter with a downcast look. "But, yeah, I understand, boss."

"That's the attitude. Besides, they'd send you somewhere where there's no signal, somewhere medieval—"

Sophie broke in and said to Dieter, "A dungeon...fine for dark, sexual adventures but no place for an innocent like you..."

Dieter turned and smiled at Anouk. "Maturity has its price."

She beamed approval back at him.

Jim looked at Anouk and continued with the lecture. "I don't want him in a cell next to Private Manning, lost somewhere behind the wrath of an angry Pentagon bureaucracy. They've lost Iraq, now Afghanistan—they're plenty deranged by now."

Anouk nodded in understanding and repeated the words, "*assez dérangé.*" (Plenty bothered.)

Jim smiled and added, "Keep him on open tweet."

"*Oui, monsieur,*" she said with the beautiful grace of a gifted hostess.

"Yeah, losing wars out on the far rim of the empire crushes morale," said Jack with a note of philosophical wistfulness. His face took on a look of faraway recollection. "Yes, I remember the end of empire. We sent the Tommies into Suez, and Eisenhower said he'd start selling the pound sterling. Money talks, and the

Tommies walked," said Jack, recalling the 1956 Suez Crisis, which ended the illusion that Britain was some sort of world power. Jack turned to Anouk and Sophie and cheerfully added, "Remember that, ladies, when someone offers you a 'special relationship.'"

"Or make sure you're sitting in Eisenhower's seat," said Sophie with a shrewd and calculating smile. "The golden rule: 'she who has the gold makes the rules.'"

"I'd never quite heard it said that way," said Anouk with a smile and a dawning realization about how Sophie viewed the game.

Jürgen jumped in, throwing a barb at Jack. "Your boy Tony seems to have forgotten the lesson with the Americans. He trotted along like the good, little poodle he is, right into Iraq with the Americans."

"Not my boy Tony. Margaret was always my girl. She popped the Big Bang on the City in the 1980s," he said, mentioning the deregulation of the old boys club that dominated banking in London.

"I thought you made your name dodging exchange controls?" said Jürgen, recalling the postwar exchange controls that kept money locked away in England. Jack had been a master at evading the rules. It all changed when Thatcher knocked over the financial-controls regime with her iron handbag. "Margaret put some sunshine into your shady game," said Jürgen.

"Yes, well, one door closes, another opens. I always danced better in the open markets; I like the up-tempo beat."

"*Bien dit.* Well said," murmured Anouk. "Finance is life, so rich in lesson."

"Yes, some lessons don't flash across the computer screen," said Jack. "Oh, by the way, just where are you going, Dieter?"

"Palo Alto. We're going to cruise the coffee shops of University Avenue, catch up with the latest in social media, tweet our way from one hot spot to another, and visit the culture—an international confab of the info elite..."

"Stay away from the dark creatures," said Jack with a flippant wave of his hand.

"Congratulations, Anouk, you can explore the future on the streets of California. That's where it's always invented," said Sophie. "A real adventure."

"For now, you two are excused to the local coffeehouse," said Jim, nodding at Dieter and Anouk. "It's been a good morning's work."

Dieter and Anouk walked out of the Rubber Room, deep in animated conversation over their upcoming trip. The others watched them go.

"Looks like you found a leash for our boy genius, Jim," said Jack.

"Yeah, and I didn't even plan it," said Jim.

Jürgen, looking at the computer screen, broke in, "Here comes a press release about Crédit Générale..."

"Oh, what does it say?" asked Sophie.

Jim and Jack looked at one another with blank expressions on their faces, shrugged their shoulders, and said in innocent unison, "Yes, what does it say?"

Jürgen started to read from the computer screen: "Crédit Générale has announced that it reached an agreement to strengthen regulatory accounting procedures over derivatives trading with authorities in Paris, New York, and Brussels based upon an audit of unreported losses for an undisclosed amount in the wake of the financial crisis...and so on."

"Does it say who made the announcement?" asked Sophie.

"Just says a spokesman in the chairman's office," replied Jürgen.

"Oh, I probably know him," said Sophie. "His fingerprints are all over the announcement."

"It didn't say much," said Jürgen.

"That's the fingerprint," said Sophie with a bright smile.

Jim and Jack looked at each other and shrugged their shoulders but said nothing.

"I have planned to have lunch with Sophie," said Jim, changing the subject. He turned and smiled at Sophie.

"Yes, and then you're going to take me to the train station, right?" asked Sophie. "I have work in Paris tomorrow."

28. Gare de Cornavin

Jim and Sophie walked along the smooth, polished surface of the vast cement-floored landing standing at the head of a half a dozen train tracks dead-ending in the massive stone train station at Genève-Cornavin. They walked to one of the far platforms at the edge of the vast structure, where the long-distance TGV train to Paris was boarding. Coming to the head of the track, they turned and walked along the platform running like a long finger alongside the passenger carriages. Above them a narrow roof ran the length of the concrete platform. Beyond the edge of the roof was the sky, blanketed with a low-lying cloud, heavy with moisture, carrying the winter cold into the streets of Geneva. They walked past the carriages until they came to the first-class section and stopped.

Sophie turned around and faced Jim as she took a position at the bottom of the steps going up to the carriage. She had on a wide-brimmed hat, sloping to one side like a 1940s film star; a smart dark-blue overcoat trimmed with fox fur that came down to her midcalf; soft, polished black boots, and a light wool scarf, with a light-blue and red pattern setting off the overcoat. Her brown hair tumbled down onto her collar. She smiled radiantly and said to Jim, "Thank you for everything. It's been a much more exciting four days than I would have thought."

"All's well that ends well," said Jim. "Can I see you next week in Paris?"

"Yes, that would be fine. I am having meetings with some UMP policy people Thursday afternoon before meeting the steering committee on Friday morning. So how about next Thursday evening at Brasserie Lipp?"

"Yeah. The holidays are coming..."

"Yes, I know, but I can't commit to anything until after the steering committee meets, and I may have to discuss my plans with my family before I can truly make any further commitments...so much is coming together...so much I've worked for these many years. I hope you understand." She tilted her head and smiled charmingly, if not a little distantly, at him.

"Well, yes," said Jim, a little flustered. He didn't seem to fit so clearly in her plans as he had hoped. "Yeah, I guess so...there's also our future..."

"Yes, there is a future. We'll discuss that next week in Paris." She stood up on tiptoe and pursed her lips, kissed him good-bye, and said a businesslike, "Time to go." She turned and walked up the steps. At the top she looked back, smiled, and blew him a kiss. Then she entered the carriage.

29. Vienna

The black Mercedes limousine drove down the Ringstrasse in Vienna in the gathering gloom of late afternoon. A sharp chill was in the fall air. Ulrich looked out the side window and watched the limousine swing into the entranceway in front of the Hotel Imperial. Well, yes, the years had flown by. He recalled the hotels, the capital cities, the endless rounds of trade negotiations with the eastern countries—and the rendezvous, so many, such good times.

It had been over twenty years ago that he had first met her; he had been a young trade emissary negotiating natural-gas contracts during the last years of the old Soviet state gas authority, before it had been sold off to the oligarchs. She had been in public relations, so she said, and Ulrich laughed to himself at the memory. The limousine glided to a stop, and a doorman approached and opened the door. A porter went to the rear of the car and got Ulrich's bags and took them into the hotel. Ulrich walked through the big plate-glass door, a doorman holding it open and tipping his hand to his hat in salute as Ulrich strode through.

Once inside, the warmth of the lobby flushed his cheeks, and Ulrich scanned the lobby. She said she would meet him here. Then, from over across the room, he saw her sitting in a big, spacious chair. She stood up, a smile brightening her face, and she waved a gloved hand. She walked over as Ulrich watched the slow sway of her hips, her bosom just pushing the bolero jacket outward, the blouse setting off her well-presented roundness, a discreet choker at her throat. The blondish, platinum hair sculpted her handsome face.

He hoped she would understand. He wanted to keep their rendezvous, but their last little meeting in Prague had resulted in some unfortunate consequences, really rather minor, but they would have to be much more private this time, more discreet.

Ulrich gave the rest of the room a quick once-over. Yes, over there were the two gentlemen, both heavyset. Yes, they looked pretty much like the two men his wife had described to him. There was one with a brush-cut flattop coming down to a brutish forehead; the other was as bald as billiard ball, making him look like some latter-day Goldfinger in a cheap suit. Ulrich sighed; it was unfortunate that they were so clumsy, but possibly today it would be a help, make them easier to brush off. Behind Ulrich's bluff manner was a mind of extraordinary calculation.

As the woman came up to Ulrich, he held out both his hands, a beaming smile across his face. "Irina, so nice to see you again. I've been looking forward to this. Just like old times' sake."

"Yes, Ulrich, for me, too. The old times...I don't get out the way I used to when I was younger"—she batted her eyelashes at him—"and in demand."

"Let's go into the cocktail lounge and have a drink," said Ulrich.

"Yes, by all means."

Ulrich held his arm out and guided her toward the cocktail lounge over on the far side of the lobby. The waiter came up, and Ulrich said rather cavalierly, "Champagne."

"Oh, my favorite," said Irina.

"Irina, there's something we have to talk about. Now you know that nothing we've ever done or will do will ever compromise how I do my work. I am completely resistant to influence, and all those clumsy blackmail attempts over the years by the buffoons in the baggy gray suits have been most amusing to my superiors back in Bonn and now Berlin."

"Oh, I know that, Ulrich. That's what has always made it so much fun to be with you, a certain innocence in a corrupting world. You have always been my most special assignment—more enjoyable than marrying for money or some other crass, bourgeois pursuit."

"Well, tonight I can't stay in your suite here in Vienna. You'll have to stay in mine."

"Oh, my, what happened?"

"Well, last time, that rendezvous in Prague...in your suite...there were other eyes, and your associates put the video on a CD—I'm sure you didn't know—and the clumsy oafs went to my villa outside of Berlin to try to influence me. But unfortunately I wasn't there to intercept them."

"Oh," said Irina, a cloud coming over her face. "They spoke to someone else?"

"Yes, my wife."

"Oh my," said Irina, putting her hand up to her mouth. "I didn't know. She must have been terribly upset with you."

"Oh, no. We have had certain understandings over the years...what happens on the road stays on the road."

"So understanding."

"Well, yes. Of course, what happens at the spa stays at the spa."

"Well, yes, I could always understand that...a woman's privacy."

"Exactly. But those clumsy oafs upset the cart."

"What happened?"

"They were brandishing the CD around in front of my wife, who was trying to shush them up and get them to leave, when one of my granddaughters—she's sixteen..."

"Yes, just coming into her sophistication."

"Anyway Kirsten grabs the CD out of the oaf's hands and hands it to her sister Krista, who's fifteen and can run like a deer..."

"Yes, fifteen, a fun-loving age..."

"Anyway, she runs away with the CD—"

"Your wife couldn't stop them?"

"No, she told the Russian oaf, 'Now you've done it. You better get out of here.' She shooed them out the door."

"Yes, the service has definitely lost its skill at field craft since the old days. So many mistakes these days."

"I came home from another trade mission. My wife was cross with me. She said, 'I'd recognize it anywhere, that big white heinie of yours, bobbing and weaving in the candlelight...don't you have any sense, Ulrich?'"

Ulrich looked at Irina and turned his palms up. "What could I say?"

Irina nodded sympathetically and explained, "Well, there has to be some light, or the pictures won't come out...so always the candles..."

"So she says, 'The girls got the CD. They uploaded it to the Internet; you're now a YouTube hero.'"

"Oh, my," said Irina. "That's troublesome."

"It gets worse."

"It does?"

"The girls put the video on their cell phones. They go to an exclusive girls' boarding school. You can imagine...in the dormitory...at night..."

"Yes, the girls would."

"They call it *Herr Diplomat and the Russian Swallow*."

"Well, it could be worse; you could be with a—"

"Then spreading across all the boarding schools, like wildfire, is a new game, *Fifty Shades of Tartar*—"

"Yes, the girls write successive chapters themselves...outdoing one another for tawdriness."

"Yes, apparently about a Cossack with big black boots and a riding crop...and not much else."

"Yes, I've heard...at the best schools—"

"So then I get a phone call from my daughter-in-law. She's very prissy, very correct, and she says, 'Herr Renke, I got a call from the headmistress at Kirstin's and Krista's school. They're upset...seems the school is having a career day...and normally the girls all want to be runway models or fashion designers and the intellectual ones museum curators and art historians—'"

"Yes, that's why we send them there."

"So she says, 'Well, the headmistress says all the girls wrote down this year that they want to be trade negotiators on their career-day forms.' And could I explain this?"

Ulrich again turned his palms up before continuing. "My daughter-in-law told the headmistress that, yes, the girls had become interested in their grandfather's travels to distant capitals, the museums he gets to see, the symphonies he attends, and watching the Bolshoi."

"Well, your daughter-in-law is quick."

"The headmistress said, 'Frau Renke, you might look at your daughters' cell phones the next time they're home.'"

Irina winced.

"Then the YouTube video..."

Irina cringed.

"The chancellor's office was not amused."

"Yes, the minister's daughter," said Irina, mentioning Angela Merkel, whose father had been a Lutheran pastor.

"Precisely, she exacts a price. I was told I had to get a good price on this natural-gas contract. The energy minister said rock bottom or *der heinie* would be in *Der Spiegel*."

"None of us would benefit from that," said Irina.

"So tonight we have to go to my room—no cameras."

"I'd love to. I'm getting a little old for the movies anyway."

"The energy minister was generous. He said I could put the swallow on the expense report. He asked if you'd like to accompany me on to Bulgaria—a bonus for your understanding."

"Oh, you know I would." She reached over and squeezed Ulrich's hand. "Such a loving relationship, full of understanding. Why, yes, I'd love to go to your room. I'll draw you a bath. I brought your favorite bubble bath. Just like the old days." Then she looked off into the distance, a moment of reflection coming across her face, and said, "Seems strange that something so simple as a telephone could so change the culture."

"Yes," said Ulrich. "Well, what counts is we're together again." Ulrich leaned back in the chair with smug satisfaction. Then a thought flashed in his mind; he leaned forward to Irina and whispered, "Did you bring them with you?"

"Of course." She looked around furtively and then pulled her handbag forward between them and opened the top to show three rubber duckies inside.

Ulrich clapped his hands. "Oh, goodie, we can play hide the ducky. You know how much I enjoy it."

"Yes," Irina said then paused. "Let me wave my friends good-bye."

"Yes, by all means, they've caused enough trouble already."

Irina stood up and looked at the two Russians across the lobby. She waved her hand good-bye slowly and shook her head back and forth in the universal sign of negative. Their faces fell. She gave them a final wave and then reached down with her hand to signal Ulrich to get up. The couple turned and walked across the lobby toward the elevators.

The two Russians stood there dumbfounded. The bald one said, "We missed in Geneva; now we've missed in Vienna. There goes the dacha on the Black Sea."

"That was our last chance. No Lagarde list, no video, no leverage." The brute's face fell with disappointment.

The other Russian just watched as the beautiful Irina glided across the lobby, her hips swaying this way then that way, her arm around Ulrich's waist. "Seems sort of unfair. They lost the war."

"Yeah, let's go into the bar. Our turn to have a drink."

The two Russians walked across the lobby into the bar and headed for a distant corner table, one hailing the waiter. "Vodka."

The waiter brought over two glasses of vodka and set them down on the table. One Russian crinkled his nose and said, "Bottles, man, not glasses. Two bottles."

The other Russian held the little glass up in front of his face and twisted it around, giving it a close inspection with a cross-eyed stare, distaste clouding his face, and said, "Tumblers."

The waiter scurried away and brought back two bottles and two big tumblers.

"Now tell me again," the one Russian said to the other, "that job the director promised us if things didn't work out—again."

"Gate guards at a refinery down in the Crimea. Nice climate. We'll make friends down in the village. Steady work…so much better than the Siberian retirement plan under the old regime…a nice little uniform like a refrigerator repairman…"

"Yes," said the other Russian, taking a long pull on a tumbler full of vodka. Then he held the tumbler out in salute to the other Russian and said, "Gate…"

The other Russian clinked his glass and said, "Guards."

Washington, DC

In the large office, all of Washington and its public buildings were spread out behind the plate-glass window behind a vast desk. Behind the desk sat a tall, silver-haired lady, stylishly dressed, impeccably coiffed. The intercom buzzed; a light flashed on one of the telephone lines. The silver-haired woman picked the phone up and asked, "Yes?" She listened then brought the phone down and held her hand over the mouthpiece and whispered to her aide, "Paris. Personal."

"*Oui, madame,*" said the aide as she set some papers down and left the office, softly closing the door behind her.

"*Maintenant,*" said the silver-haired lady. She listened and nodded in understanding. "*Oui, Sophie d'Auverne, un bon choix,*" she said. (Yes, Sophie, d'Auverne, a good choice.)

The silver-haired lady continued listening. She nodded and said, "Yes, time for the highest levels..."

The voice on the other end of the line asked some questions.

"Yes, Angela appreciates competence."

The voice continued; the lady listened.

"Berlin? The media?" The lady paused and then laughed. "No, it will be like Jackie Kennedy shopping in Paris. She'll be a real hit."

She listened some more, smiled to herself, and said, "Au revoir." She set the phone down in its cradle and buzzed for her aide.

30. Brasserie Lipp

Sophie came through the door, approached the tuxedoed maître d', and said, "I believe I'm expected at table seven."

The maître d' looked at her and smiled broadly; lots of pretty ones went to table seven. "*D'ailleurs, par ici, madame.*" (Indeed, this way, madame.) He turned and walked into the downstairs dining area. There was dark paneled wood on the walls, between a dazzling array of mirrors, and parquet floors with brass and polished mahogany everywhere—all offset by white linen tableclothes and glistening glassware. He stopped and turned his arm into an empty seating space at a banquet and said, "Madame." The two men sitting behind the table half stood up and mumbled, "*Avec plaisir.*"

Sophie reached across the table and shook the security flic's hand and said, "So nice to see you again." She turned to the other man and said, "Whom do I have the pleasure of meeting?"

"You know who," he said with an impish twinkle in his eye. "Philippe Lagrande. It is I who does not know who I have the pleasure of meeting…if I were younger—"

"We would be the closest of friends," said Sophie with a twinkle in her eye.

"Ah, sometimes the trials of old age are almost unbearable," said Lagrande, now pushing eighty, with a mop of white hair and the sharp features of what had been the look of a matinee idol.

"Philippe, may I present Sophie d'Auverne," said the security flic.

Lagrande reached his hand across the table, shook Sophie's hand, and said, "My colleague has just been telling me about you. You won an African warlord in a catfight in a disco in Bamako, because you were better than the Moroccan *putain*?"

"In my imagination…"

"My," he mused. "There was a time when a part of me would have liked to have met your imagination." He laughed.

"If it was the exciting part of you, then my imagination...well..." said Sophie, and she smiled deliciously.

"Checkmate," said Lagrande, and he tilted his head and looked at Sophie, searching his memory, and then asked, "Any connection with Inès d'Auverne?"

"*Ma* grand-mère."

Lagrande flashed his eyebrows; a smile broadened across his face. He recalled, "Yes, during the De Gaulle years, she circulated at the highest political levels. There were rumors..."

"Possibly they were true," said Sophie softly. "I have read her memoirs. She led an exciting life. I believe her imagination led her on many quests."

"Those memoirs might make a great intrigue—politics between satin sheets, money on the night train to Switzerland—someday," said Lagrande.

"Someday," said Sophie, gently closing off the subject.

"She's a cool one," said the security flic to Lagrande.

"She looks like she would be more fun when she's a little warmed up," said Lagrande in an open aside to the security flic, his eyes locked on Sophie.

"I mean with finance," said the security flic.

"Do I look like a bank clerk?" said Lagrande out of the side of his mouth to the security flic, laughing, his eyes still on Sophie. "I never mean finance." He looked at Sophie and asked, "So the granddaughter is part of the *haute gouvernement*, the finance ministry?"

"I was part of the Sarkozy government. So now I'm in the government in exile."

"And you got caught up in a little adventure with our Russian friends?"

"Yes, I hid a small computer chip with a big list inside a piece of costume jewelry and put it in a safe-deposit box in Geneva for safekeeping. Apparently there were hidden eyes that saw me depart from the ministry—"

"Sophie," the security flic broke in. "We took care of the hidden eyes last week. The Mouse was retired—quietly."

"Yes, the Mouse," said Lagrande. "I've been hearing about her for years; I almost thought she was some kind of myth. Any remorse?" asked Lagrande, turning to the security flic.

Paul A. Myers

"Heartbroken. She really liked—how do we say—being serviced by the Russian spy service," said the security flic.

"They always do," said Lagrande with knowing wink at Sophie.

Sophie shuddered. "The two I saw...urghh..."

"Rough pieces of work, eh?" said Lagrande with a laugh. "Not diplomatic grade?" He took a sip of wine and then changed the subject and asked, "Why Geneva?"

"My gentlemen friend—"

"That's the poodle I was telling you about," said the security flic. "Actually he wasn't such a bad guy after the fourth magnum of champagne."

"It was his champagne...his villa," explained Sophie to Lagrande.

Lagrande laughed, asking, "What does he do?"

"Investments. His fund was long Greek bonds."

"They won big last week, I think."

"His hedge fund banked ten percent of the total."

"Wow," said Lagrande, obviously impressed. "They cashed in on the big bazooka. That beats arms dealing any day."

"Well, the good news is that the 'bazooka' is mostly made up of German money," said the security flic with an air of resignation.

"Oh, well, they call it honest work," said Lagrande with a sigh. "Only in the James Bond movies does the spy get the good-looking girl...and my novels, of course."

Something caught Lagrande's eye; he looked up, and his eyes darted toward a man standing at the entrance to the room. He smiled and said, "A well-dressed poodle, I presume...Italian tailoring, I believe?"

Sophie turned her head around toward the entrance and saw Jim following the maître d' toward their table. She turned back to Lagrande. "Yes, Italian for the clothes...the man's New York. I asked him to meet me here; we're having dinner together—there are some open items to discuss."

Lagrande waved Jim into a seat next to Sophie. The security flic held his hand out to Jim and gave it a shake as he said, "Nice to see you again, Mr. Greek Bond, king of the big bazookas." He smirked at Sophie.

207

"I felt pretty small talking with those Russians. You guys really made our day," said Jim with heartfelt feeling. The security flic pumped up a little bit at the compliment. Turning to the older man, Jim said, "And you must be Philippe Lagrande?"

"The one and the same," said Lagrande.

"We've heard so much about your books the last couple of weeks. Sophie turns out to have had a couple dozen in her bottom drawer at the finance ministry."

Lagrande's face sharpened, and he whistled. "That's a new one."

"The girls liked to read them on their breaks...at the finance ministry," said Sophie.

"To get ready for something after work?" asked Lagrande. Then his face turned saturnine in expectation, a wolfish hopefulness infused his tone, and he asked, "Or at work?" A secretary rocking back and forth on the lap of the finance minister danced in his fertile imagination. He tucked the thought away for another day, another page.

Sophie laughed and leaned forward. "Possibly some of both..."

"Yes, some of both...that might work," said Lagrande, contemplating the writing possibilities.

Sophie smiled and said, her timing perfect, her face a picture of tact, "It has been a pleasure meeting you, Philippe." She nudged Jim toward the aisle; he stood up, and she slid across the banquet and followed. Sophie reached her hand across the table and shook the security flic's hand and then Lagrande's, saying, "We must do this again." Jim waved his hand and nodded at the two Frenchmen.

Lagrande and the security flic watched Jim and Sophie leave. The security flic leaned over and said, "As I was saying, he was all right after the fourth magnum of champagne. After the sixth, I almost had her talked into dancing on the tabletop, but she turned that little nose up and pouted. '*Pas avec le gouvernement.*'" (Not with the government.)

"Yes...the little vixen." Lagrande sighed.

"*Le gouvernement*...like I was the post office. What I do for a pension," said the security flic.

"Yes, possibly a real tease," said Lagrande. "Tell you what. In the next novel, she'll dance on the table and then take the French spy chief on a ride he won't forget. And oh, yes...the finance-ministry secretaries...during work...after work...*individuelle...ou...ensemble sexuelle...*" The writer smiled and looked off into space, contemplating the many possibilities.

A waiter came over, and Lagrande, his eyes returning to the table, circled his finger for another round. He leaned across the table and said, "Now tell me about Mali, Jacques."

Upstairs

Jim and Sophie met the maître d' at the top of the staircase to the second floor and followed him toward a table along the wall. The maître d' held his hand out, and Sophie slid into the banquet along the wall, while Jim took a chair across the table. She set her Longchamps handbag on the cushion beside her. The maître d' handed them menus and departed. Sophie looked around the room, and spotting some men at a table across the way, her face brightened in recognition. "There are some acquaintances from Sciences Po," she said. "I'd better walk over and say hello. I'll be just a few minutes, Jim." She stood up and walked across the room, Jim's eyes following her as she went. The three men were late-middle-age academic types, wearing tweed jackets and wool sweaters. The voluble one had a gold chain around his neck; it danced on his shirtfront as he waved his arms this way and that.

Jim watched as she chatted. A born networker, he thought. He pulled his iPhone out and brought up the *Financial Times* for a quick update. After a few minutes, she gave the three men a small wave and walked back and sat down and said to Jim, "One was my professor in money and banking when I was a student there. The others came later, but I have met them on occasion when Strategic International hires them to consult."

A waiter came up, and Sophie said, "*Un verre du vin blanc.*"

"The same," said Jim. He set his iPhone down and said, "Just been catching up with the *Financial Times*."

"And what is the Pink Lady saying?"

"Well, the prime minister of Bulgaria cancelled two Russian-backed 'grand slam' energy projects—one a big oil pipeline, the other a nuclear-power project. He laughs and asks journalists to name any other prime minister in the world who has cancelled two projects out of three with Moscow."

"That's quite true. Russia's strategy to have an energy stranglehold on Europe is in tatters," said Sophie.

"Bulgaria has let natural-gas exploration contracts to UK and US companies," said Jim.

"That will diversify future energy sources, but the truly fascinating development is Bulgaria's new contract for natural gas with Gazprom, Russia's biggest natural-gas company. The new ten-year contract allows Bulgaria to reduce purchases to zero after six years, and the Bulgarians won a twenty percent price cut. Who would have thought that would have been possible a year ago? The geopolitics of these developments are fascinating; it breaks up the Russian plan to control the flow of energy into Europe. President Putin's scheme isn't working out," said Sophie.

"Jürgen is really surprised. We've been following the Russian energy stocks—they've been rising while world energy prices have been falling—weird."

"And you don't know which way to jump?"

"Exactly. Jürgen knows the German trade negotiator who went to Bulgaria. He seems to have been some sort of catalyst for the Bulgarians."

"Yes, Ulrich von Renke. He's one of their best."

"You know him?"

"Of course. Strategy International keeps close tabs on all these negotiations...a bad deal can change the whole geopolitical equation."

"Yes, but Jürgen said he was accompanied by a mysterious Russian woman, who had been high up in the KGB—a favorite of Putin personally, back in what they call 'the good old days.' Whatever that means."

"Yes, Irina."

"You know her, too?"

"Yes. She's been what we call a 'friend' of Renke's since back when she was, shall we say, a 'friend' of Putin's."

"Wow, she gets around," said Jim. "Jürgen thought the fix might be in. Bulgaria has been understanding of Russian interests over the years."

"Yes, I could see how you might have that fear."

"So if we went short on Russian energy stocks, it seems it ought to pay off. But we don't know."

Sophie took a sip of wine, a certain glow of contentment on her face, a conspiratorial smile breaking across her face. "Let me share with you…"

"Please do."

"This is outside our consulting services. Normally, we share our conclusions with our clients—but nothing that might betray the sources."

"Of course."

She leaned forward and said in a low voice, "A diplomatic package went from Berlin to Moscow. In the pouch—our source said it went to Putin's office unopened—there was a letter, handwritten from the chancellor herself. It said, 'She's ours.'"

"Who?"

"We presume the woman Irina."

"And?"

"Putin opened the package. Apparently, he was stunned. He went into his office and closed the door and sat there transfixed all afternoon—no visitors, no calls—and he simply stared at a rubber ducky sitting in the middle of his desk."

Jim smiled and then laughed. "Who said the pastor's daughter doesn't have a sense of humor?"

Sophie laughed and said, "Please keep this to yourself. Our source is close to the top."

"Yes, you can count on me."

"So," Sophie said, eyes twinkling, "President Putin's plans for Russia to be the new energy superstate are on hold, if not quashed. Our clients have been in the know about this ever since Renke left Vienna for Bulgaria."

"So, Russia's energy strategy is a one-trick pony. But how to play it?" said Jim. "Dieter's just not getting a strong signal."

"Neither are we," said Sophie. "Of course, the overall effect will be to make Germany even stronger. Ultimately, that means a stronger Europe…and a powerful Angela. She will have completed the journey from *das mädchen* to *machtfrau*—from political maiden to power lady—in just two decades."

"Yes, the changing faces of power…" mumbled Jim, and he took a sip of wine.

Sophie looked across the room toward the stairwell and, to her surprise, saw Alain Renier entering the room. She smiled at him.

He recognized her. Then he saw Jim. Startled, he froze.

"There's Alain Renier," said Sophie. "He looks like he saw a ghost."

Jim gulped and turned around and followed Sophie's gaze to Alain. Jim made a weak smile. Sophie followed Jim's eyes, with great amusement spreading across her face. She stood up and waved with her hand for Alain to come over.

Alain trotted up like a dog, barely maintaining his composure, while Jim stood up like a schoolboy being called out by his teacher. Sophie said to Alain, "Jim and his hedge fund are clients of Strategy International. I believe the two of you already know each other?"

"Why, yes," stammered Alain. "Crédit Générale tries to keep in contact with a wide circle of people outside of traditional banking circles. I am, of course, intimately involved...with liaison..."

"Yes, I know that, Alain. I was particularly impressed by the press release Crédit Générale put out about settling with the regulatory authorities about the unreported losses on the derivatives. We at Strategy International were deeply impressed. I was also speaking to the UMP steering committee this afternoon. I'm meeting with them again tomorrow. I told them how deeply impressed Strategy International had been with the way you handled the matter with the Americans."

Alain's jaw dropped in open-mouthed wonder at Sophie's knowledge about what had been a deeply camouflaged process, buried under layers of public-relations obfuscation, of covering up with the Americans.

"To come in well below Deutsche Bank—less than three billion euros was the rumor—and without involving the finance police, and your alternative-valuation technique was so much more sophisticated than that crude arrogance exhibited by the Germans. Well, people in the know at the highest levels know genius at work."

"They do?" mumbled Alain.

"Yes," said Sophie with smooth assurance. "Anyway, I recommended to the steering committee that you would be the best candidate to represent the UMP at Frankfurt on discussions of how to set up and operate the new European Central Bank regulatory authority—supervising the two hundred largest banks in Europe demands experience and skill. The government has to include some representatives from the UMP in the delegation, don't you think?"

"Well, yes," said Alain. "I'm flattered at your opinion."

"Your intimate relationships with the Germans are absolutely critical to the government in this matter," said Sophie. "Even if they don't know it yet."

Alain nodded in agreement. He knew it was all true.

"The chairman complimented me on the recommendation and said, 'Yes, even the Socialists know they need Alain.'"

Jim's shoulders eased, and Alain relaxed. Sophie continued, "Jim was just telling me how impressed his firm was with a few top officials at a big French bank and how they bought shares in their bank when its price was at its lowest ebb. Jim's fund, Bermuda Triangle, knows things like that and how that attracted additional investment from some of the savviest of the big London and American funds."

Jim looked at Sophie dumb struck. He had not said anything of the kind.

She smiled benignly at him. Jim turned to Alain and explained, "My conversations with Mme d'Auverne have been only at the most general level. We only trade on information properly obtained though the types of channels all institutional investors rely upon on a daily basis."

"Yes," said Alain. "All large investors pay close attention to the big banks. We're not always sure whether to welcome such interest; some of the hedge funds have been known to be, shall we say, inaccurate in their opinions—possibly trying to profit from unsubstantiated rumors."

"We trade only on hard facts and detailed analysis," said Jim. "Why recently, we got into your bank, Crédit Générale, at the lows after carefully studying the public information. Indeed, Mme d'Auverne concurred in our finding."

Sophie smiled at Jim and then turned back to Alain and asked, "One question. Your use of Professor Vannier"—Sophie nodded in the direction across the room where the Sciences Po professors were talking—"Did the Americans bite? Vannier's position seems like a weak chip. Didn't the Americans see through it?"

Alain relaxed, and a self-assured smile spread across his face. "Yes…a weak chip…but if played skillfully…"

"By you, of course…" added Sophie.

Alain nodded at the compliment and continued, "Played skillfully in the back channels…voila…a settlement satisfactory to all interests."

"Very good, Alain. We can all see that France will be well represented at Frankfurt," said Sophie.

Jim looked at Alain and said, "Alain, there has been less communication between me and Mme d'Auverne than this conversation would suggest. Bermuda Triangle much values discretion in its business dealings."

"My experience, Jim, is that Sophie knows everything," replied Alain with a laugh, "in the back corridors…"

"From the first napkin…" said Sophie with a broad smile.

Jim's jaw dropped; he was dumb struck as he mumbled "From the first napkin?"

Sophie turned to Alain and added, "You'll have no problems with us on our understandings of what went on at Crédit Générale, Alain. So please don't let us keep you from your rendezvous." She held her hand out and shook Alain's by way of saying good-bye.

"Always a pleasure," said Alain as he took her hand, made a deep bow, and gave the hand an air kiss. He turned and walked across the café and joined several of his colleagues, deep in boisterous conversation at a table with a couple of open bottles of wine.

Jim and Sophie sat down. Jim asked, "Just what was all that about?"

"I could say 'you tell me,' but that would be dishonest."

"So you're going to tell me you're just clever."

"No, I'm going to tell you that Édouard has known about you and Alain since the first napkin."

Jim said with amazement, "How?" He paused, collected himself, and then said, "You're good. How'd you figure it out?"

"Édouard did an old-fashioned investigation. Lots of shoe leather. Found the Sciences Po guy who consulted with Alain."

"And this guy just told him?" asked Jim incredulously.

"Of course not. Édouard asked him about JP Morgan and how they might have understated their derivative losses."

"And the professor was only too happy to show off," said Jim.

"Édouard is a student of human nature," said Sophie with a laugh. "Now, my turn—how'd you do it?"

"Dieter cracked the encryption. We were reading the SEC guys' reports back to New York."

"Did the Americans buy the French professor's scheme?"

"No, they saw right through it, according to Dieter."

"But you didn't short?"

"No, for a couple of reasons. Alain wanted to only go long. 'Can't be faulted for buying your company's stock when it's in trouble,' he said. Confidence and all that. And it was pretty small potatoes all in all."

"You can't go against a big bank. They have the government behind them. So it's only smart to play the long game with big banks. We're just trying to game the system, not cheat the system." He looked at Sophie and said, "You might not believe this, but there is a difference."

"I know there is." She took a long sip of her wine and set the glass down. She shifted the conversation. "Thank you. Speaking of Édouard, he has a request. He greatly admired how your managed accounts work in Monaco. By the way, the casino manager is one of his oldest friends."

Jim's eyes opened wide. "He is?"

"Yes," she said. "And Édouard would like to know whether it would be possible for him to transfer some of his retirement funds to Bermuda Triangle's managed accounts in Monaco."

"Consider it done," said Jim, relieved. Then he thought to himself for a couple of moments. "I would, of course, like to strengthen our personal contacts with Édouard in return. He's resourceful, unusually knowledgeable..."

"This is regardless of our relationship, right?" asked Sophie, a hint of warning in her tone.

Jim caught the tone, thought for a moment, and said, "Business is business, of course."

"Good," said Sophie. "And by the way, Édouard and Jack go way back. He said Jack could work around exchange controls like no one he ever saw. It was no problem for the French, but the British at the time might not have been so understanding."

"Yes, he was a bank manager for British banks all across Europe in those years, and when the English money went offshore, he was there."

"Yes, Édouard has confidence in him," said Sophie with finality, another item on the agenda crossed off. Then she fumbled about and looked at Jim, directly and with great sincerity, and said, "I have something else on my mind. I'm meeting with the steering committee of the UMP tomorrow for lunch, as I said. More than Alain is on the agenda."

"Yes, your future political career," said Jim understandingly.

"Then I'm leaving for Auverne in the afternoon for the weekend. Grand-mère may not have much time left."

"Leaving for Auverne tomorrow..." repeated Jim in a soft voice, incredulous and disappointed. Without me? he thought. He was stunned.

Sophie sat and watched his reaction—calm and detached. "Yes, after my meeting with the steering committee, I would like to meet with you and explain...the choices I'm making, catch up on loose ends."

"I didn't know I was a 'loose end,'" said Jim. His face fell even further; he sensed something was unraveling.

"Possibly a poor choice of words on my part. Tomorrow I would like to explain to you where I think my future is going. It has been planned this way for many years now."

"Well, you're a pretty busy girl," said Jim in a downcast way.

"Yes, I am. I don't apologize for that."

"Just what is your future, if I may ask?"

"Of course you can. I have been what is called a 'technocrat.' That is not always meant as a compliment. Some in the UMP feel I should get some firsthand political experience, as I mentioned before."

"So you're going to be a politician?"

"That has been proposed."

"Are you going to the National Assembly as a deputy?"

"No, the UMP thinks I should stand for the European Parliament."

"From where?"

"Either here in the Île-de-France region or from Normandy. They want to discuss this further tomorrow."

"Why?"

"They feel I should get firsthand budget experience in both Brussels and Strasbourg. And they want to strengthen their presence in this area at that level."

"So this is about more than a budget analyst coughing up a billion in savings?"

"Jim, I can list ten billion before you finish your wine. France needs to do sixty to a hundred billion a year."

"Oh, a big deal?"

"A real reordering of priorities, yes. So I would be gone from Paris a lot. I wanted you to know that."

"So? I already travel a lot. I don't see that as a problem."

"Neither do I. However, they want a real time commitment from me. You might not approve."

"I didn't know my approval was in question," sighed Jim. "I didn't know budgeting was such a big deal to them."

"An overall fiscal framework for the Eurozone is going to be put together in the coming years. This is the most important step in the deepening of European integration—ever. Budgeting is going to be a big deal. Money always is in politics."

"So you will be a UMP budget meister?"

Sophie laughed. "Yes, you could say that. The UMP wants, in the coming elections, to present to the French people an aura that the party can provide a government with deep expertise and competence in the new world of Eurozone fiscal policy. François Fillon and Christine Lagarde already present a highly experienced and competent face to the public. They want to build on this image."

"Yes, I see. And you would be part of this?"

"Possibly. I have to prove myself."

"I thought you were their poster girl?"

"At this level, you have to prove yourself every day. Just like you and the market. Every day is a new day." She set her glass down and looked seriously at Jim. "And I don't want to be anyone's poster girl. I have worked for years to garner the experience and competence for this opportunity. I want to put it to service at the highest level. Understood?"

"Yes."

"I've already put one husband down, so to speak, over this issue."

"Yeah, I understand...I guess."

"Good. May I suggest we meet at Le Bistrot de la Banque tomorrow afternoon, around two?"

"Yes, of course."

Sophie smiled. "Good. I knew you'd understand."

"Understand? After what I thought we had?" said Jim like a hurt puppy.

Her phone beeped, and she looked down at the screen and remarked, "Oh, my car and driver are outside. I must go." She stood up and coolly said, "*À demain.*" (Until tomorrow.) She picked up her handbag and departed.

He sat there, his dismay settling in around him like a winter mist; Jack's words slammed into his consciousness—"She's a great actress." Was she? There were things more important than money, he now knew. She had proved that. He shook his head back and forth, deep in emotional confusion. Just what was the signal? His love wasn't just part of the noise; was it?

31. Encore, Auverne

Jim watched the long black limousine swerve into the taxi lane next to Le Bistro de la Banque. The chauffeur came around and opened the rear door, and Sophie alighted, stood up, smoothed her skirt, and started walking over to Jim, a big smile broadening across her face as she came up to him. She held out her hand, palm down, in a friendly if slightly distant handshake.

"So nice we could meet. I didn't really mean for this to be good-bye."

Jim looked at her skeptically, a hurt look in his eyes. "Yes..." He let the word drift off into the breeze.

"I'm leaving for Auverne for the weekend then the holidays. Grand-mère has only so much time left. It is time for the closest family to be near."

"Yes, well, have a nice time."

"Now, don't be like that. Some things are not meant to be, other things are—"

"How should I be? I'm really disappointed. No, I'm crushed."

"Now, I think we do have a future together..."

Jim looked up sharply.

"*Mais, d'abord,*" continued Sophie. "Certain understandings must be arrived at; certain considerations must take precedence over other concerns for a relationship to endure. *N'est-ce pas?*"

"Sure. Your political career *über alles.*"

She made a pout and looked at him with eyes that said he wasn't getting it.

"Well, am I right or not?" he asked.

"My political career is in furtherance of something more important than just me. That was the point of all those steps from the Hôtel de Ville to the Matignon. During those years, you made money, and I moved up the ladder."

"So?"

"I'm coming into my time. You will be a banker; I will have need of your *conseil.*" She smiled and turned wistful. "There will be other times when I will be gowned and slippered and on the arm of a handsome man under the chandeliers at the *Palais Élysée*, waiting to greet M. Président."

He looked at her, not quite understanding where the conversation was going.

"With you?" she said and added parenthetically, "*Peut-être?*" (Perhaps.)

"OK, maybe. Back to politics. Your friend Christine will become president of the Republic, and you will be a minister."

"*Peut-être,*" she said, tentatively; her face clouded with doubt. "More likely, Fillon will be president. He keeps a tidy cabinet, a smooth sense of decorum. The *machtfrau* likes him. Christine will go to the bank or possibly that big, new job at Brussels." She shrugged her shoulders and said, "Or remain *la reine* at the International Monetary Fund. Who knows?"

"Sarkozy?"

Sophie shrugged her shoulders: "Encore? Sarkozy at the Élysée and Fillon at the Matignon? Why repeat? Does it matter? Whoever is in Berlin will be driving the Euro car."

"But you will be a minister, won't you?"

"I will be at that level—somewhere. And I will have power—somewhere. Its exercise requires the greatest discretion and skill."

"Just what are you going to do with your power?"

"Enjoy it." She wrapped her arms around herself and gave herself a nice hug and shivered with imagined delight.

He laughed and asked, "Anything else?"

Sophie pouted in that cute, little way. "Restore fashion to its centrality in our culture."

"Of course."

"And there will be the larger work; the European Parliament is growing in power."

"Yes," said Jim, "the *haute cooperation.*"

Sophie glanced away with a sort of faraway look on her face and said, "Angela, Christine, and possibly another will be in power at the White House."

"At the White House—which one? Hillary, Elizabeth?"

"Does it matter?"

"Probably not."

"But we do have an agenda."

"We? I keep trying to figure out just who 'we' are."

She tossed her head in dismissal of the question. "We have experience. We will have power. We will get the job done right—step by step,"

Jim knew it was a favorite phrase of Angela Merkel's. "For example?"

"We'll start with Europe. It needs a redo. Some institutional furniture needs to be moved around. Possibly a spring housecleaning."

"I can agree with that."

"You must understand; the political world is messy because the real world is. Putting all these people in Europe together into something that works is a long and messy process, but it's the future of the world we live in. We must succeed."

"I think I understand; you're the signal swimming through the murky noise of life."

"Good," she said with finality. "*Vous comprenez*." She tilted her head, made her most winsome smile, and said, "*Maintenant*, I'm on my way to Auverne." She looked at Jim.

Jim simply stood there; he didn't know what to say. She knew where she was going; where was he? He looked at her—before his eyes her expression decomposed into one of love and longing. What is this all about? he thought.

"You must come with me," she said, in a slightly commanding tone. Then she batted her eyelashes, not quite submissively, and said, "The first of a lifetime of weekends together...then a life together..."

He looked at her with frank astonishment.

"Later, we will have much time together. That is what Auverne is for—fidelity and loyalty. But first there is the work, important work, for you and for me."

He nodded imperceptibly in the affirmative and mumbled, "Yes, the work." His mind was stumbling over what Sophie had just said: an invitation to share a life with her.

She saw it all sink in and sealed it, saying, "Good." She turned halfway around and took a couple of steps toward the waiting limousine. She stopped and looked back over her shoulder, tossed her hair, and said, "By the way, no collars, no cuffs." She smiled beguilingly. "You're the toy." She laughed lightly.

"Huh?" said Jim, standing there in open-mouthed astonishment.

"Your partner Jack questioned my mentor. You didn't think he wouldn't tell me?" She laughed. "I have many admirers"—she looked at him—"of long standing, but all that was when I was a girl, chasing my adventures."

She turned and started toward the waiting limousine. He stood there and watched—dumbfounded. She turned and looked at him. She patted the front of her thigh like she was beckoning a dog, the skirt gently rippling underneath her hand's pats. She pursed her lips: "*Viens avec moi.* Come with me. You don't want to wind up as some wannabe dodging taxes in the Cayman Islands, do you?"

"*Non, madame.*"

She smiled. Jim nodded in acquiescence and walked past Sophie toward the limousine. The chauffeur opened the rear door, and he ducked his head and got in; he slid over to the left side of the seat. Sophie came up and moved smoothly into the right side of the rear seat. The chauffeur closed the door and went around and got in the driver's seat. He looked in the rearview mirror at Sophie, his eyes asking for instruction. She nodded to proceed. Precedence was established.

An hour later, the limousine was driving down the country roads of Normandy in the falling light of the late afternoon, a winter shower leaving the tawny leaves glistening with moisture in the setting sun. Jim leaned back in the seat, relaxed, and said with a laugh, "I'm impressed with how self-confident the leadership of the new Europe is."

Sophie smiled at him, and then she too leaned back in her seat. She looked out the window and said softly, "Yes, aren't we?"

The limousine pulled up the long, treelined drive at Auverne in the last glimmer of twilight, the broad, flat stones in front of the portico mirror black in the dark shadow of the large house. The splendor of the château was beautiful. Jim squeezed Sophie's hand; she leaned over and kissed him on the cheek. He whispered, "We're here."

"We can have such a good time together."

"Yes, isn't it pretty to think so."

End

Paul A. Myers

Sources

THANKS to Arlette Gamelin for inviting my wife and I for a delightful week at her beach-side condo at Cala Bona on Majorca. Arlette told us about how the Guardia Civil had a plan to close off Costa de los Pinos at the crossroads in case civil unrest overtook Spain, securing all the ministers' villas secluded on the hillsides of the peninsula. This tale of intrigue emerged at dinner on the esplanade of Cala Bona over a fine bottle of rioja wine—red at its best. As the wine flowed, the truthfulness of the story grew ever more apparent!

Editorial Services

CreateSpace—Editorial evaluation and line copyedit. Excellent services at an economical fee.

BOOKS

Haskell, Eric T. *The Gardens of Brécy: A Lasting Landscape.* Paris: Les Éditions du Hiuitième Jour, 2007. (Available from the Department of French Studies, Scripps College.)

Hemingway, Ernest. *The Sun Also Rises.* New York, Charles Scribner's Sons, 1926. (Ironical allusion to the ending of the classic expatriate novel.)

Lewis, Michael. *Boomerang: Travels in the New Third World.* New York: W. W. Norton & Company, 2012.

The Big Short: Inside the Doomsday Machine. New York: W. W. Norton & Company, 2010.

Liar's Poker. New York: W. W. Norton & Company, 1989. (Source of the famous quote of John Gutfreund's "One hand, one million dollars, no tears.")

Mallaby, Sebastian. *More Money Than God: Hedge Funds and the Making of a New Elite.* New York: Penguin Books (a Council on Foreign Relations Book), 2010.

Villiers, Gérard de. *Panique À Bamako* (French Edition). Paris: Éditions Gérard de Villiers, 2012.

Le Chemin de Damas (2) (French Edition). Paris: Éditions Gérard de Villiers, 2012. (The excerpted phrases "read" by the heroine in the accompanying novel are paraphrased and further fictionalized from Google Translate's English translation of the Look Inside feature on Amazon.com.)

Gerard de Villiers died October 31, 2013. Obituaries were published in the *New York Times*, *Daily Telegraph*, and *Le Monde* (in French).

MEDIA

Larry Elliott and Decca Aitkenhead, "It's Payback Time: Don't Expect Sympathy—Lagarde to Greeks," *The Guardian* (Manchester, UK), May 25, 2012. (Used as the article referenced in the first chapter by both Jim Schiller and the Russian energy minister.)

Robert F. Worth, "The Spy Novelist Who Knows too Much," *New York Times Magazine*, January 30, 2013. (Profile of Gérard de Villiers, prototype for fictional novelist Philippe Lagrande.)

Hugh Schofield, "Get out of Afghanistan: France's Million-Selling Spy Writer," *Sunday Times Online*, October 7, 2007. (Gérard de Villiers on why the West will lose in Afghanistan.)

Julia Amalia Heyer, "Corruption Continues Virtually Unchecked in Greece—'We Are Greedy and Asocial,'" *Spiegel Online International*, October 16, 2012.

"Lagarde List: 24,000 Eurowide names held by UK Govt; 130,000 names held by French Intelligence," admin. Darker Net, October 31, 2012. (...from the information underground and the deeper web.)

Marcus Bensasson & Lucy Meakin, "If You Bought Greek Bonds in January You Earned 80%: Euro Credit," Bloomberg.com, December 21, 2012.

FINANCIAL TIMES ARCHIVES

Masa Serdarevic, "Greek Elections: Be Afraid, Be Very Afraid," May 3, 2012.

"Person in the News: Christine Lagarde," May 27, 2011.

Kerin Hope, "Greece Warned of Public Finances Collapse," May 27, 2012.

Sam Jones, "Hedge Funds Battered by Euro Crisis," (lecture, hedge fund convention in Monaco, June 19, 2012.)

Robin Wigglesworth and Sam Jones, "Hedge Funds Tiptoe Back into Greece," October 8, 2012. (Quotes the bench mark 10-year bond as more than doubling in price since nadir in May to above thirty cents on the euro.)

Ralph Atkins et al. "Investors Warm to Greek Debt Buyback Plan," December 3, 2012. (Estimates value of bond buyback at thirty-three cents; hedge funds are "going to make a killing—200 percent profit in six months.")

Neil Buckley, "Energy: Pipeline Tie-In Reinforces Fears of Reliance on Russian Supply," December 4, 2012.

Tom Braithwaite, Kara Scannell, and Michael Mackenzie, "Deutsche Hid Up to $12bn Losses, Say Staff," December 5, 2012.

Patrick Henkins, Daniel Schafer, and James Wilson, "Regulator Sat in on Deutsche Audits," December 6, 2012.

James Wilson, "Police Raid Deutsche HQ in Tax Probe," December 12, 2012.

Lionel Barber and Michael Steen, "FT Person of the Year: Mario Draghi," December 13, 2012.

Joshua Chaffin et al.

"'Grexit Dead' as €34bn Loan Agreed," December 13, 2012.

Sam Jones, "Greek Bond Bet Pays Off for Hedge Fund," December 18, 2012. (Quotes thirty-four cents on the euro as the buyback value.)

Neil Buckley, "Energy Battle," December 17, 2012. (Bulgaria's prime minister Boyko Borisov and the geopolitics of natural gas and energy.)

John Authers, "How Hindsight Capital Did It Again in 2012," December 21, 2012. (Looking back at how to have played the markets: buy Portuguese government bonds; short Greek bonds to midyear, then buy; short Eurozone banks to midyear, then buy Eurozone banks midyear.)

James Mackintosh, "Small Hedge Funds Outdo Elite Rivals," March 5, 2013.

NEW YORK TIMES ARCHIVES

Landon Thomas Jr., "Hedge Funds, Expecting a Bigger Buyback, Snap Up Greek Debt," DealBook, November 30, 2012.

Gretchen Morgenson, "JPMorgan's Follies, for All to See," March 16, 2013.

Landon Thomas Jr, "Concerns Mount That Investors Might Balk at Debt Buyback in Greece," DealBook, December 5, 2012.

Landon Thomas Jr, "Greek Bond Buyback May Have Been Cheaper Under Collective Action Clause," December 23, 2012.

Adam Nossiter and Peter Tinti, "Militants Battle Malian and French Troops in Liberated Town," February 10, 2013.

Marc Jarsulic and Simon Johnson, "How a Big-Bank Failure Could Unfold," May 23, 2013. (A discussion of Deutsche Bank's insolvent US subsidiary during the financial crisis.)

Doreen Carvajal and Raphael Minder, "A Whistle-Blower Who Can Name Names of Swiss Bank Account Holders," August 8, 2013.

Peter Eavis, "Unreliable Guesswork in Valuing Murky Trades," August 14, 2013.

OTHER SOURCES

Jason Kingsley and Isaac Narell. "Jazz on the Bridge." YouTube video. http://www.youtube.com/watch?v=AnuRCKAd8KE.
Jason Kingsley classic jazz standards webpage: http://www.classicjazzstandards.com/.

Figure 7 Jason and sax player on the bridge at Ile St-Louis.

Illustrations

Cover image, *Paris Couple*, Shutterstock 93281119, standard license.
Ministry of Finance, Paris. Wikipedia.
Christine Lagarde, official portrait, Wikipedia.
The Elephant Celebes, Max Ernst, 1921, original in Tate Gallery, London. Wikipedia. Public domain in the United States; fair use claimed for low-resolution image.
Jason Kingsley and Isaac Narell on the Bridge, fair use claimed for low-resolution image from the Internet.

Esplanade at Cala Bona, photograph by author in June, 2013.
Author photo by Wahyuni S. Myers.

Author

Paul A. Myers lives with his wife, Minche, in Claremont and Corona del Mar, California. When not writing, he works as a sole practitioner CPA. He is a graduate of the University of California, Santa Barbara, and has an MBA from the University of Santa Clara. Part of his misspent youth was spent as chief financial officer of a high-tech public company in California's Silicon Valley. He is a past copresident of the Scripps College Fine Arts Foundation.

Paul A. Myers at Monaco.

See author's web page at **myersbooks.com.**
See author page at Amazon.
Follow on Facebook at myersbooks and Twitter at @myersbooks.
E-mail author at <u>myersbooks@gmail.com</u>

Made in the USA
Monee, IL
26 April 2022

95442025R00134